# Finding Grace

## LAUREL RIDGE SERIES, BOOK #2

TARA BAISDEN

STERLING RIDGE PRESS LLC

Cover designed by Sterling Ridge Press LLC

Published by: Sterling Ridge Press, LLC www.sterlingridgepress.com
ISBN: 978-1-966093-02-2

First Edition: November 2024

For permissions, contact: tara@tarabaisden.com or visit www.tarabaisden.com

# About The Author

Tara Baisden is a Contemporary Inspirational Romance author who proudly calls the beautiful state of West Virginia her home. Nestled on a sprawling mountainous property, she is surrounded by the peace and serenity of nature. Her days are happily spent in the quiet of country life, writing heartwarming stories of love, faith, and second chances. Tara also enjoys quilting, working in her garden, tending to her beloved pets, and soaking in the beauty of her surroundings.

With deep roots in West Virginia, family is everything to Tara. One of her favorite pastimes is gathering on the front porch with loved ones, sharing stories, laughter, and enjoying the simple, meaningful moments that life offers. When she's not crafting her novels, Tara can often be found exploring the rich history of her home state, visiting local historical sites, and, of course, stopping by every bookstore she passes! Her passion for reading and discovery always fuels her next adventure.

Tara is the author of the Laurel Ridges Series of novels, which includes: Season of Hope, Finding Grace, His Perfect Plan, and Love Redeemed, all of which have been beloved by fans of inspirational romance. Her novels reflect her love for faith, family, and the timeless beauty of West Virginia.

Known for her sweet and clean romances, she creates characters that feel like family and settings that make readers want to visit again and again.

You can find out more about Tara and her latest releases at www.tarabaisden.com or follow her on social media for updates and behind-the-scenes glimpses of her writing process. Stay connected—you won't want to miss the heartfelt stories of love and family she has in store!

# Also by Tara Baisden

**<u>Laurel Ridge Series</u>**

#1. Season of Hope

#2. Finding Grace

#3. His Perfect Plan

#4. Love Redeemed

# Dedication

To my friends and family, who have made this chapter of my life an absolute joy, I owe you more than words can say.

And to all those who've faced life-altering moments, stared down the chaos, and decided to rewrite your own story: this one's for you. Here's to marching full steam ahead, with laughter, love, and a bit of poetic justice.

# About Laurel Ridge

**Welcome to the fictional town of Laurel Ridge, West Virginia!**

Nestled deep in the heart of the Appalachian Mountains, Laurel Ridge is a place where time slows down, allowing visitors and residents alike to enjoy life's simple pleasures. With its quaint, brick-paved streets, historic storefronts, and the ever-present backdrop of rolling hills and dense forests, Laurel Ridge is a hidden gem that attracts tourists looking for both serenity and adventure.

## A Rich History

The town was founded in the early 1800s by pioneering settlers who were drawn to the fertile land and abundant natural resources of the region. Laurel Ridge began as a small logging community, relying on the towering forests that covered the surrounding mountains. The New River, one of the oldest rivers in the world, provided an essential transportation route for lumber, as well as a lifeline for the early settlers.

As the years passed, the town evolved from a logging outpost into a thriving hub for craftspeople and artisans. By the late 19th century, it had developed a reputation for its hand-crafted furniture, textiles, and pottery, all made by skilled locals. The town's proximity to the New River also made it a destination for adventurous souls seeking to kayak, fish, or hike along the riverbanks.

## A Place of Renewal

Though the logging industry faded by the early 20th century, Laurel Ridge adapted to the changing times. Its natural beauty and deep connection to West Virginia's mountain heritage drew travelers from near and far, transforming it into a beloved tourist destination. Local shops, run by generations of the same families, line the town square, offering handmade goods, locally sourced foods, and, most of all, warm hospitality.

The town's signature event, the Harvest Festival, began in the 1930s, celebrating the craftsmanship, music, and traditions passed down through the generations. Each year, visitors flock to enjoy live Appalachian music, taste locally grown produce, and witness demonstrations of old-world techniques like blacksmithing and weaving.

## A Town of Faith and Community

At the heart of the town stands Laurel Ridge Community Church, a small, white clapboard building with a steeple that reaches toward the sky. Built in 1876, the church has been a pillar of faith and strength for the community for over a century. Its bell, crafted by the town's original blacksmith, has been ringing on Sunday mornings ever since, calling townsfolk to worship and reminding everyone of the enduring values of faith, hope, and love.

The church's history is intertwined with the town's, serving as a refuge in difficult times and a gathering place in moments of joy. Over the years, the church has grown to include an outreach center that supports local families and tourists in need, providing everything from free meals to spiritual counseling. The church's welcoming atmosphere reflects the town's deep sense of unity and service.

## A Growing Tourist Haven

Today, Laurel Ridge has grown to a population of around five thousand people, yet it has managed to retain its small-town charm. Its thriving tourist industry draws visitors year-round. Tourists can stroll through mom-and-pop shops, and dine at the beloved Martha's Diner, famous for its homemade pies and retro charm. The town square, with its white gazebo surrounded by flowering bushes, is often the site of outdoor concerts and farmers' markets, creating a sense of nostalgia and small-town pride.

For nature lovers, the New River offers breathtaking views and the thrill of adventure, whether it's fishing in its crystal blue waters or hiking along the rugged trails that weave through the wilderness. Tourists and locals alike cherish the scenic beauty, often finding peace in the simple pleasures of watching the river flow or taking in the panoramic vistas of the Appalachian Mountains.

Laurel Ridge, with its rich history, strong community spirit, and natural beauty, is more than just a tourist destination—it's a place where past and present blend seamlessly, offering everyone who visits a chance to experience the best of West Virginia's mountain heritage.

You'll find that Laurel Ridge is a town that captures the heart.

**Welcome to Laurel Ridge. I hope you fall in love with this charming small town and its residents.**

# Contents

# Chapter 1

From her corner office, Grace Anderson watched shadows stretch across the steel and glass horizon of New York City, remembering how she used to savor this view. Now the large wraparound windows felt more like a fishbowl, exposing her to the countless eyes in neighboring skyscrapers. Her mahogany desk, once a symbol of achievement, was now just another piece of furniture to be cataloged and left behind. Cardboard boxes, their flaps opened, contents hastily thrown in, littered the space, a testament to the abruptness of it all. The room, once alive with her ambition and spirit, had grown cold, resembling the unnerving stillness of a hospital ward.

The vivid details of the framed photo she held in her hands presented a frozen moment in time. Her moment. She stood mid-laugh in the photo, teeth gleaming, eyes shining, the fire of accomplishment bright behind them. Her hair, styled just so, framed her proud smile as if it had been a scene from a film. Success incarnate.

To anyone else, it would look like just another glossy snapshot of triumph: a woman at the peak of her career, holding a polished globe-shaped plaque that glittered with importance. "PR Executive of the Year," it read. In that moment, she had been on top of the world.

Yet as she stared at the image now, she felt not pride but nausea. She felt no connection to the triumphant expression in the image, no sense of pride in the sleek, confident woman dressed in her signature power suit. Years of sacrifice, late nights navigating corporate wars, failures, and triumphs—all encapsulated in that lifeless image.

Her hand twitched, as she gripped the frame tighter, fighting the urge to hurl it across the room. What good were any of the late nights, the fireworks in board meetings, the press releases? For what? To stand here, wrapped in this failure, a queen with no crown?

The bitterness surged up her throat before she could suppress it. "A cautionary tale," the press had recently called her. The great fall of Grace Anderson splashed across every headline, dissected on morning news shows, on social media, in whispers over casual brunches. How quickly they'd turned on her.

What worsened it, what made the pain unbearable, was the betrayal. It hadn't just been professional. No, it had come from somewhere closer. More personal, more piercing. Grace's grip tightened around the frame until her knuckles whitened.

Tom. Her uncle.

The prodigy who had taught her everything. He'd guided her, reassured her when deals went south. He had held her hand when the conference rooms rattled with uncertainty.

And now? Now look at what he had left her with.

A sham.

How naïve she'd been, even as she'd stood next to him in those board room meetings, speaking on behalf of their family's legacy—blind, trusting.

What had that trust earned her? Ruin. Complicity by association. The corporate scandal of mismanaged funds and backroom deals, and sure, Tom had signed the papers. But the questions circled back to her. What had she known, and when had she known it? How could the head of PR, the woman praised for controlling every narrative, have avoided seeing this? She was the niece; they'd whispered their doubts like they were truths.

One huge mistake by her uncle, one perfectly hidden lie, and her entire identity dissolved before the world's eyes. The betrayal festered. She had been left holding the bag. And the world too gladly assumed she had helped stitch it together.

Her stomach twisted with a fresh wave of disgust. The photo frame in her hand felt dead and heavy, a mockery of her former pride. She turned it over roughly and shoved it into a box without bothering to wrap it. Let it shatter.

The salty tears of humiliation stung her eyes. Five years ago, this office had symbolized limitless possibility. Grace had stood in this very spot as the newly promoted Vice President of Public Relations. She had been at the pinnacle of her career—shaping narratives, controlling crises, and ensuring the company's image shone brighter than ever. Every skyscraper beyond the gleaming windows had felt like a reflection of her success, towering reminders of how far she had climbed.

But now, as she stood amid the cardboard boxes and sterile silence, her office felt like a mockery of all she'd lost. The glittering cityscape outside the windows that once brought her a rush of pride now loomed like a distant world she no longer belonged to.

*Why didn't you see the signs?*

Her mind wouldn't quiet. Her spine curved inward, shoulders too heavy to remain straight under the weight of the grief wrenching through her chest.

Her office door creaked open, and Grace flinched at the sound. Maria, her assistant, stood hesitantly in the doorway, her face lined with worry, as though she couldn't figure out how to broach the inevitable.

"I'm sorry, I don't mean to...interrupt," Maria said as she walked toward her. The envelope in her hand marked with bold, merciless letters: "Termination of Benefits."

"Thank you, Maria," she said, her voice caught somewhere between defeat and numb exhaustion.

Grace let the envelope fall onto the desk with a soft, fluttering sound. It didn't need to be opened. She knew its contents. Finality. A door slammed shut.

The world around her blurred as her watery gaze anchored on the floor beneath her feet, rock-hard and unforgiving. She willed herself to replay her last moments in the boardroom, the scene that had settled this inevitable fall. Draped power suits with no loyalty, no depth. Every gaze burned into her as she'd given her resignation. Her concession.

And Tom? He was sitting in jail.

Could she forgive him? That question clung to her like an anchor, sinking her lower and lower with each breath. She still didn't have an answer.

Why didn't I see it all unfolding?

Grace sank into her office chair and buried her face in trembling hands. The scandal hadn't just obliterated her career—it had stripped her bare and left her standing in the rubble of something she could no longer identify. Her career had crumbled under the weight of her uncle's choices.

There was no stopping the tears. Silent, cleansing streams flowed down her cheeks. No one was there to see. No one to witness her vulnerability.

For so long she had carried an armor... the armor of self-reliance, of sharpness. Now, alone, she didn't need to carry it anymore. Her hands slipped down from her face. She forced simple, slow, even breaths. Her career was over. There was nothing left to hold on to. Yet somehow, deep beneath the exhaustion of it all, a flickering spark crawled to life.

Not hope, not yet. But something—some small part of her wasn't ready to let this city, this failure, own her.

Grace stood. This was the last day in this office, the last walk out of this building. But maybe this wasn't the end of her after all. Maybe this was the beginning.

The thought pulsed under her skin as she took a step toward the door. The clatter of the elevator resounded through the hall as she walked down it with steady, determined strides. There was only one last layer of this day left—the press, waiting hungrily, cameras pointed and ready downstairs.

At the base of the building, the elevator chimed softly as Grace stepped out into the marble lobby. And there they were. Gleaming lenses, microphone cords tangling at feet, pens rifling against notepads. Vultures.

"Ms. Anderson!" the first called out. "Will you be making a public statement?" Flashbulbs flickered like lightning strikes.

"Is your uncle going to face charges? Were you complicit?"

More flashes, more questions. The crowd pressed in, a seething mass of curiosity, and accusation... judgment.

Grace's pulse quickened, her grip on her purse tightening as she forced herself to move forward, one agonizing step after another, their voices swarming in her ears.

"What can you tell us about Tom's involvement, Grace?"

*Just keep walking.*

*Keep moving.*

Outside, a cab veered into view, and she raised her arm stiffly. The cab stopped with a screeching halt. Grace flung herself into the back seat and slammed the door behind her, hands trembling against the vinyl seat.

"Where to?" the driver's voice felt a million miles away.

"92nd and Lexington," she said.

As the cab rolled forward, merging into the ceaseless tide of New York's streets, Grace stared out the window. The skyline stretched endlessly, glass and steel twisting and gleaming against a world that no longer felt like it was hers. The stretch of avenues, the towering skyscrapers—they felt foreign now. Everything swept past like blurred echoes of a life she once had claimed... but not anymore.

She was done. Over. And tomorrow, she'd be gone. For good.

# Chapter 2

The cab pulled to a stop in front of her high-rise building, the familiar gleam of glass and marble reflecting the early evening sunlight. Phillip, the door attendant, tipped his cap as she exited the taxi, his smile thin and strained.

"Good evening, Ms. Anderson," he said, warmth tucked behind formality. But Grace noticed a flicker in his eyes—perhaps pity, or, worse, judgment. She pursed her lips, nodding without offering words in return.

She entered the marble lobby and moved through it as if on autopilot, her heels tapping out a hollow rhythm against the floor. The chandeliers overhead shimmered, their light soft and cold, casting long shadows against the sleek tile. Her building—usually a sanctuary—now felt more like a museum. And she was the artifact, displayed for the world to examine and discard at will.

As the elevator doors slid open on the top floor, Grace reached for the doorknob of her condo, but her fingers trembled when they grasped the metal. How many times had this door been the boundary between herself and the chaos of her corporate life?

Today, she felt no safety in closing it behind her.

Inside, everything was the same, yet foreign. The soft whir of the air conditioner, the pristine perfection of the furniture, the carefully curated art on the walls—all felt distant, like a life that belonged to someone else.

Grace ventured deeper into the condo. Normally, this space was invincible—fortified by her success, a polished fortress of luxury. But right now, it felt cavernous, hollow. She sank down onto her couch, rubbing the heels of her palms against her eyes.

Her stomach churned when her gaze fell on a glimmering crystal award in the room's corner—a testament to the heights she had once reached. Meaningless now.

The TV remote rested on the coffee table, a device that connected her all too easily to the world outside—the world that now relished in tearing her apart. She stared at it for a long moment, torn between the urge to disconnect and the compulsion to check in.

She pressed the power button.

Like clockwork, her face filled the screen. The words 'Grace Anderson, Former PR Exec for Peak Enterprises Falls from Grace' looped beneath the footage of her smooth but unsmiling exit from the office building earlier. She could feel the weight of the analysts' words. Their voices, dissecting her life while perched behind polished desks, became an unbearable hum in her ears.

With a shaking hand, she clicked the TV off, plunging the condo into a silence so thick it seemed to wrap itself around her throat.

She stood and made her way to the bedroom, driven by the only impulse she could feel: escape.

Grace flung open her walk-in closet doors, revealing her tailored blazers and carefully pressed suits. None of them felt like her anymore. The crisp collars and sleek lines seemed like costumes from another life.

Grace grabbed her suitcase and carry-on bag off a shelf and set them aside. She dug through a drawer, locating a pair of simple leggings and a worn t-shirt—the kind of clothes she hadn't worn in years in public, not since her college days before ambition had wound its demanding tendrils around her.

The heavy silence of the condo echoed around her as she stripped off her tailored, expensive armor. As she tugged on the leggings and t-shirt, a strange sense of detachment washed over her. It felt like shedding the skin of someone else, peeling back layers of expectations she was no longer willing to meet.

But even as she changed, she caught sight of herself in the full-length mirror across the room, and the reflection hit her harder than expected. Messy. Muddled. Not the sharp, polished executive everyone had come to expect.

Grace swallowed the lump rising in her throat. She turned away from the mirror and walked toward the bathroom.

The bright, sterile light from the vanity mirrors illuminated her face, revealing the smudge of mascara under one eye. Lines of exhaustion etched into her skin after days of endless press coverage and sleepless nights. How long had she been hiding in here? Hiding behind a face she'd painted with the promise of perfection every single day, hoping that if she looked the part, she'd feel the part.

She yanked open the cabinet under the sink, grabbing a makeup remover cloth from a plastic tub.

The cold cloth touched her skin, trailing across her cheeks, blotting out the foundation, the blush, the carefully contoured illusion of competence. Swipe by swipe, layers of concealer and perfection dissolved, revealing a bare and weary face beneath. The face staring back at her now was raw, vulnerable.

Free of the weight of makeup, she sighed—a deep, trembling sigh—before pulling open the top drawer and grabbing a hair tie. With a quiet determination, she raked her hands through her long, tangled blond hair. Tugging it back into a messy bun, not caring how loose or how uneven it looked.

Grace took one last, long look in the mirror. She brushed her fingers against the small scar on the side of her neck—a relic from a childhood accident, a reminder that imperfections had always been a part of her, no matter how much she tried to hide them beneath a polished exterior.

Grace stepped out of the bathroom, her bare feet sinking into the plush carpet as she moved into her bedroom. The cool air prickled against her skin.

Sitting on the edge of her bed, Grace reached for the open laptop perched on the nightstand, her fingers hovering over the keys. She wasn't sure what she was looking for—not yet, at least. Her mind flitted from one idea to another, thoughts of remote getaways or secluded hideouts offering a temporary escape. But then something deeper, something more purposeful, began to form.

Not just anywhere. Her cabin.

The thought sent a calming ripple through her, her racing heart slowing as it conjured memories long buried. The cabin in West Virginia. The one her Aunt Imogene had left to her after her passing. Grace hadn't been there since her death. She had been too consumed with carving out her career and keeping her image flawless to give it much thought.

But now, the memories drifted back, vivid and warm. She could picture it—standing solitary in the woods. Perched near the sprawling New River. The cabin had been the backdrop of many of her childhood summers, a place where fireflies lit up the dusk and time seemed to stretch endlessly. With Aunt Imogene, there had been no pressure, no expectations. Just love—simple and unconditional.

Grace closed her eyes and drew in a long, steady breath. The cabin was where she wanted to be. Far away from the relentless roar of New York—maybe there, in the quiet, in the trees and the fresh mountain air, she could find herself again. Not the person she pretended to be, the woman the world now sneered at, but the real Grace.

She opened her eyes, resolution settling in.

She searched online for airline flights, and without hesitation, booked the earliest one-way ticket she could find.

Grace moved quickly, tossing clothes into her suitcase with little thought. Once finished, she set the bulging case by the door and turned to her carry-on, perched at the edge of the bed. She slipped her laptop into the padded sleeve. A book on entrepreneurship followed, along with her Kindle. She hesitated for a moment, her gaze sweeping over the room as if it could whisper what she might be forgetting. With a sigh, she grabbed a charging cable, a few flight essentials, and slid her travel journal into the side pocket.

Slipping the strap of the carry-on bag over her shoulder, the weight of the bag felt strangely liberating. She grabbed her suitcase as she left her bedroom, and a sense of calm settled over her.

In the kitchen, Grace plucked a bag of coffee from the shelf, grabbed a couple of crisp apples, and tucked a bag of granola inside her carry on.

She gave the sterile, luxurious room one last sweeping glance.

Grace reached for her suitcase and headed for the door, ready to leave this suffocating world behind.

This chapter of her life was done.

***

"JFK," she murmured to the cab driver, her destination the only certainty guiding her forward.

The taxi merged into the flow of city traffic as dusk settled over the skyline. She stared out the window, the familiar rush of the city passing by in blurs of color—shining lights, towering skyscrapers, the endless chaos. None of it mattered anymore.

At the airport, the city's noise flared. Grace moved through the terminal with singular purpose, her footsteps steady against the polished tile. This time tomorrow, she would be tucked far away in a secluded cabin in West Virginia, where the towering mountains—and the memories of summer nights with Aunt Imogene—might just shield her from the relentless pressure threatening to suffocate her.

It wasn't running away, not exactly. It was returning to something simpler. Something true.

And maybe... just maybe... that would be enough to put the pieces of herself back together.

# Chapter 3

Grace steered the rented SUV on the meandering road, guided by the steady voice of the GPS. The sprawling West Virginia landscape unfurled around her, with rolling hills and dense forests painting the horizon. The road twisted and climbed, each curve requiring focused precision as she navigated the narrow, winding path through the heart of the countryside.

Her thoughts looped back to the scandal. The news headlines. The whispers. They all thought she must have known. That, beneath the perfectly ironed power suits and flawless presentations, she'd been complicit in the web of deception spun by her uncle.

Tom.

His name struck her heart like a chord strummed too hard, the vibrations lingering uncomfortably. Grace gripped the smooth leather of the steering wheel tightly as the image of him flashed before her. Her uncle. A family member. That fact made the betrayal burn even deeper.

She hadn't known what he had been doing behind closed doors. There had been no obvious signs, nothing that screamed he'd been siphoning millions into offshore accounts.

Her fingers tightened around the steering wheel as the SUV rounded another curve, pulling her mind back to the present. The road looped through thick forest and mountainous terrain as the voice of the GPS cut through her thoughts. "Turn right onto Laurel Ridge Road."

She followed the instructions, the SUV lumbering up a steep incline that made the engine groan in protest. As the road narrowed even further, anticipation gnawed at her insides. Laurel Ridge Road twisted itself around the hillside like a coiled snake. The road curved and climbed, each turn revealing another stretch of thick forest or a sudden drop into mist-covered valleys. No streetlights, no signs of life, just wilderness pressing in from all sides. This place was raw, untamed---trees clustered so tightly that they almost became foreboding.

The forest finally gave way to a large clearing, and there it was—Aunt Imogene's cabin, standing quiet and resolute among the trees. It hadn't changed much from the last time Grace had been here, just after the funeral. The same weathered logs formed its walls, the soft patina of age giving it a kind of wisdom.

The stone chimney stood proudly, with just a dusting of moss at its base, blending harmoniously with the woods surrounding it. The porch, weathered lightly from years of mountain air, its worn wood lending a rustic charm that whispered of long-ago stories.

A single, faded flower pot sat tucked beside the wooden steps leading up to the front porch—the only splash of color against the earthy grays and browns of the structure.

Grace turned off the engine, releasing a long, slow breath.

Grabbing her purse and carry on from the passenger seat, she stepped out of the SUV. The air, a little cooler here, pinched at her exposed skin, but it wasn't unpleasant. It was cleansing.

She opened the back hatch of the SUV and unloaded her suitcase.

She walked toward the porch, her shoes thudding softly against the cobblestone path.

Grace rummaged through her purse, her fingers brushing past her wallet and lipstick until they landed on the cool, comforting weight of the cabin key. Aunt Imogene's key.

It was just a key—nothing special—but currently; it was a lifeline. Simple, imperfect, just like everything in West Virginia, and yet so different from the world she'd just left behind. Holding it tight, Grace couldn't help but feel the symbolism coil around her. This key offered more than access to a cabin—it was a choice. The choice to take control of her life.

This key, this cabin—it represented something raw, something Grace hadn't tasted in what felt like years. Freedom.

# Chapter 4

The cabin looked exactly how Grace had hoped it would because of the cleaning service she had hired to maintain it after her aunt had passed—tidy, and well-kept.

Stepping inside, her shoes tapped softly on the wood floor, the sound comforting. The feel of the cabin was softer than the city—both literally and metaphorically. Grace couldn't help but kneel and run her fingers along the edge of the braided rug in the center of the living room. It was the same one she'd sprawled on during hot Appalachian summers, playing cards with Aunt Imogene as a little girl or, more often, reading under the dappled sunlight that flooded in at just the right angle.

Grace's eyes wandered across the room, landing on the plush couch. Its rich fabric and plump cushions seemed to beckon her, promising comfort and warmth. She could imagine herself lounging there during long afternoons, sinking into the soft embrace of the upholstery, the perfect place to read a book or bask in the glow of the nearby fire.

Antique lamps stood on side tables at each end of the couch, complete with stained-glass shades.

Nearby, shelves lined one wall, filled with books and bric-a-brac, haphazardly arranged yet oddly endearing. She scanned the spines of the novels and imagined the quiet evenings one might lose themselves in any of the stories housed here. The knick-knacks, brass trinkets, ceramic figurines, a tarnished pocket watch, all added a personal touch, as if each one held a memory.

But what caught her attention, and made her heart swell, was the fireplace occupying an entire wall. The stones, larger than her fists and smooth to the touch, shimmered. Every stone in the fireplace had its own distinct earthy hue, meticulously cleaned and polished to a lustrous shine. An old iron poker leaned against it, ready and waiting. Firewood stacked high in a heavy iron rack. Nearby, a box of kindling overflowed, with matches perched just in reach.

In the far corner, placed beneath a window, was a wide and welcoming recliner. Its plush upholstery offering comfort, a perfect spot to relax and unwind. Through the window nearby, the trees towering outside wavered in the breeze. Grace imagined sitting there, sinking into the soft cushions, gazing out at the wilderness through the glass. The gentle rustling of leaves and the occasional wild animal would be her only company.

Everything about the cabin tugged at her. None of it was high class, and yet, everything felt perfect in its own unrefined way. The cabin, like the wilderness surrounding her, provided shelter for body and soul.

Grace moved into the main bedroom and shrugged her jacket off, letting it slip to the floor in a soft heap. She sat on the edge of the wooden four-poster bed, running her hand along the edges of the quilt that covered it. A handmade masterpiece of intricate patterns and vibrant colors. Sturdy wooden posts rose at each corner, giving the bed an almost regal air.

On either side of the bed sat small tables, each home to a decorative lamp with intricate, etched glass shades. She pulled the chain dangling from the one nearest her, and a soft light illuminated the space, making the room feel cozy.

Across the room stood a dresser made of heavy oak, the grain strong and rich, its surface adorned with delicate carvings that spoke of both craftsmanship and care. The oak had a timeless quality, its solidity anchoring the room in a sense of history.

Her gaze drifted towards the closet. A generous space. The doors were open, revealing the rows of empty hangers aligned inside. There was a sense of abundance in its size, a welcoming invitation to belong here, in this charming room.

Determined to unpack, she brought her suitcase into the bedroom.

Silk blouses, tailored trousers, pencil skirts that once epitomized her professional stature. Grace knew she had packed hastily, shoving whatever she could into the suitcase yesterday, but she should have packed a few more pieces of suitable clothing for a mountain retreat getaway.

"I'm such a fool," she muttered to herself in frustration.

Glancing around, her gaze landed on the Bible that rested on the side table next to the bed, pages stained yellow with age. Grabbing the book, she fanned it open to a random passage. With a small sigh, she shut the book and shook her head.

*No, not tonight.*

Lost in thought, she left the bedroom and wandered into the kitchen.

Her fingers trailed along the edge of the counter, feeling the worn yet smooth surface beneath her touch.

A few delicate cracks spider webbed across the cream-tiled back-splash, weaving subtle stories of time and use.

Opening the kitchen cabinets, Grace's eyes skimmed the weathered shelves, their cream paint chipped at the edges, as though they had stood witness to countless mornings and quiet, solitary nights.

Reaching for a glass, Grace paused for a moment, fingers resting on the elegant arch of the wooden cabinet door as it hung open. The slight creak of hinges broke the stillness as the door clicked back into place.

She turned to the faucet, the old-fashioned kind with porcelain handles, and let the cool water fill her glass. The worn ceramic sink had light scratches, remnants of a life washed away over time, yet it felt comforting.

Grace glanced back before leaving the kitchen to relax in the cozy recliner near the living room window.

She sank into the seat and peered out the window. The sky was a deep, flawless blue. Thick clouds moved in waves across the horizon. Tall trees, their trunks dark and weathered, stood like silent sentinels, their leaves swaying gently in the morning breeze.

She sat in silence, her gaze fixed on the forest beyond the glass, yet her mind was far from this moment. It was crowded with the sharp edges of old meetings, clashing voices over tense emails, endless arguments that seemed to gnaw at every fiber of her being. Her body ached from the sheer force of holding herself together for so long, her muscles tight, as if any release would be its own form of surrender.

In her corporate life, silence and stillness had been an enemy, an anxious void she could only fill with action—with talking, with doing. Now, as she listened to the deepening hush of the cabin, she wondered—was there a part of her that could find peace in this stillness, or would it swallow her up?

Grace closed her eyes and kneaded her temples, the low throb of exhaustion settling deeper into her bones.

She reminisced about a summer long past, when she was just twelve, a time marked by simplicity and ease. Days were spent wandering the meandering trails nearby with Aunt Imogene, learning to quilt, preparing small meals in the cozy kitchen, and gently rocking on the porch with a book nestled in her lap. The cabin and the surrounding wilderness had embraced her then, its presence not suffocating but comforting—a true sanctuary teeming with wonder. Yet now, the girl who had danced with fireflies in the soft, fading light of summer felt as unattainable as a distant memory.

Grace sighed. She wasn't that carefree, untouched girl anymore. Life had carved out the innocence, leaving behind someone else. Someone jagged and shaken.

Feeling exhaustion settle in, she forced herself to stand, legs trembling from both the journey and the weight of the last week. Stumbling toward the bedroom, she barely registered the soft creak of floorboards underfoot. The bed inviting in a way she hadn't felt in days.

Grace collapsed onto the mattress, not bothering to change out of her traveling clothes. She lacked the energy to put in the required effort.

Her breathing slowed as she sunk deeper, chasing the fleeting hope that sleep might bring the peace the waking world could not. Grace surrendered. Drifting into a restless, fractured slumber filled with swirling dreams and fragmenting nightmares.

# Chapter 5

Grace stirred in bed, disoriented. The quilt had twisted around her during the night. She wrestled with the fabric before freeing herself. Sitting up, she ran a hand through her hair, feeling the slight knots left from a fitful sleep.

Grace pushed herself out of bed, the weight of sleep still clinging to her limbs, and padded over to the window. A wild breeze swayed the tops of the pines, their deep green needles whispering secrets that slipped through the silence of the early morning. She marveled at the sheer quietude of it all, straining her ears as if to catch the faintest trace of city noise, something familiar, a cue that the world was still spinning beyond those trees. But there was nothing. No cars honking. No people bustling in the rush of another day in the city that never slept. Just the soft rustle of leaves, the occasional trill of a bird, and an early morning calm that swirled like a long-forgotten lullaby.

She turned away from the window and grabbed the bag of coffee she had packed, and made her way to the small kitchen.

Glancing around, she spotted an old percolator. It looked like something that might have been handed down from generation to generation or retrieved from a historical kitchen exhibit. The relic of a coffee maker sat on the stove, its metal surface reflecting the faint morning light, glinting almost smugly.

Grace eyed it warily. She leaned in closer, picking it up like it might suddenly sprout legs and scamper away. The contraption was bulky, awkward, and ancient compared to the sleek, button-filled machines she was used to.

"How hard can it be?" she muttered to herself, eyeing the various parts. Some kind of strange metal tube poking out of the middle with a basket on top.

There were no automatic buttons, no digital screen telling her the exact temperature, no options for a standard brew or a double shot of espresso. Just this metal canister glaring back at her like the ultimate boss of an old-school video game, determined to humble her.

*Okay, it can't be that complicated. I've learned more difficult things, right?*

She sighed, grabbing her cellphone she had left lying on the counter. "How to use a percolator," she mumbled out loud as she typed the words into the search bar. The results popped up, each website littered with cheerful phrases like "a classic brewing method!" and "rediscover simplicity!"

*Rediscover simplicity? More like rediscovering confusion.*

Grace scrolled past the history lesson some coffee enthusiast felt the need to include.

"I don't need to know when it was invented. I just want coffee before noon," she grumbled.

Settling on a short DIY tutorial, without a single historical fact, she skimmed the steps, realizing with a touch of relief that it wasn't rocket science.

"Okay," she said, pepping herself up. "Water goes in the bottom. Coffee grounds go in the top basket thingy. The tube in the middle does... something important. Check, check, and... check."

Grace glanced over at the mismatched set of mugs hanging from copper hooks on the backsplash—one had a chip in it, another had something resembling a Christmas tree with a lopsided star, and a third declared "World's Okayest Boss".

She grabbed the boss mug.

*You can do this Grace. You're a highly functioning adult, after all.*

Grace turned the knob for the front right burner on the stove as she placed the percolator carefully on top, adjusting it like it was a priceless heirloom at the British Museum. Then she waited.

And waited.

The percolator just sat there, not... percolating.

"Come on," Grace muttered. Glaring at it as if that would intimidate it into action. "Do what you're supposed to do. Become coffee."

Just as hope was fading, she heard a sound. It sputtered and gurgled, and then, with startling enthusiasm, it began to bubble.

Grace leaned back as she fumbled to lower the heat like it was a ticking time bomb as the percolator lid clattered with the force of it brewing. The gurgling reached new heights. She wondered if she'd accidentally summoned the ghost of mornings past or unleashed a caffeine-filled volcano.

But after a few moments, everything settled. The bubbling became rhythmic, and she sighed with relief.

The smell of coffee wafted up, rich and smooth. "Okay," she murmured, backing away like she'd just accomplished a daunting science experiment. "That wasn't so bad." She glanced at the percolator with newfound respect. Or at least less suspicion.

Soon she poured the steaming dark brew into the mug, marveling at the simplicity of it all. It looked and smelled... delicious.

*Mission accomplished.*

Grace raised the mug to her lips, blowing on the surface of the coffee as she smiled to herself. "Not too bad," she said, tipping the cup in the percolator's direction, "you win this round, but I'll get the hang of you yet."

She cradled her mug of coffee, lost in her thoughts. The bitter taste of each sip was overshadowed by its comforting warmth. Wrapping her hands around the mug, she wandered to a window, her breath fogging the glass as she took in the tranquil morning once more. The steady warmth of the coffee seeped into her fingertips, chasing away the morning chill, but it did little to silence the restless thoughts swirling in her mind.

In the stillness, Grace felt a pull to go, to do something, to be productive. But she was here and not in the city now. There was nothing chasing her, no emails to check, no meetings to attend. She could just... be.

She took another sip, focusing on the liquid warmth as it spread through her, grounding her in the present moment, even if just temporarily. Today, Grace decided she would face the small-town world she had chosen to come to with all its quirks and challenges head-on. Grace weighed her options for the day.

Grocery store stat. She needed to buy a small electric coffee pot as well, not wanting to deal with a percolator every single morning. A Keurig would be even better.

# Chapter 6

The drive into town was brief, the winding roads slowly revealing the town of Laurel Ridge nestled among the vibrant autumn tapestry of the hills. The postcard-perfect town spread before her. Brick paved streets framed the scene. Blooming fall flowers in colored pots lined the sidewalks. At the center of it all stood a white gazebo in the town square, timeless and proud, surrounded by charming storefronts. Their weathered signs, each hand-painted, swayed gently in the breeze, inviting visitors into the life of this quiet town.

Grace pulled into a small parking lot off Main Street, her thoughts barely able to keep up with the bursts of scenery unfolding before her. She parked the SUV and sat for a moment longer. It was an idyllic scene, almost too perfect to be true.

The tension of the past few days eased, slipping away as the town's quiet charm and gentle warmth wrapped itself around her. Stepping out of the SUV, Grace inhaled, catching the inviting scent of freshly baked pastries and rich coffee wafting from a bakery. Nearby, a small group of older men lingered. Their laughter rang out across the brick-paved street, loud, carefree, and unlike the stiff, restrained exchanges that had come to define her world back in New York.

Grace wandered past shop windows, where behind each pane of glass, the enchanting glow of light seemed to offer a distinct atmosphere. A world within a world.

The glint of something rustic caught Grace's attention through the window belonging to a store named Antique Finds & Second Chances.

The bell above the door gave a cheerful jingle as she entered, ushering her into a world of worn linens, old dresses on mannequins, and row upon row of items with history etched into their very fabric. The scent of beeswax polish hit her nostrils.

A cheerful, portly man in an apron greeted her from behind the counter. "Good morning! Anything I can help you find today?" he asked, his voice as thick as molasses and filled with warmth.

"Just looking, thanks," Grace replied with a small smile, leaving the man satisfied, as he went back to arranging a set of tiny porcelain dishes on a shelf.

Grace browsed the store for a few minutes, her fingers grazing the tops of wooden cabinets and the backs of chintz-covered chairs. Each item belonged to another time, another life, reminding her of her own fragmented narrative.

She picked up a small, wooden hand-carved jewelry box, cradling it in her palms. The etchings that adorn the edges, meticulous and elaborate, showcasing an impressive level of detail. The jewelry box transported her to another time, awakening the memory of sitting cross-legged on her bedroom floor in her parents home as a teenager. In front of her sat a small wooden jewelry box with delicate carvings. Aunt Imogene had given it to her for her birthday.

Content with her small find, she made her payment at the counter. The man's parting words were simple, "You have a good day now, miss." But the way he said it, the genuineness underneath those words, struck her.

Outside, Grace wandered to a diner she had spotted earlier. The sound of clinking dishes and quiet chatter floating through the wide-open windows. Martha's Diner stood at the corner of the street. A charming little place with a plethora of autumn flowers crowded into mismatched pots near the entrance and a neon sign shaped like a coffee cup glowing resiliently despite the time of day. A large, red-and-white striped awning hung over the windows.

Grace hesitated at the threshold, her fingers brushing the cool metal of the handle. In the city, she would have had her pick of any trendy cafe offering organic everything and chai lattes as a given. Here, the scent of fried eggs and bacon hung in the air. Her stomach growled, leaving little room for doubt. She needed food.

As she pushed the door open, an enthusiastic jingle from the bell overhead greeted her, louder, livelier than the one at the antique store, calling out a greeting all on its own. The smell of brewed coffee wrapped around her. Patrons occupied booths deep in conversation, hunched over plates of assorted breakfast foods. Old photographs decorated the walls, capturing local milestones from long ago.

Grace took a seat at the counter. A woman, maybe in her early sixties, with a welcoming, round face and salt-and-pepper hair pulled back neatly in a bun, delivered her water with a smile so genuine it could have lit up an entire city block.

"Hey there, sweetie! Welcome to Martha's," the woman beamed, her voice a symphony of cheer mixed with the hoarse remnants of laughter, "My guess is that you're new around here?"

"Uh, yeah, sort of," Grace replied. "Just visiting for a while."

"Well, you've made a fine choice coming to Laurel Ridge. I'm Martha." Without missing a beat, Martha handed over a laminated menu, adding, "Today's special is our buttermilk pancakes—best you'll taste this side of the New River!"

"Thanks, Martha," she murmured, her eyes scanning the menu options. Hearty, old-fashioned comfort foods she hadn't eaten since she was a child.

"Course, sweetie. Take your time looking at the menu," Martha said, and then went on to navigate the diner, interacting with customers in the same friendly manner.

Grace noticed how content the patrons were, each fully immersed in the moment. The men in worn flannel shirts sitting in a corner booth. Their laughter rolled out in easy waves. A young couple near Grace chatted, oblivious to the outside world.

The warmth and ease of the diner settled into her bones.

Martha returned with a steaming mug of coffee, and Grace nodded her thanks. She glanced down again at the smaller menu inset, deciding on the special. It had been ages since she'd allowed herself this kind of indulgence.

"Pancakes, please, Martha."

"You got it, hon," Martha replied, scribbling her order on a ticket pad as she sidled off to place Grace's order.

Grace sipped her coffee, enjoying every taste of the rich beverage.

The bell above the door jingled, and she instinctively glanced back.

A man, in his mid to late thirties, entered the diner with ease, catching Grace's attention. He was dressed in worn jeans and a plain blue flannel shirt, sleeves rolled up to the elbows, showing tanned, muscular arms. His hair, dark and thick, lay tousled and fell carelessly across his forehead, as though he'd been working outside and had ruffled it into submission with his hand.

Grace observed the man as he approach the counter, smiling as he greeted Martha.

"You're out and about early, Ben," Martha said, setting down a cup of black coffee for him, her tone almost maternal. "Didn't think I would see you this morning."

Ben grinned, accepting the coffee with an easy nod of thanks. His voice was deep, just shy of gravelly. "And miss having breakfast with you? Not a chance."

Martha snorted. "Charmer," she chided, before returning her focus to Grace just as Ben took a measured sip of his coffee, pausing for just a moment to glance at her, a trace of curiosity flitting through his eyes.

Grace felt her cheeks warm and managed a polite smile. She had seen more than her fair share of attractive men in the office, but none quite like this. Rugged, yes, but there was an energy about him that drew her in.

For a split second, she thought he might introduce himself. Instead, Ben nodded her way, a twinkle in his eyes and a warm smile on his face.

"Let me just guess," Martha said. "Three eggs scrambled, crispy-fried hash browns, bowl of grits, and sausage patties, right?"

Ben laughed, "Martha, you've read my mind."

He turned, leaving the counter, and headed towards the corner of the diner, where the men Grace had seen earlier called for him. Their gestures clearly showed that they'd saved him a seat.

Ben effortlessly integrated himself into the group, his laugh joining theirs. It was comforting to witness a life being lived so easily. A stark contrast to the razor-sharp intensity of the professional world she had adopted.

But as much as Grace tried to return her focus to her own meal just delivered piping hot by a happy and smiling Martha, a part of her kept thinking back to her brief interaction with Ben. His face with that brief flicker of recognition before they had parted ways. Though, how could he know her? She puzzled over that perplexity, even as she tried to convince herself it didn't matter.

As she poked at her pancakes, snippets of conversations going on around her entered her periphery, offering her glimpses of small-town life.

"… pasture's holdin' up on the ridge—might bring out the herd soon." One older gentleman boasted, his voice lifting like bits of hay in a breeze.

"… school auction's next week. Ya know, Betsy's already started rallyin' donations with the usual crowd…" A woman in a bold yellow shawl—maybe a teacher?—spoke with authority.

"… reckon fall clean-up's near, best get all the hoses pulled an' yards ready…" another said to his pal.

Grace listened, almost seeing their stories unfold like small uncut movie reels. A myriad of lives intersecting over individual moments that seemed simple and profound all at once.

"Enjoyin' those pancakes?" Martha asked.

"They're wonderful. Thank you, Martha," Grace said.

"So, what brings you to our little corner of the world?" she asked, eyes twinkling.

"Just… taking some time off from work. Looking for a change of pace." Grace said, keeping her reply vague and hollow.

Martha nodded as she wiped down the counter next to her with a knowing smile.

"Smart gal," Martha remarked. "Ya know…this place has a way of finding folks when they need it most. You'll see."

Grace smiled, unsure how to respond, and part of her admired the woman's perceptiveness.

Martha gathered Grace's plate when she was finished, left her bill, and continued on her way without another word.

Grace busied herself retrieving her wallet, drawing out the cash to cover the bill, but was too lost in contemplation to notice Ben walking towards the counter again until he stood beside her. That lock of hair still falling over his forehead.

"I sense you're a visitor. I hope you're finding the town to your liking so far," he said, his voice breaking the silence.

Her smile felt weaker than it should've as she glanced up at him. "It's... different. I'm visiting from the city. But I like it, yes."

Ben chuckled, nodding in agreement. "Different's a good word for it. You... seem familiar somehow, though. Mind if I ask where you're from?"

"New York," Grace said.

"New York, huh? Well, down here is another world entirely," Ben said.

"Yeah," Grace replied with a smile. "It really is."

He nodded, lifting his cup in a small, polite toast of sorts. "Welcome to Laurel Ridge, then. And if you're interested in seeing a little more of the area, come visit me at Adventure Tours, just up the road a way." With that, Ben turned and left.

Grace watched him leave, feeling a wave of nostalgia wash over her. She had almost forgotten how relaxed and welcoming the people of West Virginia could be. Growing up in Charleston, just a few hours away, she was no stranger to easy-going conversations and friendly banter. But after years of navigating the fast-paced life in New York, those simple, genuine interactions felt like a distant memory.

# Chapter 7

G race sat on the back porch, her legs tucked underneath her in a rocking chair, which creaked as it swayed in rhythm with the gentle mountain breeze.

The gorgeous New River, at the edge of the backyard, spread out like a feast for her eyes. The water snaked around, gleaming like a silvery blue ribbon as it cut through the rugged valley, its shimmer breaking here and there. Small rapids rumbled over hidden rocks.

She had to admit—being here had its perks. The view alone made each moment feel like it was wrapped in a kind of solitude and elegance she couldn't find back in the city.

Her lips curled into a soft smile, but the act felt unused, like stretching an old, forgotten muscle. She wasn't used to stillness, relaxing, or even admiring God's creation at leisure anymore. For the last ten years, she had been a person who thrived on deadlines, schedules, and meetings marked with tension. Surging adrenaline with every corporate emergency.

She sighed, taking in the crisp mountain air, and told herself again that she should be grateful for the opportunity to rest. Really rest and to think. Away from New York. Away from the scandal.

Tom.

Her uncle's name flickered through her head like an image she had tried to bury but couldn't.

Tom had always been the golden uncle, the one whom the entire family championed—the embodiment of success and ambition that Grace had admired deeply. But when the scandal erupted, her world crumbled like a sandcastle swept away by an unrelenting tide.

The media coverage of the entire mess that Tom had created had been relentless. The glossy headlines, as cold and aggressive as any corporate adversary she'd ever known. When the paparazzi had finally caught up with her, sticking microphones in her face and cameras flashing so bright she couldn't see straight, Grace had felt small. She had never experienced anything like that before, and all she wanted to do was crawl under a rock and hide.

A soft breeze swept across the porch, rustling the trees and playing with strands of her hair that refused to stay tucked behind her ear. The mountain air was a blend of the sharp pine, dusted with the floral fragrances of late season wildflowers and earthy autumn scents. It filled her lungs, but did little to fill the hollow pit that had taken up residence deep inside.

Her phone screen lit up, vibrating gently on the table beside her with a persistent soft ping. Grace recognized the familiar sound—the ringtone she had assigned to her parents.

For a moment, she hesitated. She could ignore it, pretend she hadn't heard. She looked away, stalling for a moment. But the phone buzzed again, insistent. She sighed and picked it up.

"Hi, Mom," she said, her voice steady.

"Grace! I'm so glad to finally reach you! I've been worried sick," her mom responded, her voice tinged with concern. "You didn't return my messages, and... well, with everything that's been happening..."

"I know, I—needed some time." Grace's voice trailed off as she rested her forehead in her palm.

"I understand. I really do." Her mom's tone, although concerned, carried understanding—an acknowledgment that Grace needed space. "But, honey, your dad and I have been so worried. We've been following the news about Tom, and it's just been so overwhelming."

Grace's stomach clenched at the mention of Tom. "I know."

Her mother sighed, a sound laden with both empathy and sorrow. "We just never expected any of this, Grace. It feels unreal. Your dad and I are trying to make sense of it all, and the media... they've been relentless. We're just so worried about you and Tom."

Taking a breath, Grace closed her eyes. "It's all been... a lot. I should have been more alert. I should have known or sensed something was going on..."

"You're not responsible for Tom's choices. Please remember that," her mother interrupted her. "Where are you right now? It sounds so quiet..."

"I'm at Aunt Imogene's cabin," Grace said, her voice softer yet firm.

"Oh, Imogene's? That place is such a treasure!" Her mother's tone shifted, nostalgia sparkling through. "What a perfect getaway! But, Grace, is it really the best place to be right now? I worry you might be isolating yourself."

Grace smiled despite the moment's heaviness. "I understand why you'd think that, but it's quiet here, Mom. I just need some time to step away from everything. The noise... the questions."

"I get that, I do, but I just want you to know we're here for you. You can talk to me or your dad about anything, you know that."

"I know. I just really need space to think. Everything feels so heavy right now. I'm still... sorting things out," Grace said.

"I'm worried about you," her mom admitted softly. "Please stay safe. You're in my heart, sweetheart. No matter the distance or what's happening, you're never truly alone. I love you."

"I love you too, Mom," Grace replied, closing her eyes to take in the weight of her mom's words, feeling the warmth they provided amid her storm.

"Just keep in touch. If you need anything or just want to talk, I'm here," her mom said, a soothing reassurance.

"I will, Mom. I promise."

As the call came to a close, Grace unwound with relief, the connection to her mother a lifeline.

The rocking chair swayed gently as she placed her phone on the small table, her gaze shifting toward the river flowing beyond. Sunlight danced across the landscape, illuminating everything in its warm glow. Then something caught her eye—a flash of movement. Leaning forward slightly, she adjusted her position in the chair.

From her vantage point on the back porch, the river unfolded like a shimmering ribbon, its steady rush a mere stone's throw away. Brightly colored rafts bobbed over the water's surface, laughter bubbling up from the groups of paddlers, the joyful sounds blending seamlessly with the murmur of the current. In the lead raft, she spotted a familiar figure, confidently guiding the group with an unmistakable ease. It was him again—Ben, the man from earlier that morning at Martha's Diner. He navigated the raft as if the river were an extension of his own being, his presence as effortlessly connected to the water as the very earth beneath her feet.

Grace blinked, sitting up straighter as curiosity piqued inside her. He stood out, his tall silhouette was visible even from this distance.

Ben looked completely at ease as he signaled toward the other rafts ahead of him, pointing out areas of the river and guiding them around large rocks and swift-moving currents. He was smiling. That same relaxed smile she had seen in the diner this morning. It looked even easier now, like the river itself was his second home.

Grace watched, captivated by sheer curiosity.

The rafters drifted farther down the river, slowly shrinking until even Ben was little more than a dot on the horizon.

Grace's rocking chair slowed to a near stop. The peaceful sounds of the birds flitting through the nearby trees, the river's steady rhythm tumbling in her ears.

Grace settled back into the rocking chair, the lens through which she saw her world shifting ever so slightly.

For the rest of the afternoon and into the evening, as the sun dipped lower, she stayed on that porch, eyes fixed on the unseen horizon, trying to work through the questions swirling inside.

Questions about herself.

# Chapter 8

Grace open one eye, wincing at the chill that had settled into the cabin overnight. She yanked the quilt closer and huffed. No matter how inviting a fire in the hearth seemed right now, the idea of wrestling with logs before even a sip of coffee made her groan.

Easing out of bed, Grace grabbed the maroon sweater she had tossed aside the night before and padded into the kitchen, grimacing as she glanced over at the ancient percolator. She had endured its subpar performance yesterday, but a gal can only take so much.

"Shoot. I forgot to buy a more modern coffee pot yesterday," she muttered under her breath.

"Come on, we can do this, you and me," she said, as if words of encouragement might magically infuse the percolator with some modern efficiency.

Spooning coffee grounds into the filter basket, Grace set it to work and leaned back against the countertop. The groaning of the machine rumbled up from deep within, producing a sound halfway between sputtering and wheezing, as though it resented being forced back to life.

Grace shook her head with a resigned sigh. Short of a fresh latte delivered to her door, this would have to do. As the coffee started bubbling, its process as sluggish as her own awakening, she opened the fridge and shot a dubious glance inside. She had forgotten to grocery shop with actual meals in mind yesterday, grabbing apples and oranges more out of habit than hunger. It wasn't even eight o'clock, and she already missed the city's endless breakfast options.

Grace shut the fridge door and opted to wait for the coffee. She would have to make another trip into town and remedy her errors. With coffee in hand, she set about pacing the length of the cabin.

Her steps echoed back at her from the walls—rhythmic footsteps that cracked the silence but did little to fill the space. Restlessness coiled around her shoulders; the stillness of the cabin felt isolating. Grace didn't quite know what to do with herself. The pace of New York had yet to drain from her muscles, a sharp contrast with the sluggish tranquility surrounding her now. Wasn't this what she had wanted? All this peace and quiet... time to think?

Except, now that she had it, she didn't know what to do with it.

Sitting down at the small wooden dining table, Grace reached for her phone out of habit, seeking distraction in the usual sites—news, emails, social media. But after swiping and tapping in futile frustration, a reliable connection was just not happening this morning.

"Fantastic," she muttered, tossing her phone next to her empty mug. No signal. No emails. Completely cut off.

She pressed her palms against the sides of her face, willing away the tightening knot of anxiety she felt creeping in. This wasn't how she'd imagined cabin life. She had naively pictured herself here, free from the world, and yet all this uninterrupted solitude was making her feel as though she were missing out on her former life. Her mind wandered back to her career—the constant buzz of meetings, deadlines, the thrill of crisis management. The ladder she'd climbed so high, only to be struck down as easily as sweeping a lone chess piece from a board.

Groaning, Grace picked up her Kindle. Yet, page after page, her thoughts refused to align with the words. The storyline—the slow life of a small New England village unraveling in fiction—seemed to mock her, as if to say, this isn't your world. You're a stranger in it.

She set the Kindle aside and resumed her pacing, this time on the front porch. Birds flitted and chirped among the trees—carefree and unburdened. Their chatter, at first a welcome novelty, only grated on her nerves now. It was as if the natural world outside this rustic cabin knew a secret she wasn't privy to, one that conspired against her.

Enough was enough. Grace needed human interaction, and badly.

Back inside, she dressed quickly, grabbed her purse, and threw on a light jacket.

The drive into town was short. The winding roads seemed a little more familiar and less daunting. The early fog of the morning was lifting, revealing the lushness of the surrounding trees dappled in sunlight under the vivid sky.

In town, many shops had already opened. She drove around the town square in search of something sensible she could do. A mega store would be nice. An extra blanket for chillier nights. Clothes ... she needed more appropriate clothes ... and a real coffee pot.

Her thoughts turned toward a homemade breakfast at Martha's Diner, again. And with more than food on her mind, she wanted to get details regarding that Adventure Tours place, or whatever Ben had called it, as well.

Inside the diner, the crowd was in full swing, early risers trading gossip for bacon and eggs. The warmth of familiar scents wrapped around—bacon, coffee, pancakes.

"Hey there, sweetheart." Martha's congenial voice broke her reverie, a coffeepot in one hand and a welcoming smile on her face. "Back already?"

Grace smiled. "Looks like it." She adjusted her jacket and made her way to the counter, sliding onto one of the swivel seats.

"Want your usual?" Martha asked with a twinkle in her eye. "Figured those pancakes might've won you over, eh?"

"Not today, I'm afraid. I want something lighter. I'll take scrambled eggs, a side of fruit, and coffee, please."

Martha grinned, as though Grace had made the best decision possible. "Bless your healthy little heart," she commented warmly.

As Martha turned to relay the order, Grace felt nerves bubbling up. "So, um, Martha..." she began, "I've been thinking of, you know, exploring a bit more around town."

Martha didn't seem to think much of it. "Oh? What kind of exploring have you been thinking about?"

"Well, someone mentioned a place," Grace continued. "Adventure Tours, I think it was called. I thought I might check it out."

"A tour, huh? They offer hiking tours. Their kayaking tours are the best. I think Ben has some other tours as well, but I can't remember them all." Martha said with a curious note in her voice.

"Yes, something like a tour might be fun. I guess. I'm not sure what I want to do. Just something."

Martha's expression softened as she smiled. "Ah," she said with a warm chuckle, "Looking for something to do, fill up a little restless space. Honey, you won't regret it. Ben's tours are pretty popular. He runs a quality operation out there. Takes his clients on fishing trips, kayaking adventures, hiking tours, and even camping trips near the river."

Upon hearing his name, Grace straightened almost instinctively.

"Where can I find it?" she pressed.

"Just go over the bridge headed out of town and follow the signs." Martha said. "That'll lead you right to the headquarters!"

Grace focused on her coffee cup, taking a sip to steady herself. "Thanks, Martha."

"Don't mention it."

"So… is there a mega store nearby where I can grab a coffee maker, an extra blanket, some comfy clothes, and groceries?" she asked, trying to sound hopeful.

Martha let out a hearty laugh, wiping her hands on her apron. "Oh, honey, the nearest Walmart is about an hour and a half away. You'll get there just in time to forget why you even went!"

Grace's eyes widened in shock. "An hour and a half? For a Walmart? Where am I, the middle of nowhere?"

"Pretty much," Martha winked. "But don't worry, we locals survive just fine."

Grace shook her head in disbelief. "But—but how do you live without the convenience of a mega store?"

Martha chuckled again. "The hardware store is on Main Street, just down from the bakery. You can snag yourself a coffee maker and blanket there." She gave Grace a playful smile. "Who needs Walmart when you've got Earl's Hardware? He's got everything… well, almost everything."

Grace raised an eyebrow. "A coffee maker and a blanket from a hardware store? That's a new one for me."

"Hey, it might not be a fancy place, but it works," Martha grinned, unfazed.

"Okay, what about clothes? I was hoping to pick up some yoga pants or, you know, maybe something soft and comfortable?"

Martha lit up with amusement. "Well, Mountain Chic Boutique just around the corner will have what you're looking for—that is if jeans, flannel shirts, or comfy t-shirts are okay! Beth's got all the essentials for small-town life. Yoga pants? I'm not sure if I even know what those are!"

Grace couldn't help but laugh at Martha's cheery words. "Jeans, flannels and t-shirts it is, I guess. I feel like I'm going full lumberjack out here."

"Don't knock it 'till you try it!" Martha chuckled. "Once you've pulled on one of Beth's flannels, you'll be shocked you ever wanted anything else. It's basically a small-town luxury."

# Chapter 9

Grace stepped out of her SUV, her eyes focused on the clothing store Martha had suggested earlier. Nestled between Leslie's Blossoms, a florist, and Bubbles & Bliss, a shop specializing in candles and soaps, the wooden sign hanging from the eaves swayed gently, declaring without pretense or pomp: Mountain Chic Boutique. Below it, in softer, hand-painted letters, the motto followed: 'Where style meets comfort—in the heart of the mountains.' Through the display window she spotted an array of colorful, neatly arranged flannel shirts, jeans, and casual wear.

On a mission to find more suitable clothes while here in Laurel Ridge, Grace pushed open the heavy oak and glass door. The scent of lavender and cedar flooded her senses. The space smelled fresh and earthy, far removed from the sterile, over-perfumed department stores in the city. Soft acoustic music floated through the air, blending with the low hum of customers murmuring and hangers clinking as people shuffled through the racks of clothing.

"Good morning! Oh, wait... don't tell me—you must be Grace, right?" A woman's lively voice burst through the serene atmosphere, and Grace looked over to meet the expectant gaze of a warm and boisterous woman in her late forties. She stood behind a large wooden counter, her blonde hair tied back in a loose, messy ponytail. Gold hoop earrings dangled from her earlobes, swaying as she spoke. She wore a taupe colored blouse and stylish jeans, an outfit that screamed laid-back-but-sophisticated. Her wide smile radiated excitement, as if welcoming an old friend rather than a first-time visitor.

Grace blinked, caught off guard. "Y-yes, I'm Grace, but how did you—"

The woman chuckled. "Oh, honey, word gets around faster than a wildfire in Laurel Ridge. Martha called a little while ago. She mentioned we had a visitor staying in town and that she had referred you to come see me. I mean, no offense, but you do have a 'fresh-from-the-city' look about you. Call it intuition."

Grace couldn't help but laugh, caught between amusement and mild embarrassment. "Well, I suppose I'm not exactly blending in just yet."

The woman made her way around the counter, extending her hand. "I'm Beth Rutledge, owner of this fine clothing store. And might I say, you've come to the right place? We'll get you in some comfy clothes in no time."

Grace shook Beth's hand, feeling a sense of comfort flood over her. There was something about Beth's presence—warm, welcoming, and just the right touch of Southern charm—that put her at ease. It wasn't forced or overly polite, just ... real.

"Thank you. I do need a new wardrobe, something more... appropriate for my stay here." Grace glanced around the shop, feeling overwhelmed. The city's fast pace and ultra-trendy fashion felt worlds away.

"Well, honey, you're in the right place," Beth declared, placing her hands on her hips and surveying Grace with an appraising eye. "Now, tell me, what exactly are you looking for?"

"Honestly, I'm not sure," Grace admitted. "Definitely jeans, comfortable t-shirts... Martha recommended flannels, so I guess those too. I kind of forgot to pack more casual clothing. Pretty much all I have with me are business clothes—skirts, blouses, you know, typical office attire. Not exactly something I'd wear hiking or spending time outdoors."

Beth raised an eyebrow and gave a theatrical tilt of her head, her eyes sparkling with something akin to amusement. "Well, that won't do at all! Girl, you're in Laurel Ridge now, not hosting some big city board meeting. You need clothes that'll let you move and breathe, something practical that won't remind you of crunching numbers or squeezing into a subway car."

Grace smiled, already feeling lighter. "That's exactly what I need."

"Well, you are speaking my love language now!" Beth waved for Grace to follow her as she meandered through the store. "We've got the essentials, and then some, to get you properly outfitted while you're here."

The boutique was cozy and eclectic. Wooden beams stretched across the ceiling and plush throw rugs beneath the racks of clothing. Unlike the impersonal clothing stores in New York, Mountain Chic Boutique had character. It was filled with lovingly crafted displays of sensible clothing.

Beth led Grace to a section of jeans first, all of them folded meticulously on rustic wooden shelves. "Alright, now, jeans are a thing of beauty," Beth began with a wink as she pulled out a pair of dark-wash, straight-leg jeans. "These are durable enough for hiking, but comfortable enough for lounging around in. Trust me, girl, you'll want a few pairs of these." She handed the jeans to Grace. Then, motioning to a nearby shelf, she added, "We've also got these soft boyfriend jeans, a bit more relaxed. You'll love 'em."

Grace ran her fingers over the soft fabric, a small smile forming as she realized how much more comfortable these clothes would be compared to the stiff, tailored pantsuits she was used to. "These are nice," she admitted.

Beth chuckled. "Oh, sweetie, you're here to relax, not run board meetings. Trust me—a bit of comfort goes a long way. Ditch the business suits for a while. A soft pair of jeans and some cozy shirts are much better."

Grace nodded

"Now, let's see..." Beth continued, moving toward the next rack, "T-shirts!"

Grace followed, her eyes scanning the variety of soft, inviting tees displayed with care on wooden hangers. Some shirts featured whimsical prints—mountain landscapes, trees, peaceful bears lounging under a sky of stars with sayings like "Let the Outdoors Inside" or "Adventure Awaits." Others were simple solid colors—greens, blues, and other earthy tones.

Beth grabbed a few of the solid-colored tees and handed them over to Grace. "This material is as soft as a cloud, no joke. And the colors are perfect!" She gave an exaggerated wink.

Grace chuckled, running her fingers along the fabric and marveling at its softness. "These are nice."

"I knew you'd like them," Beth said, hanging a few more options over her arm. "You'll want a variety of colors for all those hikes Martha mentioned. And, speaking of hikes... let's get you some of these!" She said as she walked toward another rack displaying lightweight flannel shirts.

"This here is a Mountain Chic Boutique specialty," Beth explained, holding up a pastel flannel with rolled-up sleeves. "Breathable and light, but still warm enough for the cooler mountain air, as we edge further into fall. Trust me, layering is key around here. You never know when the temperature's going to pull a fast one on you."

Grace smiled, gripping the flannel with a surprising sense of excitement. While back in the city, she had always chosen sharp lines, immaculate blouses, and nothing less than perfectly tailored suits. Here in Laurel Ridge, she was already feeling drawn to the soft, layered approach that Beth was re-introducing her to. The flannels seemed like a perfect balance between laid-back and prepared.

Beth tilted her head, watching Grace explore the clothes with growing interest. "It's funny, right? You think you need your life so tailored, so perfectly buttoned up in the corporate world. But here? It's like nature forces you to untangle yourself." Beth paused, letting the words hang in the air before flashing another quick smile. "Alright, now how 'bout we pick out some yoga pants to seal the deal?"

Grace raised an eyebrow playfully. "I hope you know, city girls don't belly-crawl into workout clothes lightly."

"Honey, once you try on these yoga pants, you'll never wanna go back to whatever brand you're used too," Beth promised as she led Grace to the next display. "They're soft, stretchy, and can work just about anywhere—from hiking to lounging to impromptu dance parties. And when paired with a flannel, it's even better!"

Grace was already reaching for a pair of black yoga pants from the neatly folded stack. They looked perfect for relaxing and exploring the great outdoors. The lightweight material whispered beneath her fingers, promising both comfort and mobility.

While Grace contemplated grabbing a couple more pairs of yoga pants in other colors, Beth leaned in, hands on her hips and eyes glimmering with mischief.

"Soooo," Beth began, drawing out the word as if savoring the taste. "You're new in town, just here for a little while, right? Any particular reason? Or are you doing a 'find yourself in the mountains' kind of thing?"

Grace hesitated for a second, unsure how much she wanted to share.

"I guess you could say I needed a break—a chance to reset, clear my head. I've been working non-stop for years, and it was starting to catch up to me. I figured getting away from the city might help me, you know, breathe again."

Beth's teasing smile faded into something more reflective. She nodded slowly, taking in Grace's words like she was absorbing not just the surface meaning, but the layers of aching exhaustion beneath. "Oh, sweetie. You don't have to explain a thing. Sometimes, life has this way of draggin' you through the mud and what you really need is a good ol' rinse in the clean, cool rivers of West Virginia." She paused, then added with a laugh, "Literal or metaphorical. Your choice."

Grace chuckled, feeling the tension ease away. "You know, I think that's exactly what I need."

"Well, the mountains have a funny way of bringing out the truth in people," Beth said. "It's like you can't hide from yourself when you're surrounded by all this raw beauty. No skyscrapers, no deadlines, no noise. Just you, God, and a whole lot of time to think."

Grace nodded. "Yeah, I've already realized there's no escaping my thoughts out here in the peace and quiet."

Beth tilted her head ever so slightly, her gaze softening into something a little more knowing. "And maybe... you're not supposed to, sweetie. You've gotta stop sprinting sometime—and when you do, well, that's when God starts workin' on your heart. Turning things over that you didn't even know needed turning."

Grace felt Beth's words settle over her like a quiet invitation to release the firm grip she had on herself. The thought that this impromptu vacation might open up more than just vistas of scenic views left her introspective.

"Maybe you're right," Grace admitted.

Beth smiled, recognizing a woman in need of renewal without forcing her to admit it. "You'll get there, honey. These mountains have a way of showing you what you need when you least expect it," Beth said as she rested a hand on Grace's arm.

Grace nodded. "Thanks, Beth."

"Anytime, darlin'. Now, come on! Let's get you into a fitting room and make sure those pants fit you like a dream. We don't have all day to chat—you've got some struttin' around town to do in your fancy new clothes!" Beth's infectious grin returned, along with a playful wink.

The back-and-forth between them had Grace feeling lighter than she had in days. Maybe she had been mistaken about one thing—this town wasn't just a quiet bowl of serenity. It was filled with vibrancy, with welcoming people who didn't see her as a stranger walking through for a brief stay but embraced her as if she'd been part of their community all along.

Grace stepped into the fitting room, holding an armful of t-shirts, flannels, yoga pants, and jeans—all of which felt like tiny pieces of a new identity she hoped to build. Before she even closed the door, Beth's voice rang out, her energy unable to be contained.

"And sweetheart, don't forget! You wear those clothes like a mountain queen. Own it, girl. Own it."

Grace grinned as she shut the door behind herself. She gazed at her reflection in the mirror—hair slightly out of place, face showing the wear and tear of recent stress, but her lips turned up into something genuine.

Beth's words danced through her mind as she started trying on clothes.

Stepping out of the fitting room, Grace twirled in one of the flannel shirts paired with jeans.

Beth clapped her hands, looking at her like a proud stage mom. "Now there's a girl who's ready to own Laurel Ridge."

Grace beamed. And for the first time since arriving in this sleepy town, she believed her.

# Chapter 10

Grace parked in front of Earl's Hardware, glancing up at the wooden sign hanging above the door. It swayed in the breeze, declaring the shop's no-nonsense purpose in bold, block letters: "Hardware Store." She had to chuckle. The simplicity of it was endearing.

She pushed open the door, and yet another bell jingled above her head, announcing her presence.

*This town has a thing with bells.* She thought to herself.

The smell of polished wood, freshly cut lumber, and a hint of metal assaulted her senses. She paused for a moment, taking it all in. It was vast but cozy, filled with everything from tools to home goods. Shelves were stacked high with neatly organized rows of nuts, bolts, paint cans, and even, to her delight, an aisle boasting an assortment of kitchenware.

"Good mornin'!" a friendly voice boomed, interrupting her brief admiration of the unexpected orderliness of the store. A large man came into view from behind a nearby shelving unit, wiping his hands on a well-worn rag that hung from his apron. His face, round and ruddy from a lifetime spent outdoors, lit up with genuine warmth as he approached her.

"Well, you're a new face!" he said, his voice thick with the twang of someone who'd never spent a day outside the mountains. He extended a hand, calloused but gentle. "Name's Earl Smith. Been runnin' this place for—well, longer than I care to admit."

Grace smiled and took his hand, feeling grounded by the man's unassuming presence. There was something about Earl that made her feel like she'd known him for years, despite meeting him just now—that small-town charm radiating from him like the heat of a summer sun.

"Grace Anderson," she introduced herself, hoping she sounded confident, though a part of her felt awkward in this tiny haven of tools and country comforts. "I'm... visiting Laurel Ridge."

Earl's eyes twinkled with amusement. "Ahh, the city gal who's trading in skyscrapers for treetops for a little while. Martha told me about you. She said you stopped by the diner."

Grace grinned, not the least bit surprised. "That sounds about right. Martha's great—and yes, I think I'll be here for a little while, trying to... figure things out."

Earl nodded, his expression softening. "Well, you came to the right town for that. There's no place better than here to take a little break from life, believe me."

She cleared her throat, trying to shake the emotion that threatened to rise.

"I'm thinking you're right," she said, her voice a little quieter than before.

Earl smiled. "Now then," he said, clapping his hands together as if to shift the mood from reflective to practical. "What can I help you find today, Miss Grace? Martha said you might be lookin' for a few essentials."

Relieved for the change of pace, Grace nodded. "Yes. I'm looking for a coffee maker—a simple, electric one. And a blanket. It's... cooler at night than I expected."

Earl chuckled. "You'll find the nights here can surprise you. Even in summer, the mountain air can turn crisp when the sun goes down. A good blanket'll do the trick."

He motioned for her to follow, leading her through the winding aisles of his store like a tour guide welcoming her into a hidden, well-loved world.

"This place is incredible," Grace blurted out without even thinking as they passed by wooden bins on shelves filled with everything a person could need. "I wasn't expecting...all of this."

Earl glanced over his shoulder, pride clear in his beaming smile. "It ain't fancy like what you're used to, I reckon. But we've got everything you might need here, whether you're fixing up your kitchen or gettin' ready to tackle those mountain trails. I've been at this long enough to know what folks need, even when they don't know it themselves."

Grace continued to follow, her curiosity piqued as they turned a corner, arriving in the small appliances section of the store.

"Here we are. Got a couple of different brands of coffee makers," he said as he tapped a finger on one box. "This one's as basic as they come. Just an on-and-off switch, no bells or whistles. But it'll get you your coffee, strong and hot, every morning without fail."

Grace looked at the sleek, no-frills design and smiled. Simple was perfect. After her enlightening experience with the percolator, she wasn't looking for anything complicated. "That's exactly what I need," she said, not bothering to second-guess herself.

Earl nodded approvingly and handed the box to her. "Good choice, Miss Grace. Practical and straightforward. That's the way to go. Now, let's get you that blanket."

As they made their way across the store, Earl continued chatting, his words flowing as if he were with an old friend. He shared a tip about navigating the weather and bits of simple country wisdom that Grace found refreshing.

"You know," Earl said as he guided her through the aisles, "this town ain't as big as some might think, but it's filled with good folks. People look out for each other around here. It's a different sort of life, slower and simpler than what I reckon you're used to. But maybe that's just what you need right now. You know, a chance to breathe."

Grace nodded. "It does feel... different. But in a good way."

Earl looked back at her, his expression kind but cautious, as if he were trying to measure her words against what he sensed from her. "You don't owe me an explanation, but something tells me you've got a lot more goin' on up here," he lifted a hand to tap his temple, "than just wanting some peace and quiet."

Grace swallowed, looking down at the coffee maker in her arms as if it might distract her. She didn't know Earl. In fact, she didn't know anyone in Laurel Ridge anymore to air out all her thoughts and feelings and yet, here she was, in a hardware store of all places, having what felt like one of the most insightful conversations she'd had in a while.

"I've been through... a lot recently," she admitted, her fingers tightening around the box. "I thought coming here might help me figure out what's next."

Earl nodded. "Sometimes life kicks you, hard. Leaves you wonderin' and wanderin'. But you're here now, Grace, and that says more than enough about what you're hopin' to find. You'll get there."

His words settled over her like a warm coat during winter. Grace let the sentiment sink in as they arrived at a display stacked with blankets of various sizes, styles, and thicknesses.

"You said one good blanket, right?" Earl asked.

Grace smiled, grateful for the shift in conversation. "Yes, I just need something to get me through the chilly nights. What would you suggest?"

Earl stroked his chin, narrowing his eyes as though considering each option carefully. "Let's see here," he mused, rooting through the stacks until he pulled out a thick, deep-blue blanket that looked as soft as a cloud. "Now, this one's made of fleece. Thick enough to keep out the mountain chill, but not so heavy you'll feel you're buried under it. It's been one of our bestsellers for years."

Grace reached out to touch it, feeling the velvety texture beneath her fingers. It definitely had the cozy factor she was looking for. "This is perfect," she said, already imagining snuggling beneath it in front of the cabin's fireplace. Once she gathered the energy to actually build a fire, that is.

Earl nodded, pleased with himself. "Good, good. Glad I could help. Anything else on your list, or have we got you covered?"

"Well, maybe you could help me with something else." Grace hesitated. "There's a lovely fireplace in the cabin where I'm staying. I'd really like to use it, but I'm not exactly sure how."

Earl scratched the side of his head, clearly trying to hide a grin. "Well, that's somethin' you don't hear every day, 'specially 'round these parts. Your tellin' me you've never lit a fire before?"

Grace let out a small laugh, feeling her cheeks warm. "Not unless you count candles. I searched online and found some brief instructions on how to work the fireplace, but I'm a little nervous."

Earl chuckled, "Fireplaces are a little more... demanding than a cinnamon-scented candle. You might just burn down the entire cabin if you're not careful!"

Grace pursed her lips in mock seriousness. "That's exactly what I'm trying to avoid. So, I was wondering if you had any tips. Or... something to make it a little easier?"

Earl straightened up and rubbed his chin in exaggerated contemplation, as if lighting fires was a life-or-death universal challenge. "Well, first thing is, ya gotta know your wood. You don't wanna use green wood. It's still got moisture in it, and it'll just smoke like the devil's takin' a drag. What you want is seasoned firewood. Nice and dry."

"Seasoned wood, okay," Grace repeated, nodding with exaggerated seriousness, as if committing it to memory.

"And kindling," Earl added. "You're gonna want plenty of that. Little sticks, twigs, some smaller splits of wood to get things going. Big logs ain't gonna catch fire on their own, no matter how much you try to sweet-talk 'em."

Grace groaned jokingly, rubbing her head. "And here I was, practicing my best fireplace pickup lines."

Earl laughed, shaking his head. "Well, that might work in some places, but a fireplace doesn't fall for charm too easy." He pointed toward a shelf in the store's corner. "I have some fire starters. Little packets you can stick under the wood. They'll give ya a jumpstart. Once the kindling gets going, you'll wanna add the bigger logs, but not before it's good and strong, or you'll just smother the whole thing."

Her eyes lit up. "Fire starters sound perfect! I'll take a few of those, please?"

"Sure thing," Earl replied, shuffling over to grab a few. "Trust me, even folks who've been doing this for years use these sometimes. Ain't no shame in it." He handed her a pack of small, waxy-looking cubes.

"Thanks," Grace said, taking the fire starters. "I'm not sure if I could've figured this out on my own. I've had enough mishaps lately. The last thing I need is to accidentally burn down a forest."

Earl suppressed a smile. "Well, I'm sure Smokey the Bear doesn't want a spare job right now. He's near ready for a long winter's nap, huh?"

Grace laughed. "Agreed."

"Anything else you need help with?"

"I think this covers everything for now," Grace said as they made their way to the checkout counter.

"By the way," Earl drawled as he rang up her purchases, "once you get your fire going, there's something mighty satisfying about sitting back and watching the flames. Warms ya up, both inside and out. Might do ya some good to just sit back and enjoy a quiet fire of the evenin'."

Grace smiled. "I hope to do just that, Earl. I really do, and thank you."

"My pleasure," Earl responded. "You take care, now—and if you need anything else, you know where to find me."

Offering a grateful smile, Grace gathered her bags and headed toward the door, the tiny bell jingling as she stepped into the sunlight once more.

# Chapter 11

Grace parked the SUV again and cut the engine, leaving the windows down just enough to let the mountain breeze trickle through. She inhaled, filling her lungs with the clean air.

She'd driven here without thinking much, just following the directions Martha had given her. Adventure Tours sat on the banks of the New River. Grace could see the flowing river from where she sat. The main building had a cozy, lodge-like feel, a destination for anyone seeking outdoor adventures. The gentle sound of wind chimes made the place feel welcoming and enchanting.

As she stepped out of the SUV, Grace hesitated, unsure whether to walk straight in or linger for a moment to take it all in. Several cars were parked nearby, but she noticed there weren't many people mingling around.

Inside, the store gleamed under warm lights, which highlighted the rustic interior. It was a treasure trove of rugged adventure gear, most of which Grace had never seen up close and in person, let alone used. The scent of cedarwood clung to the air, mingling with the earthy smell of leather and faint whiffs of motor oil from all-terrain vehicles on display toward the back of the store.

Mountain bikes of every size and model hung from heavy steel hooks, some fat tire bikes for rugged trails, and others sleek racing models for the more daring riders.

Nearby, shelves were crammed with tents that came in every shape and size: lightweight models for backpackers, sturdy ones for family camps, and even ultralight shelters suited for mountaineering expeditions. A display table boasted waterproof backpacks, carabiners, and coils of climbing rope.

There were racks of fishing poles, each categorized by type—fly rods, spinning reels, and a variety of other setups. Beneath them, tackle boxes brimming with colorful lures, sinkers, and bobbers that promised hours of patient, sunlit days by the water.

As Grace wandered, she came upon an aisle of thick soled hiking boots, all neatly arranged beneath maps that covered almost every inch of wall space behind them.

She wandered to another area of the store, where metal racks displayed kayaks and canoes of bright yellows, blues, and reds, their hollow insides reflecting the overhead lights. There were oars, paddles, and inflatable life jackets hanging nearby like sentinels waiting for the next big trip out onto the water.

High above it all, the walls were lined with cured animal pelts, the soft fur glowing in the light. Wolf, deer, and beaver hides, each one telling the story of the hunts that had taken place in the wild terrain outdoors.

Polished racks on the far side of the room held rifles and hand guns in protective cases, flanked by glass cabinets showcasing hand-crafted hunting knives, along with compasses and GPS devices.

Grace paused at the center of it all, feeling as though she'd wandered into a wilderness museum, an unspoken invitation to lose herself in the adventures that awaited her outside these walls. She took a deliberate, deep breath, grounding herself for a moment.

"Well, well. Look what the rush in the river brought in."

Her pulse jumped as the warm voice tugged her thoughts back to the present.

Ben Turner. His sleeves were rolled up, showcasing muscular forearms dusted with a few freckles from hours under the sun. His brown locks were just as she remembered from their brief meeting at Martha's Diner—tousled, like he never gave them a second thought.

"Grace, right?" His voice held an easy warmth.

"Yes. Thought I'd swing by. Look around," Grace said, a little flustered.

Ben's grin widened. "Well, feel free. We've got quite a bit to offer... if you're up for some adventure."

"Okay, honestly, that is what I am interested in. I'd like to see the area a bit more," Grace replied.

Ben took a moment to ponder her words, shifting into a more relaxed pose that hinted at a playful side.

"Well, we've got plenty of options," Ben said. "Let me grab a brochure for you about our kayaking trips, hiking tours, and weekend getaways over at Old Mountainhead. It depends on how rugged or scenic you'd like your tour to be."

"I don't have a clue what type of tour I'd like. Something not too crazy ... or rugged," she replied.

Ben chuckled, his friendly demeanor putting her at ease. "No problem, ma'am," he replied. "Maybe a hiking tour or a beginner's kayaking tour?"

The corners of Grace's mouth turned up as she considered his suggestions. "A beginner's kayaking tour sounds perfect," she said, her heart picking up pace at the thought of gliding through water. "I've always wanted to try kayaking, but I've never had the chance."

Ben nodded, an encouraging smile breaking across his face. "Well, it's a great choice! The New River is beautiful, especially at this time of year. I'll make sure to keep you in calmer waters. No one wants an unexpected swim during their first kayaking experience." His playful smirk reassured her.

"Thanks," Grace said, feeling a sense of relief wash over her. "I appreciate that."

Ben grabbed a colorful brochure from a display nearby, filled with images of energetic groups paddling in bright kayaks against a backdrop of lush greenery. He handed the brochure over, their fingers brushing. A connection that was fleeting but illuminating. She felt her cheeks flush.

"So, you're up for some fun and adventure?" Ben asked with a glint in his hazel eyes that made Grace's heart race a little faster.

"Absolutely," she replied.

Ben continued, "Okay, our schedule for tours today is already full, but would tomorrow be ok?"

"Tomorrow works for me," Grace said, a mixture of anticipation and anxiety simmering within her.

"Great! I'll pencil you in," Ben said, his voice smooth and reassuring. "Just be here around 9:00 AM. I promise you're in for a memorable experience."

She admired the smooth ease with which he handled the logistics. "Sounds good. I'll bring my appetite for adventure," she added playfully, feeling herself relax further with each word exchanged.

Ben laughed, the sound infectious and warm. "Sounds good."

A moment passed where his hazel eyes scanned her, friendly yet a little appraising, before his smile shifted into something more thoughtful. "You're staying in the old Anderson cabin, aren't you?"

Her breath hitched. "I am. I own the cabin now. My aunt left it to me after she passed," she answered.

Ben nodded, his gaze lingering. "I thought I saw you there yesterday on the back porch," he said. "I remember your Aunt Imogene. She was a kind soul. Hard to believe she's been gone for...let's see...quite a while now, right?"

Grace swallowed, surprised—and touched—that he remembered. "Yes... she passed about two years ago."

"Imogene had a beautiful place. Her view from the back porch is amazing," Ben continued.

"It is," she said, and glanced around the store before continuing. "Ben, I need some help with something else as well."

"Don't tell me you want to dive into extreme sports or something."

Grace chuckled, shaking her head. "Not quite. I want to do a little hiking while I'm here, and I didn't come prepared. I need a good pair of boots. And I'm guessing I may find a decent pair here."

Ben grinned. "Yep, you're in the right place for hiking footwear. Of course, I am the boot whisperer in this area."

Grace raised an eyebrow, amused. "Boot whisperer? That sounds... well, let's just say I'm not filled with confidence."

"Hey, don't knock it till you try the Ben method. I've successfully navigated the wild world of footwear many times. Trust me, you'll be as happy as a duck in waterproofs when you're out hiking." Ben said as he led her to the aisle of hiking boots.

She laughed, "Alright, Mr. Boot Whisperer."

"Okay, first things first. You want something durable but comfortable. You're not climbing Mount Everest, but you also don't want to feel like your feet are being held hostage by a couple of bricks. Let's start with these."

He pulled down a pair of women's all-terrain boots. "These are designed for beginners, so nothing too fancy, but they'll give you enough support and protection. Plus, if you get chased by a mountain lion, you know... you can at least outrun it."

"That's reassuring," Grace said with a chuckle.

Ben handed them to her. "Try 'em on. And while we're at it, let me grab you a few pairs of thick hiking socks."

"Special hiking socks?" Grace blinked, slipping off her shoes.

"Yup, you need them to prevent, uh, something I like to call 'blisters from the ninth circle of hiking misery.' See, your boots might feel great at first, but once you've walked a few miles, even the best ones can rub like a violin on fire. Thick hiking socks cushion your feet and help with moisture control, which is a fancy way of saying they'll stop you from having to peel your boots off your feet along with half your skin."

Grace winced. "Well, that's a horrifying image. Give me all the socks."

Ben chuckled, tossing her a pair. "Try these. When you wear them, it feels like you're walking on clouds."

Grace slid on the socks and then stuffed her feet into the boots. After a few tentative steps, she turned to him, raising her eyebrows. "Whoa, these feel... solid. How do I look? Like I belong outdoors, or more like a lost tourist?"

Ben stepped back, scanned her, and then nodded with mock seriousness. "You officially look like someone who's about to ask for the Wi-Fi password at a campsite."

"Perfect, exactly the vibe I was going for," Grace said, laughing.

"Well, you nailed it," Ben said, grinning. "Anyway, break in those boots at home. Walk around, do fun activities like... vacuuming or air guitar... that kind of thing. You'll be ready for the trails in no time. Just don't wait till the last minute or your feet will revolt during your first hike."

"Got it. Break them in, or hiker misery blisters will break loose," she deadpanned.

"Exactly, and wear the socks. Don't forget the socks," Ben said.

Grace smiled, tapping her boot heals together. "Alright, these are the ones then. And I'll have you know I'll be taking all of that air guitar advice to heart."

"Good. You'll be thanking me when you're halfway up a trail, blister-free, shredding invisible chords," Ben said, heading towards the check-out counter.

Grace followed. "Thanks, Ben. You might just make a serious hiker out of me yet."

"Don't thank me," Ben said. "Just name the first mountain you conquer after me."

Grace laughed and said, "I greatly appreciate your kindness. I'm kind of at a loss for what to do while I'm visiting, apart from dawdling around town. The area is gorgeous and so full of life. I want to get out and enjoy it all while I'm here."

"Like I always say, Laurel Ridge has a way of surprising newcomers," he replied. "And hey, if you find yourself looking for more to do while you're here, just let me know. We can set you up with all kinds of tours in the area, and I can give you some tips on the best local spots to visit."

"Really? That would be very helpful," Grace replied, feeling a flicker of excitement dance in her chest. "I'd love to hear what else you recommend."

"Deal," he said, his expression shifting to a more serious note. "Say ... what if we meet at the diner around six this evening? I can tell you about some interesting things you might want to check out over dinner?"

Grace felt a thrill course through her. "That sounds great. I'd love to!"

"Perfect. Martha's Diner, six o'clock. I'll be there," he said with a smile.

With one last wave, he turned back to his work as Grace departed the store.

As she walked towards her SUV, her heart raced—not from anxiety, but from excitement.

What if this small-town adventure held the keys to the renewal she was searching for? What if, within this quaint town and its steadfast inhabitants, she found more than just a temporary escape?

As the trees and mountains enveloped her once again, Grace drove with purpose, anticipation bubbling within her. Her thoughts darted to how she could fill her time for the rest of the afternoon. She could explore more shops in town or enjoy a leisurely walk before heading to the grocery store.

Grace pulled off the narrow, winding road and parked in a small gravel lot at the base of a forested trailhead. A faded wooden sign stated that this was the start of a trail that would lead to a lookout point she'd spotted earlier on a map at Adventure Tours. The gravel crunched beneath her feet as she stepped out of the SUV, and she paused for a moment, surveying the surroundings. Tall trees towered overhead, and the trail itself was a mixture of dirt, pine needles, and small stones.

Unzipping her jacket, Grace inhaled, savoring the crisp, earthy scent of the mountains. The trail seemed well-worn, clear enough to follow, yet uneven in a few places. Nothing too daunting for her sneakers, she hoped.

As she walked further into the woods, sunlight broke through the branches, lighting up patches of wildflowers peeking through the bushes. With each step, the friendly sounds of nature welcomed her: birds chirping, leaves rustling, and the occasional buzz of an insect breezing by. Grace felt herself relax as she followed the winding path, the world around her coming to life with every step. It was as if nature were wrapping her in a gentle hug, easing the tension in her shoulders.

Thoughts about the city faded away, replaced by the stunning beauty of the area. She paused at a clearing where the trail opened into a small overlook.

Looking out across the valley, she marveled at the breathtaking view. Rolling hills in different shades of green, dotted with bright wildflowers that danced in the breeze. The New River wound through the landscape, sparkling like a winding ribbon under the sun.

A wave of gratitude washed over her, unexpected and deep.

Grace wiped her forehead with the back of her hand, feeling energized, but also thinking about what to do next. The desire to explore more bubbled inside her, and for the first time in years, she felt alive again.

Grace continued along the trail, winding through the tall trees.

She soon reached a small waterfall sparkling over a series of rocks, the sound of the rushing water enhancing her sense of peace. She stood for a moment, soaking in its beauty, allowing herself to be present in this moment. Leaning against a sturdy tree, she closed her eyes, listening, as the world whispered to her. No deadlines, no responsibilities, just endless possibilities ahead

# Chapter 12

Grace prepared for her visit back to Martha's Diner. Her pulse quickened at the thought of seeing Ben again. Perhaps the town's charm was growing on her also, or maybe it was more about the people within it. Ben, specifically.

She stood before a mirror, trying on the casual shirt she'd purchased that very day. Something too simple for her previous life, but here, it felt perfect. She added a light jacket as insurance against the evening chill. Running her fingers through her hair one last time, admiring the way her appearance balanced polished composure with an easy casualness.

A smile tugged at the corners of her mouth as she took one last survey of herself, convincing herself she was ready for the evening ahead.

Stepping out of her cabin, she locked the door behind her and hurried to the SUV. The drive to town felt a little more familiar now, a testament to just how quickly one could adapt to a new rhythm when a person slowed down long enough to allow it.

Soon, Grace pulled into the parking lot near Martha's and shut off the engine. Splotches of sunlight filtered through the trees that surrounded the town, casting elongated shadows across the brick-paved streets.

Grace checked her reflection once more before stepping out of the SUV. The low hum of chatter from the diner could be heard as she approached the entrance.

Nearing the diner's door, an uninvited voice stopped her in her tracks.

The voice, so familiar yet so out of place here, sent a chill up Grace's spine as though someone had just doused her in ice water. She froze, her fingers tightening around the strap of her purse instinctively, a flicker of dread curling around her chest. She turned to face the source of her growing unease.

Standing just a few feet away, with a smug expression that sent her heart plummeting, was Michael Clayton, a journalist she had frequently sparred with back in New York. He had always been an ambitious opportunist, the kind of man who trawled for scandals like a fisherman on a long ocean voyage. His beady eyes locked on her with the same deceptive sympathy he always used just before swooping in for the kill.

*Oh, no. Not here. Not now.*

A sharp knife of anxiety slid into Grace's gut, and her breath hitched. "Michael? What ... what are you doing here?"

She hated how breathless her voice sounded, a rising tide of panic swelling inside her. Michael's saccharine smile widened, like a used car salesman sweeping in with a weekend deal.

"Following up, of course," he drawled, his tone smooth as glass. "Wasn't easy tracking you down, Grace, but considering your... colorful history, I thought it'd be worth the effort."

The world narrowed to the point of suffocation around Grace as his words hit their mark. She couldn't tell which shook her more—the audacity of his intrusion, or the realization that her situation had caught up with her so quickly, in yet another unexpected strike.

What did he want, anyway? It wasn't like there was more blood to draw from this stone. Michael Clayton could never let sleeping dogs lie.

His gaze didn't waver as he watched her, his smile never reaching his eyes. They gleamed with veiled opportunism, sharp as a vulture's beak that had once again spotted his prey. "This must be a significant departure from the life you're used to in New York," he continued, coiling like a serpent ready to strike. "It can't be easy keeping your head above water when you're drowning in unanswered questions."

Each breath was harder, like pushing air through a sieve. The serene town dissolved behind Michael's words, bit by bit, drawing all of Grace's defenses sharply to the forefront. She battled against the impulse to flee back to the SUV, to drive away and keep running until Michael and his pointed questions no longer lingered in the rearview mirror.

Swallowing against the rising spurt of panic, Grace tried to muster her poise. "Michael, you're trespassing on my privacy right now," she said, a tremor in her voice. "Whatever it is you think you need to know, you won't find it here. Just... go back to New York."

But the journalist only flicked his gaze around, as though assessing the small town for the headline it could lend him. "Come on, Grace, don't be like that. It's just a little chit-chat—for old time's sake." From his pocket, Michael produced a slim recorder, waving it absently. "It's not every day I find my next story unraveling itself in a place like this. People want to hear about Grace Anderson after her fall."

The phrase felt like molten lava dripping into her veins. The urge to slap that arrogant smile off his face simmered just beneath her skin, barely restrained by years' worth of tightly controlled composure. But here, in this quiet place, with the sun slipping under the far-off peaks and the townsfolk wandering obliviously down the sidewalks, Grace didn't want to make an even bigger scene. She knew Michael craved and needed her reaction.

Steeling herself, she stood tall and locked eyes with him. "There is no story, Michael, not for you. Now, please... leave, before I call the police and ask them to remove you for harassment."

Michael's smirk only deepened as he took a step closer, a challenge. The scent of his cologne, sharp and overpowering, skirted the edge of her senses, reminding Grace of boardrooms and power plays.

"I don't think you'd want to cause a scene here, Grace," he said, his voice slithering around her composure like ivy slowly choking a tree of its vitality. "Do you really believe, after everything that transpired, a quiet little mountain retreat can hide you from the truth? You're too smart to think that the past just... disappears, aren't you?"

Grace was at a breaking point, her composure crumbling at the edges. A part of her screamed to run, to retreat into the shadows, out of reach of any consequence or revelation. Another side of her, a quieter, stronger side, told her to hold her ground, to refuse to let him tarnish what little peace she had gained. But before she could even decide on a response, another voice pierced the tension, and she felt herself exhale, albeit shakily.

"Excuse me. Is there a problem here?"

Grace turned to see Bean approaching.

The contrast between his understated presence and Michael's invasive one hit her in the chest like a gust of clean air blowing through a storm. Her pulse slowing its frantic race as the journalist's hold on her began to splinter.

Michael sized up the newcomer with the calculating eyes of someone assessing the dynamic that had just shifted. Grace could see the gears turning in his mind, registering Ben not just as some passerby, but as someone intent on obstructing his access to her.

"Just catching up with an old acquaintance," Michael said with syrupy charm, but Grace could see just the barest hint of alarm now flickering across his otherwise predatory gaze. "Didn't catch your name, Ben, is it?"

Ben didn't answer right away, instead stepping in front of Grace, his broad shoulders drawing a line between her and Michael that now felt nothing short of impermeable. His eyes, a steely edge as they met the journalist's brazen stare.

"It is. And how do you know my name?" Ben replied in mild tones, the words like an unsheathed knife hidden behind the curtain of calm that defined him. "Forget it. I'm not too sure I'd like to find out. You must be mistaken, though, this hardly looks like a catch-up between you and Miss Grace. Seems more like you're badgering a lady who clearly doesn't wish to speak to you. Is that how you talk to someone you call an 'acquaintance'?"

A twitch danced along Michael's jawline. Grace held her breath, noticing how the air between the three of them felt charged.

"I see how it is. You must be the local hero around here, always quick to rescue a damsel in distress?" the journalist commented, sarcasm sliding off his tongue like grease.

Ben didn't even flinch. "Only when there's someone clearly worth protecting."

Grace watched the irritation flash in Michael's eyes. He seemed less sure of himself now that Ben challenged the nature of his encroachment.

Still not missing a beat, Michael declined to break posture before the growing threat just inches away. "Be that as it may, some of us have jobs to do—information to gather," he resumed. "What happened with Grace and her uncle, back in New York, hasn't exactly reached a... satisfying conclusion to those following her story. Engagement makes the marketplace, as they say."

"Look, I have no idea what you're talking about, but I do know this, you're not a very kind person, and you're not welcome here in Laurel Ridge," Ben said, a note of disdain creeping into his voice.

Michael opened his mouth to retort, but then thought better of it, his expression shifting into something more appraising. "Hey man, I'm not here to cause trouble. I'm here to uncover the truth. It's what people like me do."

"No. You're here to exploit someone at their most vulnerable. And in a small town like this? Not happening." Despite his calm tone, Ben's words conveyed something non-negotiable. He crossed his arms in front of him.

For a brief, writhing moment, no one spoke. Grace's pulse thrummed with an odd mix of relief and suspense. Relief that someone had drawn a line against the onslaught of demands that this scrappy journalist represented; suspense, uncertain whether Michael, a man rarely known for stepping down, really would.

But Ben's posture, commanding and rooted, seemed to chip away at Michael's determination. Michael recognized what many prestigious New Yorkers had yet to learn—that, against an opponent with an immovable moral backbone, raw ambition faded into mere bravado.

Michael let out a stiff sigh. "Alright... alright," he said, waving a dismissive hand. "I can see you enjoy playing the knight in shining armor. A quaint trope to entertain, I'm sure. But mark my words, Grace, we're not finished. Not yet. People will still be watching... regardless of where you hide."

Grace's chest clenched as Michael's ugly words burrowed into her thoughts. But she stood resolutely behind Ben, willing herself not to let Michael's poison seep into her resolve.

As Michael took his leave, turning on his heels with his coattails flapping behind him, Grace felt a heavy, oppressive weight pull away from her shoulders. Ben's presence, still standing firm, felt somehow larger than it had before.

"Are you okay?" Ben asked.

It took her a moment to respond—her tongue almost too heavy against the residue of nerves still flooding her senses. "Thanks to you," she said, an undercurrent of gratitude pooling tight against her throat. "Ben... I just ...I don't know what to say. If you'd not shown up, I don't..." She didn't let herself finish.

Suspended between this dual world of standing firm and struggling to breathe, Grace blinked the world back into sense.

Ben's brow drew together, his eyes narrowing just enough to shade his gaze beneath the wide brim of his cap. "You don't have to explain anything, Grace," he reassured her, his tone tender. "I saw what that guy was doing. It was wrong, and I wasn't about to let him corner you like that."

His words settled into Grace like a soothing balm against the wound that had nearly ripped open her composure just minutes ago. She observed the man before her. Ben was more reserved and rooted than any man she'd ever known.

"Well... Thank you," Grace murmured, though her voice still held a hint of the lingering tense aftermath. "I never... expected Michael to follow me here."

"Well, it seems he needs a better sense of direction," Ben commented, inserting just a touch of humor into his observation. "He should give up journalism and try taking a spin at map-making."

A small laugh escaped Grace. So rare it was for someone to inject humor without diminishing the legitimacy of her concerns.

"Ben, how long have you been rescuing women being cornered in distress?" Grace asked.

Ben chuckled, his easy-going smile returning. "I'm going to guess you don't really want a full answer to that," he replied casually, but with a note of playful warning. "Let's just say it happens more often than you'd imagine."

The tension in Grace's chest unraveled. "Is that so?" she quipped back, the smallest part of her intrigued by the steady, dependable calm of this man who'd defended her with both ease and purpose. "Guess there's more to life in Laurel Ridge than I realized."

Ben's smile became a full, self-satisfied grin. "I'd say so," he agreed.

# Chapter 13

The cozy ambiance of Martha's Diner felt like a warm embrace as Ben and Grace settled into a quiet booth by a window. The aroma of fried chicken, mixed with a hint of apple pie and freshly brewed coffee, wafted through the space, mingling with the sound of clinking plates and simple conversation. The diner was bustling but in a relaxed, unhurried way.

"So, Grace," he began, his hazel eyes glinting with curiosity, "what's one thing about this town you've found surprising so far?"

Grace leaned back, tapping a thoughtful finger against her chin. "Besides the fact that everyone genuinely seems to like each other?" She chuckled. "I think it's how peaceful everything is. No one here seems... hurried."

Ben grinned, nodding. "Yeah, it's easy to get used to. Though, don't let it fool you—small-town folk have their own kind of hustle. It just runs at a slower pace. Gives you time to enjoy things."

"Like the stack of pancakes you had for breakfast the other morning?" Grace teased, her eyes sparkling with amusement.

"Exactly," Ben laughed. "Why rush when there's good food involved?"

The two fell into a peaceful rhythm of conversation over dinner. Ben had ordered the grilled salmon, whereas Grace had opted for a hearty chicken pot pie—a far cry from the sleek, calorie-conscious meals she'd been used to in the city.

"Have you always lived in Laurel Ridge?" Grace asked between bites of food.

Ben looked out the window for a moment before turning back to her. "Born and raised," he said with a note of pride. "I took over the Adventure Tours business not too long after my parents passed away, though back then it wasn't as big as it is now. The land, the river, and the surrounding area have always called to me. I can't imagine living anywhere else."

Grace felt a pang of envy. The connection Ben had with this place—it was something she'd never known. "You seem so... grounded."

Ben smiled, touched by the comment. "I think it's easy when you're surrounded by nature and good people. It keeps you honest... humbles you. The mountains, the river, the people here—they have a way of reminding you just how small you are in the grand scheme of things."

"That sounds... nice," Grace murmured, more to herself than him. She looked down at her plate, her thoughts swirling around the idea of being part of something larger, something meaningful.

Ben leaned forward, a note of gentle insistence in his voice. "I sense you're struggling with something. I'm not sure what, and I don't need to know. You don't have to have it all figured out right now. You're allowed to just... be."

Grace's chest tightened at his words. "I'm working on it," she admitted, giving him a small but sincere smile.

Before the conversation could go any deeper, the bell above the diner's door jingled, signaling the arrival of new customers. Grace looked up to find a tall man with neatly combed silver hair entering with a cheerful, petite woman by his side. They greeted Martha, chatting briefly before their eyes scanned the diner.

"Evening, Ben!" the man called out with a wave as he spotted their booth.

Ben's face lit up with recognition. "Pastor Eli! Claire!"

Grace tensed, unprepared for introductions. The couple made their way over, each exuding a warmth that immediately put her at ease.

Pastor Eli extended his hand to Grace, his grip firm but kind. "And who's this? A new friend?"

Ben smiled at Grace, then back at the couple. "Pastor Eli, Claire, this is Grace Anderson. She's here visiting for a little while."

Claire's face brightened as she shook Grace's hand. "Welcome to Laurel Ridge, Grace! We're so glad you've chosen to spend some time with us."

"Thank you, it's... it's lovely to meet you both," Grace said, still adjusting to the warmth of personal interactions she wasn't quite used to anymore.

Pastor Eli chuckled good-naturedly, his eyes crinkling with kindness. "You've settled in with Ben here. Good choice. He's one of the finest folks around these parts."

Grace blushed. "He's been very kind," she said, shooting a small smile at Ben, who returned it with a modest nod.

"I like to think kindness is what we do best around here," Claire chimed in. "And if you need anything while you're here, you just let us know."

"I'll remember that and thank you," Grace said, her smile growing more comfortable.

"Good, good," Eli nodded, his tone gentle and grandfatherly. "And you're most welcome to join us for Sunday service at the Laurel Ridge Community Church. We'd be happy to have you."

"Oh, well..." Grace hesitated.

"No pressure," Pastor Eli added, sensing her hesitation. "You come if you'd like to. Everyone who walks through those church doors is a friend."

Claire reached out and squeezed Grace's hand. "That's right. And until then, you just enjoy your time here in our little slice of paradise."

Grace could almost feel herself relax in response to such genuine warmth. "Thanks... I'll think about it."

"We have a harvest festival coming up soon," Claire continued, "full of food, games, and crafts. You should definitely come if you're still here!"

"There's going to be a huge pie-baking contest," Pastor Eli added with a wink. "We might even have Ben here put his skills to the test."

Grace couldn't keep a laugh from bubbling up. "Ben? Pie-baking?"

Ben rolled his eyes, though his grin remained as wide as a sunbeam. "You can thank Claire for that one. She roped me into the pie-baking competition once and once was enough."

Grace made a mental note to find out more about this harvest festival.

"Well, we won't keep you," Pastor Eli said with a smile as he glanced around the bustling diner. "Just wanted to say hello to you folks and welcome you properly, Grace."

"Thank you," she replied.

The couple bid them both farewell. Ben watched them go with an amused smile, his gaze drifting back to Grace the moment they were out of earshot.

"They're nice," Grace murmured, sipping her coffee. "Friendly."

"That's the thing about small towns. Most everyone is friendly." Ben said.

Their conversation resumed, filled with talk of mountain trails, hidden waterfalls, and local legends that stitched the fabric of Laurel Ridge together. Through it all, Grace found her previous anxieties slipping into the background, replaced with genuine curiosity and, dare she admit it, enjoyment? Ben, with his endless stories and unabashed love for the land, was a comforting presence—a symbol of stability in a world that had almost spun out of control for her.

Soon enough, the evening at Martha's came to a close. Grace and Ben walked back out into the evening air, the quiet of the night settling over the town like a soft blanket. Streetlamps bathed the sidewalks in gentle light, and crickets began their nightly serenade.

Ben stopped at the corner where their paths would diverge, turning to her with a smile. "I'll see you tomorrow at nine in the morning, then?"

"Wouldn't miss it," Grace replied, her smile wide and genuine.

"Good. I'll be ready—just make sure you are too," Ben teased, with that signature glimmer of mischief in his eyes.

"Challenge accepted," Grace shot back playfully.

# Chapter 14

Grace pulled into the parking lot of Adventure Tours. Her nerves hummed, but the sensation wasn't unpleasant, more like a quiver of anticipation before diving into something new.

Grace stepped out of the SUV, taking a deep breath, savoring the fresh air and the scent of the river. In the city, the air had always felt dense. Clogged with exhaust fumes and the static of too many lives converging. But here? It felt like a living thing, wrapping itself around her in a welcome embrace.

"Grace!" a voice called from across the lot. She turned, spotting him beneath a canopy where a few kayaks were lined up like soldiers ready for battle.

Ben waved her over, a wide smile stretching across his face, the sleeves of his red plaid flannel shirt rolled up to his elbows. There was something about his casual confidence that made Grace grin.

"Well, look at you," he teased as she approached, his gaze appraising the outfit she'd put a little more thought into than she'd care to admit. "I wasn't sure if you'd back out or not."

She rolled her eyes, though playfully, as she tugged at the hem of her flannel shirt. "What can I say? I'm dedicated," she countered. "Plus, I didn't want to miss the chance to watch you show off your skills on the river."

Ben laughed. "Show off, huh? I think you're giving me far more credit than I deserve."

"That remains to be seen. So...the New River. No sharks in there, right?" Grace said, with a nod towards the river and a sly smile.

"No sharks," Ben promised, his eyes crinkling in amusement. "We've got more fish in the water and nosey raccoons in the woods than anything out here. So as long as you don't leave any snacks exposed, you're safe."

Grace gave him a mock-serious nod. "I'll note that."

Despite the banter, there was still a flutter of uncertainty in her chest. It wasn't exactly a fear of kayaking. It was just so... out of her element. But maybe that was the point. For years, her feet had been planted firmly on the ground, ruthless in their chase for success in a shimmering cityscape. Today, she'd let herself be carried by a river she didn't control. And something about that felt freeing, yet unnerving.

Ben started hauling a brightly colored kayak towards the landing dock. Grace followed him. "I'll go easy on you," Ben said over his shoulder. "It's just a beginner's tour today, no rushing white water rapids. Promise."

"I appreciate that, Captain Turner," Grace replied, trying to tamp down her nerves with humor.

Grace helped him load their minimal gear—mostly by handing over paddles and pretending to know what she was doing, which earned her another amused look from Ben.

"We'll go tandem today. That way, I can control most of the coordination, and you won't have to worry about steering. Just enjoy the ride."

She raised an eyebrow. "You mean, 'just enjoy not capsizing,' don't you?"

"Depends on how good a student you are." He winked.

The water lapped at the dock's wooden posts, rhythmic and soft, as if calling them to it. Taking a deep breath, Grace nodded. "Alright, I'm ready."

Ben offered his hand to help her settle into the kayak, and as her palm touched his, a warmth shot through her. His grasp—calm and confident. She slid into the front seat of the kayak with relative ease, the cool plastic of the seat pressing up against her back as she grasped the sides and adjusted herself, getting comfortable.

Once settled behind her, Ben chuckled. "See? You're a natural. You haven't fallen out yet."

"Don't jinx it," she warned, still holding onto the sides of the kayak.

Ben untied the dock line and pushed them off. "Alright, Grace. Welcome to the New River."

The irony of the name wasn't lost on her. This river was one of the oldest on the continent. Time had carved its course, much like it seemed to do with everything else around here, slowly and deliberately.

The kayak glided, the soft "plop, plop" of the Ben's paddle dipping into the water, providing a hypnotic rhythm. The river was wide and glassy, its surface reflecting the burgeoning daylight while stubborn patches of mist clung to the riverbanks, draping the tall pines in ethereal white veils.

Grace exhaled, her breath mixing into the hush of the river's gentle current. "It's... beautiful."

Ben's voice, low and introspective, seemed to fit the expanse of the water perfectly. "Yes, it is. My dad always said that rivers don't ask for much. You just have to let them carry you, and they'll show you everything worth seeing."

"Your dad started Adventure Tours, right?"

"Yup," Ben answered, his paddle moving with practiced experience. "He grew up here, then lived out of state for a while. He came back here after a few years working east coast tours, wanting to bring the excitement and joy he found back to West Virginia. Dad always said Laurel Ridge deserved to be seen by the world, so he made it his mission to share his love for the mountains, the river, and the land."

There was an unmistakable fondness in Ben's voice, a quiet pride that echoed years of admiration for the man who had shaped his life.

"Must've been hard taking up that responsibility after he was gone," she remarked, struggling a little as she attempted to find a rhythm with her paddle.

"Yes. It was," he admitted, his voice softer now. "I think at first, I wasn't sure if I could do it. But the more I tried, the deeper I connected with this place. The way I see it…this is where I'm meant to be and what I was meant to do."

His comment hit home for Grace, casting a light on her restless mind. A sense of belonging. A place where things made sense, where the pieces fit together seamlessly, where no one had to chase endlessly after the next better version of themselves?

Her paddle dipped into the water again. "Do you think it's always been that simple for you? Knowing you belonged here?"

Ben laughed. "Simple? No. I'd never say it was simple. I was actually confused, or maybe a mess, as a young adult. After I lost my parents, I thought about leaving. Thought about trying to forge my own way somewhere else, somewhere bigger. I even considered moving to a city on the West coast, you know, where the 'real action' seemed to be happening." He shook his head, as if recalling a younger version of himself he hadn't thought about in years. "But every time I'd go to leave, I'd hesitate, because part of me deep down knew this was my home."

Grace shifted as she processed his words. Home. The term itself, so simple, carried such complex meaning. A place of comfort, yes. But also a place of grounding, of purpose, a point from which all things flow outward. Grace chewed on the idea for a moment, her paddle cutting through the water awkwardly.

Had she ever truly felt home? Yes—before moving to New York. Her dreams and ambitions of city life, of making a fortune and enjoying a life of luxury, had led her astray.

She peered up ahead. The mountains framed them like wise sentinels guarding a hidden kingdom. Their peaks soared into the cloudless sky, the ridgelines kissed by the sun, gilding the edges with warm light. Oak and maple trees lined the banks, some of them dipping their roots into the water, as if tasting the river to make sure it was reliable.

"I wish I had that same certainty," Grace admitted.

Ben's face softened. "Certainty is tricky," he said. "It's not something you find all at once, you know? More like it uncovers itself little by little, like a stone that gets exposed as the river wears the dirt away. It takes time. Patience."

His grin returned as he added, "Which, let me guess, is probably not something you're used to?"

Grace couldn't help but laugh. "You got that right. The city is all about immediacy. There's no room for waiting around. It's all go, go, go. If you hesitate for even a second, you're already on your way to being left behind."

"So, what happens when you finally stop?" Ben's question hung in the air, waiting for an answer.

Grace took a deep breath, letting the cool air fill her chest. "Honestly? When you stop... everything catches up to you. The noise. The pace. The mistakes. My career, my entire time in New York, was all about controlling the narrative. Making sure I shaped the story before someone else could."

"That sounds exhausting," he said.

"It was," Grace confessed as she pulled her paddle out of the water for a moment. She thought back to those frenetic boardrooms, where her voice had been sharp, commanding every gaze with precision, like a master puppeteer pulling taut the strings of her reputation. But no amount of control had saved her from the fall.

A long pause drifted between them, the only sound coming from the light plopping of Ben's paddle and the occasional call of birds from the treetops.

"You know, I'm not used to silence," she said.

"Silence can be intimidating when you're used to noise. But sometimes, it's where the best things come through," he replied.

"Ben, how did you...?" She hesitated, unsure of the right words. "How did you know who you wanted to be? What you wanted to do after your parents passed?"

Ben's paddle eased through the water, his gaze growing distant for a moment, as if he were seeing something far back in time. "At first? I didn't." He placed the paddle across his lap, the kayak drifting naturally. "For a good while, I didn't know whether I was doing what I was supposed to, or if I was even cut out for this. But I realized my dad hadn't worried about whether it was the grandest thing he could've done with his life." He gestured to the surrounding river. "Dad just focused on the small things—like taking people in need on these simple tours, showing them that this place could give offer them peace and renewal." He paused and then added, "None of us are guaranteed life will go the way we planned or hoped for. But we do get to choose how we handle what comes our way."

Grace's heart clenched at his words.

*None of us are guaranteed life will go the way we planned or hoped for. No kidding*. She thought to herself.

They continued paddling for several more moments in companionable quiet, the sunlight filtering through the trees casting dancing shadows on the water. And as the river widened, Ben guided them toward a small inlet off the main current—an area where rocks formed shallow shelves and the sky mirrored itself on the water's surface.

They stopped paddling, sitting quietly as the kayak drifted into a space between two rock formations that flanked the channel like guardians of a secret passage.

Ben spoke then, his voice lower, more reflective. "My dad called this place Reflection Cove. He brought people here all the time. Said it was a good place to just... exist."

Ben continued, "Mom and Dad would come here every Sunday after church too, and sit and read the Bible together. They'd talk and just enjoy each other's company."

"It's... incredible," she whispered, unable to find a more fitting word for the tranquility that enveloped them. "I can see why your parents must have loved it."

Ben shifted. "Yeah. Mom and Dad had this way of finding clarity in things that most people overlooked. When things seemed chaotic or pointless, Dad always told me to come here. Just sit and do nothing. Just listen."

Silence fell between them for a few moments.

"One thing I'll always remember Dad saying, 'The river doesn't chase its own tail. It just moves forward, gracefully. We could all take a page out of that book.'" Ben said, as if he were remembering a certain moment in time.

Grace let those beautiful words settle over her.

Ben's voice took on a new, playful tone, shattering the seriousness of the moment. "Okay, before I get too poetic here and turn into someone who starts quoting Emerson, I'm gonna ask you something important, Grace."

She turned his way, grabbing the sides of the kayak as it rocked, and raised a teasing eyebrow. "Something important?"

"Very important," he insisted, eyes sparkling mischievously. "It's a well-known fact that every good kayaking adventure requires snack breaks. And, I happen to have brought some expertly chosen snacks. The question is... may I share them with you?"

Grace smirked. "Now that, Ben, is a real test of our tour guide-to-customer relationship. Let's see what you've got."

Ben reached under his seat, pulling out a small cooler, his grin widening. "Prepare to be impressed."

He popped open the cooler and displayed an array of snacks: a couple of granola bars, apple slices, and—what stole her attention entirely—large, homemade chocolate chip cookies.

Grace's eyes widened in delight. "Those cookies look incredible!" She reached for one without hesitation, as if it were a treasure she had been searching for.

"Only the best for my paddling partner," he said with a wink, and grabbed one for himself.

"I can see why your tour company is so successful," Grace said, taking a hearty bite, letting the cookie melt in her mouth. "Top-tier snacks."

Ben coughed with laughter, clearly pleased with himself. "Well, I don't mean to brag, but I'm basically a snack sommelier at this point. There's a fine art to combining good food with adventure. And it's all about the cookies, really—makes or breaks the experience."

Grace smirked, playfully rolling her eyes, pretending to analyze the cookie. "Hmm, I think I detect a hint of mischief in this one. Your secret ingredient?"

"Absolutely," he replied, feigning seriousness. "Mischief is key to a successful day on the river."

As they both continued to munch, the world around them melted into the comforting rhythm of nature. The gentle lapping of the water against the kayak, the chirping of birds high above, and the soft rustle of leaves in the trees surrounded them.

"So, tell me," Ben began between bites, "if you could be anywhere else right now, where would you want to be?"

Grace paused, considering the question. "Honestly? I can't think of anywhere I'd rather be than exactly here." She spread her arms to encompass their idyllic surroundings. "For the first time in forever, I feel free."

"That's a good feeling," Ben replied. "And it's only going to get better. We can't let city life keep bogging you down."

Her pulse quickened at his words, a thrill bubbling just below the surface. Here was a man who understood resurgence, who seemed to embrace life with open arms. Was it possible that in this exploration of the river and moments shared, she might find the start of something new—something she craved?

With a satisfied sigh, Grace turned serious again. Her brow furrowed as she gazed at Ben, a faint frown curling at the corners of her mouth. "So, what about you, Ben? What does the future look like for you? You've got all this—Adventure Tours, the land, the love for what you do... Do you see it continuing like this? What's your dream?"

Ben appeared thoughtful, his expression shifting as he looked out over the shimmering water. "You know, for a long time, I thought it was all about keeping my father's legacy alive and passing it along someday. But lately, I've been wondering if there's more than just that. I've been considering expanding the business a bit more. Adding a few rental cabins. In my way of thinking, that could attract more tourists to the area. Then I've been toying with the idea of offering youth camping expeditions. You know, fun camping experiences for kids who rarely get to enjoy nature."

Grace watched him, captivated by his honesty and the passion that flickered in his hazel eyes. "Tell me more?" she encouraged.

"Well, I've always loved the outdoors. I grew up on this land, and it will always be a part of me. But the more time I spend guiding others, the more I realize I don't want to just share adventures. I want to create experiences that truly matter," he said, his words gathering weight. "I want to help people reconnect with nature, with who they are. The outdoors has this transformative power. With every experience, I want to provide a little piece of clarity, a reminder that life is bigger than the confines we build around ourselves."

The sincerity in his voice struck her. It reminded her of her own yearnings—not just for peace but for meaningfulness, for an existence filled with intention. "That's incredibly inspiring, Ben."

He shrugged, though she could see the modesty in his bashful smile. "It's just what I know."

"But you know a lot." Grace chuckled. "It must take a certain strength to share something so vulnerable with others, though."

Ben's gaze held hers. "Vulnerability is the glue, Grace. It's what connects us all. Without it, we might as well build walls and live behind them forever."

"Maybe you're right," Grace said, pondering the truths buried in his words. "I hadn't thought about it like that before. But... it's scary too...being vulnerable?"

"Sure, it can be," Ben admitted, his tone serious. "But think about how much fear drives us to hold back what we feel. Once you let it go, the river just carries it away." He glanced towards the water and the gentle swell, then back to her, a twinkle in his eye. "And besides, what's the worst that could happen? You ice skate across the surface instead of trusting the current?"

Grace couldn't help but laugh at the vivid mental image of herself slipping and sliding across the river like an awkward ice skater at the height of summer. "That would be quite the Instagram post, wouldn't it?"

"Oh, absolutely," he chuckled. "But hey, at least you'd still have that charm!"

Grace rolled her eyes playfully. There was a subtle yet growing ease in Ben's company.

After they finished their second cookie, they settled into a peaceful rhythm. Ben directing their kayak back towards the main channel of the river. Grace focused on not tipping the kayak with any sudden moves while soaking in the surrounding beauty.

"Okay," Ben said as they re-entered the wider stretch of the river. "I think it's time we level up a bit."

"Level up?" Grace asked, skepticism urging her brow to furrow in concern. "What's that supposed to mean?"

"Well—maybe not literally level up," Ben started, a playful grin forming again. "But how about we both paddle a bit more actively? I promise I'll keep it to the calmer parts of the river for a bit longer while we build some rhythm together. Then we'll hit some small rapids. It'll build your confidence!"

Grace hesitated, but the thrill of spiking her adrenaline overrode her caution. "Alright, Captain. Just guide me through it; I'll follow your lead."

Ben chuckled, positioning his paddle for a stronger stroke. "No problem. Let's pick up the pace!"

As Grace did her best to match his strokes, she found a pleasant rhythm amidst the lapping waves. Each movement of her paddle felt liberating, pulling her further away from her worries as the water sprayed against her cheeks. The afternoon sun warmed her skin.

"See?" Ben said, his enthusiasm palpable. "Not so bad, right? You're a natural!"

Grace grinned, the energy coursing through her making her feel alive. "Oh, stop it! You're going to give me a big head! I feel like I'm finally coming into my element."

"Well, I'd say the river is doing its part to help," Ben replied, guiding their path toward a bend where the water shimmered, and gentle rapids could be seen beyond, "But it takes two to tango... and you've definitely got the moves!"

They curved around the bend, where sunlight filtered through the tree canopy, creating a mosaic of dappled light on the surface of the water. Grace paddled with increased vigor, feeling like the river was a partner urging her forward, challenging her to embrace the experience fully. It was exhilarating, electric even—each stroke, every push against the water, made her feel more empowered, less like the frail, lost woman she had been mere days ago.

"Okay, let's stop here," Ben called, signaling with his hand. "Check this spot out for a moment. We're coming up to an observation deck."

The kayak came to a halt beside a rustic wooden platform that hugged the riverbank. The perfect spot for a break.

Ben pointed toward the summit above. "There—that's one of my favorite viewpoints. The view from up takes your breath away."

Grace's gaze followed his gesture. "Sounds amazing. Do you often take groups up there?" she asked, intrigued by the prospect of exploration.

"Whenever I can. It's a just a short uphill hike."

"Hiking?" she ventured, raising an eyebrow playfully. "You promised no hard workouts today!"

Ben laughed. "Just a small jaunt! Nothing too strenuous, I promise. Just think of it as a little adventure snack."

"Fine, adventure snack it is." Grace rolled her eyes, half-teasing but also smitten by the idea.

As they hopped out of the kayak and secured it to the dock, Grace felt a surge of exhilaration in her chest.

"Alright, follow me!" Ben called, already striding ahead as if the path was just an extension of who he was, moving effortlessly along the terrain. Grace fell into step behind him, noticing how his movements blended naturally with the surroundings.

They wound their way along a narrow trail, flanked by trees and the vibrant underbrush of ferns and wildflowers. The air was filled with the soft sound of rustling leaves against the backdrop of birds singing and the river rushing below—their melody enveloping them, unfurling like a welcoming embrace.

Ben looked over his shoulder, a playful twinkle in his eye. "Ya know, when I first started taking people on these trails, I often heard folks complain about the hiking itself. Some people expected a grand view without the effort," he said, a hint of nostalgia creeping into his voice.

"But I'd tell them that every step forward comes with its own re-ward—sometimes a view, other times the peace of the journey itself."

Grace smiled at his perspective. "That's a lovely way to put it. In New York, it was always about rushing to get to the destination and checking it off the list. I'd completely forgotten about enjoying the moment."

"And it's a beautiful moment we've got here," Ben replied, motioning to the tall trees encasing them like protective sentinels. "You notice how the light changes throughout the day? One moment, it's bright and vibrant, and the next, it's soft and ethereal. Just like life—it's all about how you choose to see it."

*Chapter 15*

The sun hung a little lower in the sky as Grace and Ben walked toward her SUV in the parking lot of Adventure Tours. They strolled side by side, their spirits infectious with the warmth of the day.

"Well, you know," Ben said, breaking their companionable silence, "I think you're officially ready to take on some challenging white water rapids next time."

"More challenging?" Grace chuckled and glanced at him from the corner of her eye. "You'll have to forgive me if I prefer to keep my heart rate to a reasonable level."

Ben laughed, his hazel eyes twinkling with mischief. "What's life without a little thrill? I promise I'll wear my best rescue vest for you next time."

"Such a gentleman," she teased, rolling her eyes playfully.

Grace couldn't help but feel a pang of regret as they arrived at her vehicle, their day together coming to an end. "I didn't realize how much I missed being out in nature," she admitted.

"Pretty sure that's the cookies talking," Ben said, nudging her with his elbow. "Sugar can make you feel pretty magical."

Grace laughed. "Maybe a little sugar boost is all I needed—who knew I'd have to thank a couple of cookies for grounding me?"

"We all need a magical cookie occasionally," Ben countered, his gaze drifting to the horizon. "What's a little adventure without a few indulgences?"

Grace heard her phone chime from inside the SUV. The sound was out-of-place amid the tranquility of the moment. Curiosity sparked, and she unlocked the SUV to retrieve her phone. The name on the screen halted her mid-motion—Jack.

Her heart raced, an odd mix of excitement and dread forming a tight knot in her stomach. Jack was a colleague from her corporate world—a voice from a life she wanted to leave behind. With a tight swallow, she answered, "Hello?"

"Grace! I'm glad you answered!" Jack's voice boomed through the receiver, overly enthusiastic and laden with that all-too-familiar corporate charm that sent a chill down her spine. "I hope I'm not interrupting anything too important."

"No, not at all," she said, forcing the words out with a nonchalance she didn't feel. Her mind drifted briefly to the glorious day spent floating on the river with Ben, and the overwhelming calm she had gained now felt threatened.

"Good, good! Listen, I've got some exciting news," Jack continued, his tone vibrating with triumphant energy. "We're expanding the team here, and I wanted to be the first to let you know that we're offering you a position. The President of Communications. Of course, your salary package will be spectacular, and you'd get to lead some really exciting projects!"

Stunned, Grace felt her breath catch. President. The title echoed in her mind like a siren call from the depths of her past—a past filled with ambition, success, and a reputation she had worked meticulously to carve out. But the sharp edges of that world stung.

"Jack, that's... I don't even know what to say!" she stammered, her thoughts racing as she glanced around for Ben, who was now busy unloading items from a trailer attached to a pickup nearby that had just pulled into the parking lot.

"Great! Just great! There will be a team in place to help you transition smoothly. We'd love to have you here Grace, as soon as possible—the energy in the office will be outstanding with you in it!" He continued chatting as though she were reeling in excitement, oblivious to the undercurrent of dread that had bubbled up inside her.

Grace shifted her gaze to the nearby trees, their leaves rustling in the gentle breeze, and the soft melody of birds chirping filling the air. The contrast between those peaceful sounds and Jack's upbeat, sharp voice was jarring. The cellphone grew heavier in her hand.

"That's... something, Jack," she said, trying to stall, unsure of how to navigate the conversation.

"We will really put your crisis management skills to use, especially with the new merger coming up. You'll be leading from the front." Jack's persistent tone cut through, piling on more temptations.

*But at what cost?* She thought as her heart tightened. The thought of city skyscrapers and late-night strategy meetings weighed on her chest. What had once lit her on fire, fueling her insatiable hunger for success, now seemed like a thorn in her side?

Jack kept rattling off specifics: company perks, bonuses, launch schedules. It felt like he was laying each word down like stepping stones, leading her out of nowhere and back onto a path she had once proudly walked. But now, despite the initial flutter of excitement, those stones seemed slippery, uncertain, like crossing back into a realm that had left her bruised.

"Well, give it some thought," Jack pressed, sensing her hesitation at last, though his salesman tone didn't waver. "But don't think for too long—we've got others eager to jump on the opportunity. We need you here soon. We want you Grace. We want a heavy-hitter."

That phrase, we want you, punctured the fragile bubble of her emotional space and left her reeling. She realized then that Jack didn't know the real Grace that was starting to appear. The one she was trying to find again.

"Right," Grace mumbled, her voice soft and distant. "I'll need some time to think about it."

"Of course!" Jack's voice brightened again, as if he'd already closed the deal. "I'll send you the details via email, and we can hit the ground running from there."

Grace's mouth moved, but it felt on autopilot. Her mind was drifting between visions of her past life and the gentle simplicity of the present. "Thanks, Jack. I'll check my email."

"Looking forward to hearing from you soon Grace." Jack said with enthusiasm before ending the call. As if he'd dropped a neatly wrapped package of temptation into her hands and walked away, leaving her to untangle the knots.

She stood motionless for a moment, phone still clutched in her hand.

She glanced sideways to where Ben was finishing up with the gear he was helping to unload. Absorbed in his task, his sun-kissed skin glowing in the fading early evening light.

"Everything alright?"

His voice startled her.

Grace opened her mouth to say something, then hesitated, frozen mid-thought. It felt as if she were caught between two worlds. A vice grip in one hand was trying to drag her back into the dizzying swirl of the city, while the other hand reached forward toward something quieter, something… kinder, a place where she didn't have to be defined by prestige or pressure.

Ben glanced over his shoulder when she didn't respond, lifting his eyebrow in mild curiosity.

She took a deep breath and stepped toward him. "Ben, I just… took a call from one of my colleagues in New York."

Ben straightened and turned his full attention to her. "Oh?"

Grace felt her heart hammering in her chest. "He… offered me a job. A pretty big one, to be honest."

Ben's face showed no surprise, only the calm interest that had been there since the moment they met. "What kind of job?"

"President of Communications." She tried not to sound boastful, but there was no hiding the significance of the title.

Ben was quiet for a beat, his expression thoughtful as he absorbed her words. His eyes flickered, like he was weighing something in his mind.

"And that's what you want?" His voice was steady, level.

Grace hesitated. "I don't know," she admitted.

Ben sat on the trailer's wheel well, his arms crossing casually over his chest. "Can I ask you something?"

Grace nodded.

"What is it that you're looking for? Like, big picture. Is it status? Stability? Money? Or is it something else?"

"I'm not sure yet," she said. It felt like the truest statement she had made in a long time.

Ben nodded. He didn't push, only waited, giving her space.

Grace took a deep breath, the fresh mountain air filling her lungs. "There was a time when I lived for the big things," she continued, the words flowing freely. "The title, the prestige, the money, the difference I could make in the boardroom. But... lately, I've been finding—" she paused, gesturing around her, "I've been finding peace in things that don't feel so loud. In things that actually stop the noise."

Ben's lips twitched into a soft smile. "Well, this place does have a way of quieting things down. What does your gut say?"

"My gut?" Grace echoed. "It's urging me to embrace that young college graduate once more, but this time, to choose a path I know is right for me."

Ben watched her closely, understanding in his expression, but he didn't interrupt.

She continued, her voice softening. "My sole focus after graduating was to move to the big city and leave Charleston, West Virginia, behind which, by the way, is where I grew up. All I could think about back then was escaping, making a fortune, and living a big, bold, flashy lifestyle. And now, after experiencing all that... I just want my simple, humble life back. I don't need a fancy title, I don't need prestige, and I absolutely don't want to work ten- or twelve-hour days, seven days a week, any longer. I'm exhausted. I'm worn out. All I want is to reclaim my life—and find my old self again."

Ben nodded again, standing up and taking a step closer as he uncrossed his arms.

"Here's my perspective," he said, locking his gaze with hers. "You embraced city life, believing it was what you wanted when you were younger. You've tried it. You succeeded. Now it's perfectly alright to let it go. There's no shame in this. You've simply come to realize that it's not the person you wish to be anymore."

Her breath hitched at his words, and she blinked rapidly, emotion swelling in her chest.

"Success isn't always about what you earn or the title you hold," Ben continued, his voice calm but firm. "Sometimes it's about finding yourself. Finding what fills you up, what gives you real joy. Everything else is just... well ... noise. I don't know if the answer is staying here in Laurel Ridge, or leaving here and exploring another town or community, or going back to Charleston, but I do know this—if you listen to your gut...and follow your instincts...you'll often find the right answer."

"I think you're a little too wise for your age," she teased.

"Pretty sure it's the river talking through me," he joked back, flashing that smile she'd come to rely on. "Spend enough time in reflection, and suddenly, you sound profound."

Grace shook her head, a soft smile playing on the edges of her lips. "Well, whoever's talking, you've given me a lot to think about."

"Good. You've got time," he replied. "The river's not going anywhere."

"Thanks, Ben. Really..." Grace said, her voice quieter now, but filled with sincerity. "For everything today. And for... being here for me and listening."

Ben's eyes softened. "Any time," he said.

She slid into her SUV and watched as Ben waved one last goodbye, his figure standing tall in the parking lot. For a moment, Grace let herself savor the deep sense of peace she was beginning to feel.

# Chapter 16

Grace leaned back in the rocking chair. The book she had been trying to read rested in her lap. The story's cheerful pages, unable to compete with the chaos in her mind. Her thoughts swirled, drawn again and again to the past few days, to New York.

Her hand moved to the back of her neck, kneading a knot of tension that had taken up residence there.

With a sigh, she gave up the pretense of reading, and placed the book on the weathered wooden table beside her. The cheerful cover—a sunny farm scene—clashing with the storm zipping inside her mind.

She fiddled with the zipper on her jacket.

Her foot absently swiped at the dry leaves scattered on the porch.

This vacation away from New York had seemed like an excellent decision—a quiet retreat, far removed from the demands of the city. No skyscrapers, no high-rise offices humming with expectations. Just peace. Or so she'd thought. But now the stillness was suffocating.

The phone call from Jack yesterday hung over her like a cloud she couldn't quite shake. President of Communications. Everything she'd worked toward since college came lurching back the moment she had answered his call. Her heart had raced, though not from excitement like it once would have.

Ben's words reverberated in Grace's mind.

*Success isn't always about what you earn or the title you hold. Sometimes it's about finding yourself.*

Ben's words seemed so simple. Yet for Grace, the path forward remained murky. At thirty-two, she felt she should have life figured out, but in reality, it felt like a chaotic mess.

She needed to move...do something to distract herself. Clear the clutter from her mind.

She laced up her boots and grabbed her water bottle.

The trail, beyond the edge of the property, beckoned her in with a canopy of leafy branches stretched like arms above the path. The underbrush crunched beneath her boots as the trail snaked up a gentle incline.

She pressed on, stepping over a patch of exposed tree roots with ease as the path narrowed. The familiar cool, calming numbness of exertion filled her limbs as she concentrated on the hike—breathing deeply, letting the rhythm of her footsteps drown out the noise in her head.

As she climbed, the clean mountain air filled her lungs. The higher she went, the more the noise from her thoughts faded into the sounds of the woods. Birds chirped high above, and she occasionally startled some unseen animal in the underbrush, its rustling adding a bit of vitality to the stillness.

The energy from the exercise released itself through her limbs, the familiar fatigue giving her something solid to rely on. Gradually, the path opened up and the sound of rushing water filtered through the stillness. She instinctively quickened her pace.

The waterfall.

It poured down from above, cutting through slabs of ancient rock to form a quiet pool beneath. It was a little pocket of the world, hidden away and unbothered by anything outside itself. Grace blinked, and a rush of childhood memories flooded her mind—those carefree afternoons spent wading in the gentle waters with her aunt. She remembered the joy of splashing around, the thrill of building rock formations, and the comforting warmth of the sun on her back as she surrendered to the blissful serenity of the moment.

"I miss you, Aunt Imogene," Grace said.

The water fall cascaded, each drop shimmering gold in the fractured sunlight that filtered through the overhead tree branches. The mist from the fall cooled the air, and Grace's steps slowed, tension easing from her shoulders as she stepped closer.

On impulse, she pulled off her hiking boots and socks, and rolled up her jeans.

Her feet hit the cold water, and the shock sent a jolt of clarity spiraling up her spine. But it wasn't unpleasant. No, it was something else: freeing. Each step unraveled a tight thread of tension within her. The chill wrapped around her calves, grounding her, as though the water welcomed her in, rushing past her defenses, smoothing over the jagged edges of doubt and guilt.

She crouched down, letting the current tickle her fingertips. The cool water rippled against her skin. She stood again, letting warmth radiate from the dappled sunlight overhead.

*This is peace.*

The sun warming her face. The water lapping at her legs.

Before she could sink further into her thoughts, a wave of laughter floated toward her. Her eyes snapped to attention, realizing she was no longer alone. A voice, deep and familiar, called her name.

"Grace?"

She turned in the direction of the sound, her cheeks warming as she locked eyes with Ben, who stood at the edge of the clearing, several teenagers in tow.

He smirked, amusement twinkling in his hazel eyes. The group of teens stared, equally wide-eyed, at the sight of Grace, barefoot in the water with her hair tousled.

"Fancy meeting you here," Ben said. "Didn't picture you to be the wading waterfall type."

Grace's cheeks flamed several degrees warmer, and she scrambled to recover. "Well, I'll have you know, this isn't the first time I've played in a waterfall, and it definitely won't be the last," she said with a smile.

One teenager—a tall boy with shaggy hair that looked like it hadn't met a brush in weeks—popped beside Ben, glancing at Grace with exaggerated curiosity. "Is this part of the bible study hike, Pastor Ben? Are we supposed to do... Zen waterfall therapy now?"

Grace didn't even blink, her wit kicking in even more. "Oh, absolutely. Your guide...uh... Pastor, I mean, just forgot to mention it, but really—five-star wellness package. Highly recommended."

Ben rolled his eyes, and Grace's embarrassment faded into something lighter, something that felt far more like camaraderie than awkwardness.

Ben herded the teenage crew to a comfortable grassy spot nearby. Grace, wading back to the shore and sat.

"Alright," Ben called, wrangling their attention. "Let's take a quick break before we hit the trail again. Everyone, grab something to drink and a snack."

The kids obeyed, pulling out their canteens and ziplock baggies of snacks.

"For those of you meeting my friend, Ms. Grace, for the first time," Ben said, giving her a smile and a nod, "she's our visiting waterfall wader."

Laughter, lighthearted and infectious, rippled through the group, and Grace shrugged, deciding it was better just to roll with the teasing than fight against it.

Ben pulled his Bible from his backpack, flipping through its well-worn pages until he settled on a passage, his voice taking on a quieter tone.

"Since we're here by the water, I thought we'd read from Psalm 1 today," he said, pausing.

Grace wrapped her arms around her knees. She was intrigued by how the day had unfolded and, most of all, surprised to learn that Ben was a pastor.

Ben cleared his throat, the gentle sound of the waterfall behind him adding an almost poetic layer to the scene. "He is like a tree planted by streams of water, which yields its fruit in season and whose leaf does not wither; whatever they do prospers," Ben read, his voice steady.

As he read the passage, Grace closed her eyes, images of a tree and its roots melding with her swirling thoughts. Wasn't that what she had always truly wanted? To yield something rooted in success?

"The Scriptures talk about people like us—people tied to the living water of God. Just like trees, we grow at our own pace, but we need to stay connected to our roots. Our faith is like a stream, constantly nourishing us, keeping us healthy through all the seasons." Ben said, pausing and looking over at the water beside them. "Faith like a stream. The tree doesn't question its roots. It doesn't force the water to come."

Grace's thoughts drifted, guided by the verse, back to untouched memories. She was fifteen again, sliding into the familiar wooden church pew beside her parents. The air was infused with the comforting scent of old hymnals and lemon furniture polish. Sunlight streamed through the stained-glass windows, casting vibrant patterns that danced across the congregation. She recalled the solace of those routines—the reassuring squeeze of her mother's hand during prayer and the resonance of her father's rich baritone voice rising above the rest during hymns. Pastor Robert's gentle voice echoed in her mind, reminding them all that faith was a journey, not a destination.

Grace hadn't attended a church service in years, not since she had moved to New York.

"Remember to nourish your roots," Ben finished with a friendly smile, tucking his Bible away as the kids stirred and began their usual post-reflection banter and jostling.

Ben approached her, hands resting casually in the pockets of his jeans, a grin tugging at his lips. "Not the way you pictured your hike and dip in the waterfall to go, huh?"

"Let's just say it added a delightful surprise to the agenda, Pastor Ben." Grace grinned, tucking a stray strand of hair behind her ear.

"I serve as a youth pastor at the Laurel Ridge Community Church. I genuinely enjoy it; it's my way of giving back to the community. You're more than welcome to join our youth group hikes anytime," Ben replied.

"I just might take you up on that," she said with a warm smile.

Ben's expression softened. "They're a good bunch of kids. Keep me grounded... and on my toes."

Grace smiled, stuffing her hands into her jacket pockets. "I can imagine," she said, glancing back at the teens, their laughter ringing through the trees. It was infectious, that kind of carefree energy.

Ben followed her gaze, his expression thoughtful. "You know, moments like these are what ground me in what I do. It's not merely about leading hikes or sharing bits of wisdom. It's about helping people—whether they're kids or adults—realize there's so much more to life than the constant rush to get from one destination to the next. Often, the most profound changes occur in the quietest of moments, much like the tranquility of that waterfall you were enjoying."

Grace tilted her head thoughtfully. She understood what he meant—these small, seemingly insignificant moments when the chaos stilled long enough for something deeper to take root.

Ben adjusted the strap on his backpack. Some of the teens were getting a little restless. He turned his attention back to Grace, his gaze lingering on her for just a beat longer than seemed necessary. "You know," he started, as if weighing his next words carefully, "for someone who's spent so much time in the city, always on the go, caught up in the rush, you seem to be fitting in here quite nicely."

Grace raised an eyebrow, smirking. "You think wading in a waterfall makes me a local now?"

Ben chuckled, but there was a seriousness beneath his words when he replied. "It's not the waterfall. It's the way you took the day. Let it carry you somewhere unexpected. That's something few people do. It takes a certain kind of courage."

Courage.

She hadn't thought of it that way. But now, as she stared back into Ben's steady eyes, she realized he might be onto something.

"We're headed back down the trail. You're welcome to join us for the hike back. Or... continue your solo wilderness retreat—five-star wellness package included, obviously," he said with a smile.

"Tempting," Grace replied with a chuckle. "But I think I'll keep to my own pace today."

"Fair enough," Ben said, nodding in understanding. "Either way, I'll see you around town, Grace."

She watched him gather the teens and take charge with a confidence she was beginning to admire more and more. After the group trailed off down the path, Grace sat for a moment longer, wrapped in her thoughts.

Courage.

For so long, she had believed that courage was about climbing higher, achieving more—about conquering the world on her terms, with grit and relentless ambition. But here, at this unexpected crossroads in her life, courage looked very different. It looked like standing at the edge of something new and choosing to step in without a clear roadmap.

# Chapter 17

Grace entered Martha's Diner. She paused just inside, letting the gentle warmth of the diner wrap around her like a well-worn quilt. There was something about this place—the hum of quiet conversation, the clatter of plates and silverware, the lingering scent of something baked and golden—that felt grounding, soothing.

The double doors leading into the kitchen area were propped open and allowed Grace a glimpse of Martha kneading dough, her hands moving in perfect, rhythmic motions. Flour dusted the air as she shaped the dough with practiced ease, her focus on the task at hand. Grace smiled, appreciating the simple art of it.

"Hi Grace," Martha called out as soon as she noticed Grace. "Have a seat and take a load off. I'll be right there in a jiffy!"

Grace smiled as she approached the counter, taking a seat on one of the sturdy, chrome-legged stools. Martha wiped her hands on her apron and leaned against the counter with a knowing look in her blue eyes.

"You look like you could use a good meal—and maybe more than that," Martha said, her tone casual, though her gaze held an edge of concern. "You okay? You've got that faraway look going on, hon."

Grace's first instinct was to brush it off, offer a flippant remark about being tired, or blame it on lingering stress from the tripling notifications on her phone. But with Martha, that didn't feel right. The woman had a way of cutting through pretenses with her gentle, persistent kindness.

"I'm... fine," Grace began, searching for the right compromise between truth and avoidance. "Just... trying to figure some things out."

Martha raised an eyebrow as she poured a cup of coffee for Grace.

With a sigh, Grace gave in, leaning her elbows on the polished counter. "Okay, fine. I'm a little more than 'trying to figure things out.' That much is an understatement, actually." She paused as Martha gave her a patient nod of encouragement. "I got a call yesterday. A job offer. A big one—President of Communications. Back in New York."

Martha's brow furrowed, though her expression didn't lose its soft attentiveness. "Oh .... President. And that's not exactly the news you were hoping to hear, is it?"

Grace pressed her lips together, straightening in her seat as she looked down at the counter. "It's complicated. This should be exactly what I want."

Martha moved behind the counter to pour herself a cup of coffee, watching Grace as she spoke. "Go on," she prompted, sipping the dark liquid.

"There's just... nothing back in New York for me, other than my condo." Grace admitted, her words growing softer, almost hesitant. "There's no one waiting for me. I... barely had a life outside of work." She laughed, her tone reflecting the bitterness of that truth.

Martha nodded, urging her to go on.

"I haven't shared much about what really brought me here to Laurel Ridge, but to keep it simple, I was forced to resign from my job at the company my uncle owned. He made some terrible choices, and he's paying the price for them now. The board strongly suggested I leave, and in hindsight, it was a blessing in disguise. But here's the truth: I've spent my entire career driven by success, always striving to be the very best, to make my parents proud. Somewhere along the way, I ended up in a life that left me feeling empty. Day after day, I poured everything I had into my work—long hours, endless projects—while giving nothing to myself. I never took the time to simply live. To enjoy, to experience. And now, after stepping away, I can see it clearly: I want something more. I want to create a life that's mine, on my own terms, not tied to someone else's expectations or a title that doesn't fulfill me."

Martha placed her cup down, her weathered hands wrapping around it for warmth, though her eyes remained steady on Grace. "You know, Grace," she began, her voice low and filled with familiarity, "sometimes the things we think we need—security, success, prestige—well, they might not matter as much as they once did. Life changes. We change. And it's okay to recognize that maybe what you're really seekin' now... is something else entirely."

Grace blinked, feeling her throat tighten. "I just don't know what that is yet."

"Of course not," Martha said with an easy smile. "These things take time. You don't have to rush into any decision, pressure yourself into fitting a mold that doesn't feel right anymore. Go easy on yourself, sweetheart."

Martha didn't press any further. Instead, she reached over and gave Grace's hand a light squeeze, just a moment of connection that somehow said more than words.

"Thank you," Grace said.

Martha's eyes softened with the warmth of a smile that radiated reassurance. "You don't have to thank me, sweetheart. Every person on this side of heaven is always trying to figure things out in life." She shifted behind the counter and clicked the coffee machine on to brew a fresh pot. "And besides, no one ever gets there alone. That's why we surround ourselves with community, you know?"

Grace nodded, letting Martha's words swirl in her mind. A community. That was another thing she'd never made time for back in New York.

When was the last genuine connection she'd had with someone? Not a networking contact or a colleague, but a true connection.

"I guess it's kind of hard to find that in the city," Grace admitted. "Back there, it's all about the hustle. You're valuable as long as you're grinding, producing, showing the world you've got it all together."

Martha leaned forward, her blue eyes filled with a knowing gleam. "But here," she said, "you don't have to prove anything, darling. You just have to be. That's something you won't find on any balance sheet."

Grace smiled, amazed at how effortless Martha made it all sound. Just be. Could it really be that simple?

Her phone buzzed, blinking at her like a tether to the life she'd left behind. The temptation to check it tugged at her. She glanced up at Martha and then turned her phone off.

Martha nodded approvingly. "Good choice," she said.

Grace chuckled softly. "You know, I never imagined I'd end up talking with a diner owner about... well, about everything."

"Life has a funny way of working out, doesn't it?" Martha said, sporting a knowing smile. "So... not to change the subject, but I heard through the grapevine that you're staying up at Imogene's old place on the ridge." Her smile widened just a touch. "Imogene's niece, huh?"

Grace blinked in surprise, caught a little off guard by the sudden shift in conversation. "Yes, that's where I'm staying, and I am Imogene's niece."

Martha leaned on the counter, her blue eyes twinkling with mischief. "It's nice up there." She waggled her eyebrows. "Peaceful... maybe a little too peaceful for a city girl like you?"

Grace laughed, nodding. "Yeah, I'll admit, it's an been an adjustment. The quiet is... unsettling sometimes. It's weird not hearing sirens and car horns all the time."

"Oh, don't worry," Martha said. "You'll adjust—just long enough for the wild turkeys to start up their racket at dawn. Nothing like a bunch of birds having their morning chat just after sunrise to make you wish for a fleet of delivery trucks blasting their horns."

Grace snorted into her coffee cup, unable to stop the chuckle that escaped. "Wild turkeys? That's what I have to look forward to? Fantastic."

"Oh, honey, that and more," Martha replied, leaning in. "I'm guessin' you haven't met the raccoon tribe yet. They used to think Imogene's compost pile was a nightly buffet. You won't see them... just hear 'em. They're like tiny bandits in the night." She grinned broadly. "It's West Virginia, sweetheart. Nature's constantly auditioning for America's Got Talent right outside your door."

Grace rolled her eyes playfully. "I'm already feeling so at one with nature."

Martha cackled, shaking her head. "You'll be swappin' pest stories like the rest of us by the time you're done here. Anyhow, bless Imogene's heart—she really did love that cabin. I can't even tell you how many pies she baked for me over the years. She always looked after everyone here in town. She'd be happy knowing you're up there." Her smile softened for a moment, just a brief flicker of fondness, before the humor returned to her expression. "Of course, now the real question is—have you figured out how to work that stubborn old stove in the kitchen? Or does that thing have you prayin' to it like the rest of us did?"

"Oh my goodness," Grace said, shaking her head. "I spent a good twenty minutes trying to get it to light yesterday evening. I gave up and ate cold soup from the can like a wilderness survivalist."

Martha's laugh filled the tiny diner, a hearty, infectious sound that made a few of the other patrons glance their way with amused smiles of their own. "Oh, I've been there, darlin'. The first time I used that stove, I thought it was part stove, part antique torture device. I nearly lit myself on fire just trying to cook a pot roast."

Grace wiped the corners of her eyes, catching her breath. "I might just stick to takeout."

"And what a loss that would be," Martha replied. "The town will be reeling when the news breaks that the mysterious Grace Anderson, PR extraordinaire, has been defeated by an ancient piece of kitchen equipment. I'll make sure to spread it around town tomorrow." She gave a cheeky wink, clearly enjoying herself.

"Oh, great," Grace groaned, playing along. "I'm sure that will be the only thing anyone remembers me for."

Martha leaned back, tapping her chin. "Well, we did already hear about that kayak trip with Ben, so maybe the stove won't be the most interesting story after all..."

Grace's eyes widened. "Oh no—that already made the rounds, too?"

"Honey, this is Laurel Ridge. We've got about five places to talk, and Martha's Diner happens to be all five of them." Martha said with a sly grin. "Around here, stories travel faster than gossip at a high school reunion."

Grace shook her head, but she couldn't help the smile tugging at her lips. "I guess there's no keeping a secret in this town, huh?"

"Not a chance," Martha said with a wink. "But don't worry. We save the real storytelling for special occasions. Maybe we'll pull out all the good ones at supper tonight." She patted Grace's hand. "You're one of us now, even if you don't know it yet."

Grace couldn't help but laugh. Somehow, despite her best efforts to fly under the radar, Laurel Ridge was weaving her right into its fabric—and maybe that wasn't such a bad thing after all.

"So, here's the plan," Martha said with a sudden brightness in her voice. "You're coming to my house tonight."

Grace blinked, confused. "Wait, what? Coming to your house?"

"That's right," Martha brushed her hands down her flour-dusted apron and grinned. "Every month, a few of us ladies from church get together. It's nothing fancy—just good food, good company, and, of course, some girl talk. I'd love to have you join us."

Grace hesitated. Her gut instinct was to decline, to say something about having too much to think over, or needing time alone.

Martha's smile was warm and genuine, the kind that made Grace feel like she could decline the invitation without hurting feelings but might regret not saying yes.

"What do you say, sweetheart? It's just supper and some good girl company. No need to worry about putting on airs or anything like that. Just be yourself."

"Okay. I'll come."

Martha's smile widened as she handed her a chocolate chip cookie from the tray beside her. "Good. But first, why don't you have one of these to hold you over until supper?"

Grace bit back a smile, unable to say no to freshly baked cookies.

"So," Martha said, her tone light but clearly interested. "Tell me more about your little kayak adventure with Ben the other day.

Martha leaned on the counter, the smile never leaving her face. "You know, he doesn't take just anybody on those quiet, solo river tours. He must've thought you could hold your own."

Grace tilted her head. "He did more than his fair share of the paddling, trust me. I mostly tried not to fall into the river."

Martha's laugh filled the diner, warm and genuine. "Oh, honey, I wouldn't be so modest. Ben's mentioned more than once that he appreciates someone who's willing to do something out of their element. He probably had as much fun as you did."

Grace shook her head, brushing a stray tendril of hair behind her ear. "It was terrifying at first. But I'll admit... it was amazing, too. The river, the quiet... it's something I wouldn't have even imagined a few months ago." Her voice trailed off.

Martha's expression softened, her smile taking on a gentleness, as if she understood more than Grace was letting on. "Sometimes, it takes someone like Ben—and a little adventure—to remind a person what's been missing. That boy... he's full of wisdom, more than he gives himself credit for."

Grace snorted. "You don't say. He was all philosophical about rivers and life, like a modern-day Thoreau. I wasn't sure whether he was trying to guide me down the river or solve all of life's mysteries." She shook her head. "But honestly? There's something pretty remarkable about him."

Martha hummed approvingly, her eyes crinkling with a slow, satisfied smile. "Oh, I've known that boy since he was knee-high to a grasshopper. Always had a good heart. Stubborn as a bull sometimes, but his intentions are always clear and honest."

Grace couldn't help but smile at the way Martha spoke about Ben—with the fondness of a family member, or perhaps a friend.

Martha's brow quirked as she took a sip of her coffee, her eyes still fixed on Grace. "Careful now, Grace. A girl could get quite comfortable here... between the river, the people, and a certain tour guide who doesn't seem to mind showing you the ropes."

"Whoa, let's not get ahead of ourselves," Grace said, waving her hands in mock defense, though her smile betrayed her amusement.

Martha chuckled, her eyes gleaming with quiet wisdom. "Of course, of course." She paused. "But... you know, Grace, some things have a way of falling into place when you least expect them. Like drifting down a river—you don't always know what's around the bend, but sometimes what you find can take your breath away."

"A river metaphor, huh? You and Ben have a way with those," Grace said.

Martha winked and patted her hand before straightening again. "Maybe so. Or maybe we just know a thing or two about driftin' through life ourselves."

The bell dinged above the door as a couple of locals shuffled in, greeting Martha with wide smiles and nods. Martha's attention shifted for a moment as she welcomed them.

"Well," Martha said, "You enjoy the rest of that cookie. And don't forget, dinner. Six o'clock, sharp. You don't even need to bring anything, just yourself."

Grace smiled, feeling lighter than she had all day. "Wouldn't miss it. Thanks, Martha."

"Anytime, sweetheart," Martha said, her eyes twinkling once more before she turned to tend to the new arrivals.

# Chapter 18

Grace turned into Martha's driveway, a nervous flutter deep in her chest reminding her she was stepping into something unfamiliar. This wasn't a power luncheon with colleagues or a networking event where every conversation had an angle—this was something different, something more personal. It had been years since Grace walked into a room filled with women without an agenda, not since her carefree college days when laughter and connection weren't calculated, but effortless.

Her palms felt a little clammy as she continued up the driveway. Yet beneath the nerves, there was a flicker of something else, too—excitement. The thought of relaxing, spending an evening surrounded by women who weren't trying to hurry her along or dig for something beneath the surface stirred a longing in her.

Martha's farmhouse was exactly what she expected—cozy and practical. The whitewashed exterior had the comfortable, lived-in look that invited you in without pretense.

The smell of roasting chicken drifted through the open windows as Grace walked along the sidewalk leading to the front door.

She paused on the quaint front porch, hesitating before knocking.

Grace glanced down at her casual jeans, pink flannel shirt, jacket, and tennis shoes. Had she at least dressed the part? She felt...out of place. But Martha had reassured her earlier. "Come as you are," she'd said, with that motherly twinkle in her eye.

Before Grace could change her mind and turn back towards her SUV, the door opened.

"Grace, dear, you made it!" Martha's voice boomed with genuine delight as she enveloped Grace in a hug that felt like coming home. "Come on in and join us!"

The farmhouse was clearly lived in, worn in all the best ways—comfortable, functional, and filled with heart. The living room was a cozy, inviting space. Mismatched pillows in earthy tones of burgundy, olive, and cream were scattered across a well-loved couch. In front of it, a braided rug stretched across the wide-planked wood floor, the kind you could imagine children playing on while the adults sipped coffee and chatted.

A rustic stone fireplace dominated one wall, its mantle adorned with framed photos of smiling faces and sunlit moments.

A quilt draped over the arm of an overstuffed armchair in the corner, looking as though it were just waiting for someone to curl up with it and get lost in a good book.

Bookshelves flanked either side of the fireplace, stuffed not only with books but with a mix of trinkets—ceramic roosters, glass jars filled with marbles, an antique clock that had long stopped ticking but remained part of the decor like an honored elder in the family. The faint scent of beeswax from polished wood mingled with the aroma of fresh baked bread from the kitchen, adding another layer of comfort to the welcoming atmosphere.

Martha's home felt timeless and reassuring, as though every detail spoke of years spent loving the space and the people within it.

"Come on, now," Martha said, beckoning Grace to follow her. "I'd like you to meet a few of my dearest friends."

Grace followed Martha into an enormous kitchen. The space radiated warmth and charm. Cleary, it was the very heart of Martha's cozy country home. The soft butter-yellow hue of the kitchen cabinets contrasted beautifully against the deep rustic walnut floors. Hanging copper pots gleamed above a long, worn-wood island, their surfaces glowing under the gentle light of a glass pendant lamp that hung overhead. Along the far wall, a large oak dining table nestled into the bay window, its surface weathered and smooth from years of shared meals and conversations. Soft linen curtains in a simple checkered blue and white pattern flanked the windows, fluttering in the evening breeze.

"First up, we've got Beth, whom you've already met. She's the genius behind making sure we all look far more fashionable than we've got any right to in a small town." Martha said as she gestured toward the women seated around the table.

Beth chuckled and winked at Grace. "Now, Martha, you're buttering me up. It's good to see you again, Grace. And you look like a doll in your new duds!"

"Thanks to you, Beth," Grace responded with a nod.

Martha moved on, gesturing to a young woman seated next to Beth. "And this is Leslie Williams. Her lovely flower shop, Leslie's Blossoms, is next door to Beth's shop."

Leslie's vibrant auburn hair fell in loose waves around her freckled face. She had that glowing, effortless style that was all warmth and color. "If you're ever in need of a bouquet—or just some friendly conversation—my shop's got both," Leslie quipped with an inviting smile.

Grace nodded, already picturing Leslie tinkering with flowers, hands covered in petals and greenery. "I'm sure I'll be dropping by. I could use a few tips on keeping plants alive."

Leslie grinned, taking pleasure in the banter. "Challenge accepted."

Next was Claire Thompson, who sat with her hands folded neatly in her lap, graceful and composed. "And of course, you've already met Claire," Martha said. "She's the pastor's wife and the heart of this little community. She's also the wisest woman I know."

Grace exchanged a warm smile with Claire. "So glad you could join us tonight," Claire said, her voice rich with sincerity.

Martha rounded up the introductions by pointing a thumb playfully at Rachel, who had claimed her spot, sitting on a countertop nearby. "And last but certainly not least, Rachel Turner, Ben's sister and local art gallery owner, who brings all kinds of culture to our corner of the world. Now she's a character. You gotta watch that one."

Rachel gave an exaggerated wave. "Nice to finally meet you, Grace!"

"Now girls, you be good to Grace. She's visiting Laurel Ridge, taking a break from the clutches of the big city." Martha said with her characteristic humor.

Grace's shoulders relaxed, warmed not only by the cozy kitchen but by the welcoming kindness radiating from each of these women. "Thank you for having me this evening, Martha. I have a feeling I'm going to enjoy the rest of my stay here in Laurel Ridge. Everyone has been so good to me."

Martha smiled in return. "Go on and take a seat, Grace. And Rachel, you hustle yourself off my counter and take a seat. Supper's ready, and it's been far too long since I've had such good company around my dinner table."

The women offered soft nods of agreement, smiling in a way that spoke of years of easy friendship. Bowls and platters of food circulated around the table as conversations flowed, just like the meal itself—consistently and full of flavor.

"Oh, Martha, you've outdone yourself—again," Beth said. "What's your secret? I need to know if it involves some kind of magic."

Martha laughed. "Hardly magic, dear. Just time. And a lot of butter."

"So, Grace, what do you think of Laurel Ridge so far?" Rachel asked.

"It's... different, that's for sure," she replied with a nervous laugh, drizzling gravy over her potatoes. "Not at all like New York. Slower. Way less...noise. But I'm enjoying myself."

Beth nodded. "Noise doesn't always come from just sound, does it? Sometimes, it's our own mind working overtime."

"Exactly." Grace nodded, surprised at how well Beth understood. "In New York, there's always something, or someone, demanding your attention. It's hard to decompress. But here..." she trailed off, searching for the right words. "Here, the quiet? It's almost... shocking. It's taking me a little longer to adjust than I expected."

Rachel gave her an understanding look. "The quiet can become something pretty amazing if you give it time."

As the meal continued, the warmth of shared conversation crept under Grace's skin, seeping into the parts of her that had been closed off for so long. The easy flow of words around the table shifted into a lighthearted banter of local gossip.

"You'll never guess—Earl down at the hardware store accidentally locked himself in his storage room for a few hours before anyone found him. Bless his heart; apparently, his wife wasn't too pleased when he finally got home." Beth said.

The table exploded into laughter. Grace joined in, letting her guard down even more. Beth's southern charm and the way she spun the story made it impossible not to laugh.

"And here I thought small towns were void of excitement." Grace quirked a teasing eyebrow.

"Excitement? Oh, honey, just wait until the Harvest Festival starts," Leslie said, leaning forward with a wink.

"Glad you brought that up," Claire chimed in. "Grace, I'm not sure if you remember me bringing the festival up the other evening when we first met. But I hope you come. Martha's been spearheading the potluck dinner planning for weeks now."

Grace leaned in a little. "A festival, huh? What's it like?"

"Oh, it's not one of those commercialized things like you might see in the city," Rachel explained. "It's all homemade pies, local vendors, and hayrides. A way for everyone to take a breath, step away from the usual routine, and just... have some fun."

"It's definitely something we look forward to every year," Claire added. "The kids, especially. But I think it's a real gift for us adults, too. A reminder that God instills joy in the everyday simple things—families coming together, laughter, and fellowship."

"I just may have to check this festival out while I'm here. It sounds like something I would enjoy," Grace said.

"Now, tell us about your little adventure with my brother," Rachel said, steering the conversation in another direction. "I hear you took a little private tour via a kayak on the river." Rachel grinned, clearly having heard Ben's version of events.

Grace laughed. "Thanks, Ben, for letting that get out."

"Oh, come on now," Rachel coaxed as she grinned. "Do tell."

Grace retold the story, laughing as she explained her feeble attempts to stay balanced in the kayak while Ben effortlessly guided them through the water.

"It wasn't as bad as I'm making it sound. Ben did most of the work, and I pretended like I knew what I was doing until I caught on. I was so worried at first I would tip the kayak and put us both in the river. Ben never said a word about how uncoordinated I really was," Grace admitted.

Leslie waved her hand dismissively. "That's half of the charm of learning to kayak. We all had to start somewhere."

Martha raised an eyebrow, a playful smile tugging at her lips. "Our Ben, he's a good one."

Grace nodded, her smile softening. "He is definitely a wonderful tour guide. But truthfully...kayaking on the river was wonderful. And way more enjoyable than I expected."

Their stories and laughter continued to flow around the table, tales of life in Laurel Ridge that Grace couldn't help but be drawn into—the annual Harvest Festival preparations, the mishaps of running their local businesses, and even playful rumors that floated around town like cotton in the wind. Each of these women carried a piece of Laurel Ridge with them, and with every story, Grace could feel her earlier nervousness melting away.

"So, tell us, Grace. What brought you here to Laurel Ridge?" Beth asked. The table quieted as the attention shifted toward her.

Grace swallowed, very aware that all eyes were on her.

"Well... it's a bit complicated," she began, fiddling with the edge of her napkin. "I guess you could say I needed a change. My life in New York was, um, pretty chaotic. Fast-paced. Lots of work, no real... space to breathe." Her words came slowly, like she was still trying to piece them together in her own mind.

Martha's soft, maternal smile encouraged her to continue.

"I thought coming here might give me some room to breathe," Grace confided, her voice soft but steady. "To figure things out." She hesitated for a moment before continuing, "To be honest, I was forced to resign from my job. And though it was all a shock at first, I'm seeing now that it really was for the best. I think I'm finally starting to see things more clearly—about what I want, and how I want to live my life from here on."

Before she could say more, Rachel leaned in, her tone light but genuine. "Wow, that's a lot. Bless your heart."

"So tell me, Rachel, you own an art gallery in town. Right?" Grace asked, trying to steer the conversation away from herself and into more comfortable waters.

Rachel nodded, her face lighting up. "That's right. It's small, but I love it. Art is a passion of mine. I offer pieces in my store that I create, as well as those from other artists."

Claire tilted her head thoughtfully. "Rachel was pivotal in helping grow the arts community here. She's brought in artists from all over the region."

Grace smiled, catching the pride in Claire's voice. "That sounds incredible. It must be rewarding, offering people a platform like that."

Rachel hesitated a little, brushing a lock of hair behind her ear that had slipped free from her braid. "It is," she agreed. "Though, things are a bit tough at the moment. I'm trying to figure out how to bring in more business, but... well, marketing's never been my strong suit."

Immediately, Grace went into problem-solving mode. Marketing strategies, branding campaigns, target demographics—all the things that had once consumed her twirled in your mind. And while she would rather not dive headfirst back into business mode, there was something about Rachel's situation that tugged at her. Here was someone passionate and talented, someone trying to make a differ-ence—but struggling against the weight of logistics. It was similar to her own struggles, though in a different form.

"That's actually something I know a little about," Grace said. "Af-ter I graduated from college and moved to New York, I was a marketing specialist at first, and then I moved into Public Relations."

Rachel's eyes lit up. "Really? I had no idea."

Grace nodded. "If you ever want to talk, I'd be happy to give you some ideas, maybe help with some strategies."

"I'd love that," Rachel said with a grin. "Coffee at the gallery some-time soon?"

"Definitely," Grace agreed. "How about if I pop in tomorrow?"

"Sounds like a plan. I'll be there all day. Stop by anytime," Rachel said.

# Chapter 19

Grace pulled the quilt closer, sinking into the softness of her bed. The events of the day drifted through her mind as the soft pitter-patter of rain drummed against the window as if to soothe her restless thoughts.

As her eyes grew heavier, her phone pinged.

Grace blinked groggily as her head popped off the pillow. The small screen glowed on the nightstand beside her, vibrating lightly with each ring. Disoriented, she squinted at the screen. Mom.

She sat up, frowning instantly. Why was her mother calling at—she glanced at the clock on her phone—ten-thirty at night? Her stomach sank. It could only mean one thing: bad news.

"Mom?" Grace said, a hint of concern threading through her voice.

"Oh, Grace, sweetheart!" Louise's voice came through the phone, warm but laced with worry. "I'm so glad to hear your voice. Your dad and I just saw something that... well, is upsetting, but expected."

Grace's heart sank. "What's going on?"

"It's your uncle Tom," Louise started, her tone shifting to one of gentle urgency. "He's been indicted on felony charges. The news just broke."

"Indicted." Grace felt the weight of the word settle heavily in her chest.

Louise exhaled a shaky breath, her heart aching for her brother-in-law. "Yes, honey. It's all over the news. Mismanagement and misuse of funds. I'm still having a hard time wrapping my head around him in sitting in a prison for years...let alone the fact that he stole money."

Grace closed her eyes, swallowing hard against the rising tide of emotions. Tom had been a fixture in her life, a mentor, and someone she had admired deeply. Now, his image was fractured. "I don't even know what to say."

"I know," Louise said, her voice steadying as she spoke. "Your dad and I have talked about it a lot. We're just... disappointed. We prayed for Tom, and we're still praying for him, but he has to face the consequences."

Grace nodded, even though her mother couldn't see her. "I know. It's just heartbreaking."

"Of course it is, love. There's so much at stake now, and your uncle has put himself—and everyone—into a really tough situation. It makes my heart ache," Louise said, her tone softening. "But how are you doing? Really?"

"I'm okay," Grace replied, her voice lightening, though the weariness lingered.

"Oh, Grace," her mother said, a hint of relief rushing through her words. "That's good to hear! We have been so worried about you leaving New York. We were praying you would find peace."

"I really needed to escape the city and find some clarity," Grace admitted. "Things in New York got so overwhelming, with the scandal and my job. If I'm being honest, I haven't been happy in my job for several months, long before...well, before Tom's mistake came to light."

"I'm so proud of you for stepping away, sweetheart," Louise said, her voice brimming with maternal pride. "That took a lot of courage."

Grace felt a flutter of warmth from her mother's encouragement. "Thanks, Mom. I have no plans to return. I think it's time for something different. A new beginning, if you will."

"Oh? You don't plan to look for another job back in New York?" Louise asked, her curiosity piquing.

"Nope," Grace replied, tucking a stray hair behind her ear. "I mean, I might eventually if I absolutely have to. But my savings account is healthy enough that I could take a year or more to figure out what I want to do."

Louise's voice brightened. "That sounds like a wonderful plan! Here's an idea: find a local coffee shop, and bring out the laptop! You can work remotely while getting to know your neighbors there in Laurel Ridge. I know you love that little town. Plus, if that doesn't work out, you can always come back to Charleston, right?"

Grace hesitated. "Honestly, Mom, I think I will stay here in Laurel Ridge for a while. And yes, I could look for remote work. I hadn't considered that yet. I've missed West Virginia so much. It's peaceful, and... I just feel different here." She paused, rummaging through her thoughts. "This town feels right. There's something honest about it, and that's what I need after all the chaos."

"And whenever you feel overwhelmed by the chaos stemming from Tom's troubles, just take a moment to look around you. Lean into the support of those who care about you, and remember to pray over everything," Louise said gently.

"I will," Grace agreed, the sincerity shining through her words.

"How about we end this lovely conversation with a prayer?" Louise suggested.

Grace nodded, utterly grateful. "Yes, please."

"Dear Lord," Louise began softly, Grace closing her eyes and linking her heart with her mother's words. "We thank You for this new beginning for Grace and for the peace You're placing in her heart. We ask for wisdom with the challenges Tom has brought before us and pray for his heart, Lord. Let us, as a family, draw closer together—bind us in this time and guide Grace so she feels Your love surrounding her daily."

Grace smiled with the softness of her mother's tone, filling her mind with love and warmth. The prayer flowed over her like gentle rain, nourishing her spirit.

"Let her find a home in a place that brings her joy, and guide her through this time with clarity," Louise concluded, her voice rising with hope.

"Amen," Grace said, as a tingle of emotion swirled within her.

"Goodnight, Grace," Louise rasped, her voice choked with unshed tears of tenderness and concern.

"Goodnight, Mom. I love you."

# Chapter 20

As Grace meandered along the peaceful country road toward town, her mind couldn't stop replaying the events of the night before at Martha's home. She had felt unburdened in a way she hadn't in so long. Laughing freely with the women, sharing stories, enjoying simple, hearty food—it was so vastly different from the high-stakes, polished conversations she'd perfected back in New York. There was no strategic positioning, no glitzy networking hidden beneath casual laughter. Just a genuine connection.

As she turned off Main Street, The Silver Brush Art Gallery came into view. Grace pulled up in front of the modest, blue-painted building, admiring the quaintness of it. Through the large windows of the art gallery, she could see Rachel bustling around inside.

Stepping out of the car, she grabbed her notebook, having brought it along out of habit. Not that she intended to take this get-together too seriously, but just in case. There was a part of her that itched to help Rachel solve her business problems. Grace thrived on answers and solutions, on making things better. It would be fulfilling to use her skills in a way that wasn't about climbing to the top—but simply helping a friend.

Grace entered the gallery. The quiet serenity and beauty of the space hit her immediately. The walls were a crisp white, acting as a clean canvas for the various art pieces that adorned them. Soft music played in the background.

"Grace! So glad you came." Rachel approached her, wiping her hands on a bright cobalt-blue apron splattered with paint. "Welcome to The Silver Brush."

"It's beautiful in here," Grace said, her eyes skimming the artwork that hung on the walls. They each told a story—bright oil landscapes of the mountains, soft watercolor florals, intricate ceramics arranged on shelves in one corner. "You have so much here. Such a variety."

Rachel grinned, her eyes lighting up with pride. "Most of the artists are local. I try to highlight different talents from around the region—show people what they wouldn't normally see if they just stick to the city galleries or online shopping."

Grace nodded, her gaze drifting to one piece—a vibrant abstract painting that seemed to swirl with movement. "That's part of what makes this gallery so special. I can tell just walking in here that it's got its own kind of... soul. A special feel to it."

Rachel's face softened as she looked at her, and Grace could tell those words had meant something. "Thank you," Rachel said. "That's all I've ever hoped for."

Grace walked farther into the gallery, taking in more of the pieces, but as she moved, she couldn't help but notice there was an emptiness here. "So, how's business been going?"

Rachel hesitated for just a millisecond before closing the gap and sighing a little. "It's... okay. Well, I mean, it's been tough lately. I get visitors, sure, but they usually come through town in waves—tourism helps a lot. But when the tourist season slows down, so does traffic. And locals... well," she chuckled. "They don't buy new art that often."

Grace nodded again, her mind already clicking into gear. There it was—the problem she had guessed from the moment she walked in. "It's got so much potential," Grace said, her eyes roaming over the arrangement of displays. "But it might need a little... push. Something to grab people's attention. To keep them engaged, even when it's not a peak tourist season," she suggested.

Rachel's expression shifted, her hope mingling with exhaustion. "I've been thinking the same thing, honestly, but I'm not really sure where to start. Social media isn't my thing. Marketing or branding isn't either."

Grace's lips quirked. "That's actually something I'm pretty good at. How much time do you have today?"

Rachel's eyes brightened, and she brushed a lock of her chestnut colored hair behind her ear. "I've got time. I honestly didn't think you'd want to dive into this so soon, but... oh man, I'd love your help."

Grace smiled. "Well, it seems like a good day to me to make a strategy."

With that, Grace pulled out her notebook and began writing things down. Leaning against the gallery counter, her fingers tapping on her pen, Grace asked, "Have you thought about creating a strong brand voice? A memorable identity for The Silver Brush?"

Rachel blinked at her. "Brand voice? You mean like... a slogan?"

"More than just a slogan," Grace explained. "It's about telling people what your gallery represents. You said you highlight local artists—that's powerful. That's your edge. People are drawn to stories. And you're not just selling art; you're selling the stories behind those pieces. You need to let people know what makes this gallery different from the hundreds of others out there."

Rachel tilted her head, intrigued. "Okay... like, what would that look like?"

"Well," Grace leaned forward, excited now. "You could brand The Silver Brush as the gallery where art and community meet. Something that speaks to the idea that buying a piece from here means taking home a piece of Laurel Ridge. You could focus on local, hand-crafted, unique art pieces that people can't get anywhere else. Create a tagline that highlights that connection." She scribbled down a few examples and passed the notebook over to Rachel.

Rachel studied the words for a moment and then looked back up, nodding. "I like that. I never really thought of it that way. That the story could be part of the sale."

Grace grinned. "Exactly. It's not about being flashy. It's about being authentic. That's what people connect to."

Rachel lit up, excitement replacing her previous hesitation. "Okay, I'm sold. Where do we start?"

"Let's start with a brand refresh—a strong slogan or tagline, as we've already brainstormed, and maybe creating a consistent visual theme. Your gallery is gorgeous, but galleries live and die by their visual appeal. Let's create a welcoming environment but keep it fresh, so people who walk by are intrigued enough to come inside."

Rachel nodded. "Makes sense. What do you suggest?"

"Perhaps something soft but elegant," Grace replied, scanning the room again. "You want the art to take center stage, but the branding—your website, your fliers, your social media—should echo that same subtle, artisanal elegance. I'm seeing warm-neutral tones—something that feels inviting but doesn't compete with the art."

Rachel's eyes flicked up toward the incoming light from the windows, then back down to the notebook before looking at Grace. "That could work. Yeah."

They spent the next few hours sketching out a rough timeline for how they could create this visual consistency. Grace suggested practical ways of implementing small changes without overwhelming Rachel's workload.

"Every step should be manageable," Grace encouraged. "No need to tackle everything at once. Start with the small stuff—branding, fliers, and definitely social media."

Rachel winced at the mention of social media, and Grace chuckled. "Don't worry—I'll walk you through it."

Grace's phone buzzed from her back pocket. Without thinking, she pulled it out, glancing at the screen. Jack's name blinked up at her, along with the preview of a new email:

*Still waiting for your decision. Time's running out.*

Her chest tightened.

He had been patient—well, patient for Jack. But she knew this email was his polite way of saying she needed to give him an answer or risk losing the opportunity altogether. The shiny titles, the lucrative paycheck, the prospect of her returning to New York—the life she had spent years building felt like it was clawing its way back into her present.

For a moment, Grace's vision tunneled. The walls of the quaint, calm gallery seemed to shrink, and her heart began drumming faster.

A soft voice snapped her out of the spiral.

"Is everything okay?" Rachel shot her a curious glance, her eyes filled with concern.

Grace turned her phone off and tucked it away. She forced a light smile. "Oh, yeah. Sorry. Just... something from New York."

Rachel nodded. "Work stuff?"

Grace shrugged. "Sort of. But nothing that can't wait." She didn't want to dive into Jack's message or the life-altering decision hanging over her.

"You sure?" Rachel pressed, eyebrows drawn with earnest concern.

"I'm sure," Grace replied, waving it off. "Really, don't worry about it. Right now, let's focus on you and your gallery."

***

By late afternoon, they'd covered branding and dipped into the meatier subject of promotional events.

"I'm thinking you should host something special—maybe once a month?" Grace suggested, her mind alive with possibilities. "You could create Gallery Nights where the artists can meet potential buyers face-to-face, and people will feel like they're part of something exclusive. It could be a fun experience for locals and tourists alike. Have appetizers available to encourage people to stay and linger, and maybe even live music. You turn the gallery from a retail space into an experience."

Rachel had been scribbling furiously, pausing now to look up. "I like that...community events. An experience of something that feels natural, organic even."

"Exactly." Grace pointed at her excitedly. "You're not trying to force people in—you're inviting them to experience something meaningful."

They spent the next hour hammering out the details of what a Gallery Night would look like.

After that, Grace touched on some low-budget but effective ways of promoting The Silver Brush through social media. "It's all about telling your story," Grace said, tapping her pen. "Instagram would be great for you—posting pictures of the art, sure, but also behind-the-scenes stuff. Show people how the gallery operates—give them a peek into your process, your artists. People love that personal connection."

"Do you think that'll help? I'm no expert with hashtags and all that. In fact, social media gives me a headache just thinking about it." Rachel gave a wry smile.

"You don't have to be an expert at all," Grace assured her. "It just needs to be consistent. Pictures, stories, live videos—maybe even something like a behind-the-scenes video tour sometime."

Rachel let out a slow breath, her eyes wide. "This is... way more involved than I thought. But you make it sound doable."

Grace laughed. "That's because it is doable. One step at a time. Let's start with Instagram. Do you have a laptop?"

Rachel nodded, gesturing toward a small corner desk. "Yeah, over there. It's an old thing, slower than your average cell phone, but it gets the job done." She walked over to the desk and pulled out a slightly battered laptop, opening it with a quick smile of apology. "Don't laugh, it's not exactly cutting edge."

Grace chuckled, waving off the comment. "Hey, as long as it works, it's perfect."

Rachel powered it on, and soon enough, Grace was navigating through the Instagram settings, showing Rachel the step-by-step process of setting up a business Instagram account.

"Alright," Grace said, her fingers flying across the keyboard. "First thing we'll do is set up a cohesive profile—your username is super important here. Something simple and memorable, not too different from your gallery's actual name."

Rachel watched, leaning in over Grace's shoulder. "Would the name of the gallery work, or would that be too long?"

Shaking her head, Grace smiled. "Nope, it's perfect. It tells people exactly who you are and what they're looking at. Now, for the bio..." She paused before typing, "Where the art of Laurel Ridge meets community. Local artists, curated experiences, and a touch of southern charm. How's that sound?"

Rachel's eyes lit up. "I love that! You make it sound so... inviting."

Grace scribbled down a few more thoughts in the margins of her notepad. "We can always tweak or add more down the line, but let's start here. Next, a profile picture. Do you have a simple logo or artwork that you think best represents The Silver Brush?"

Rachel nodded, turning to the shelf behind her and pulling out a small framed piece with the gallery's logo—a simple, elegant brushstroke in silver that swirled into a stylized frame with the name underneath. "How about this?"

Grace grinned. "Perfect." She snapped a quick photo of the framed piece with her phone and uploaded it to the new account with ease. "Now your official."

Rachel's excitement was palpable. "Okay, now what? You said something about posting stories?"

"Yep!" Grace began typing again, explaining the process aloud. "So for right now, you'll want to start with a few introductory posts—maybe a shot of the gallery, some of your favorite pieces, or even a picture of you working on your next display. Just little things to show people the behind-the-scenes of what you do and why it matters."

She took Rachel's phone and began snapping some images of various corners of the gallery, explaining angles, lighting, and potential captions.

Grace continued guiding Rachel through the basics of navigating Instagram. By the time they had set up their first few posts, along with scheduling a few more for the next week, Rachel was grinning ear to ear.

"Wow." Grace sat back, pushing her hair out of her eyes. "I didn't realize how long we've been at this."

Rachel let out a breathless laugh. "Same! We've been working all day, but it went by so fast." She snapped her notebook shut in triumph. "This has been incredible. I haven't felt so excited about the gallery in... goodness, months."

"Well, I'm glad to hear it," Grace said, stretching her arms overhead and feeling that familiar satisfaction of a job well done.

Rachel checked her phone and sighed. "Shoot. I almost forgot, I have dinner plans with Ben." She looked up, "Grace, why don't you come with me?"

"Oh, I don't want to intrude," Grace said. "That's your family time."

Rachel waved it off as unimportant. "Oh, please, Ben won't mind. He'll be happy to see you again, I'm sure. Plus, maybe you'll get to meet some more locals—everyone gravitates to the diner in the evening. Come on, it'll be fun."

Grace nodded, smiling. "Alright. I'll come."

Rachel beamed, tossing her things into her tote and locking up the gallery after they gathered their belongings. "Trust me, it'll be a relaxing end to a productive day."

Grace chuckled. "I sure hope so. We deserve it."

# Chapter 21

Grace and Rachel walked down Main Street towards the diner. The streetlamps casting a halo of light over the sidewalks.

Ahead, the diner's iconic neon sign blinked, swaying gently in the slight breeze. Grace took a deep breath, soaking it all in—this place, these people—it was a far cry from New York's hurried pace.

They were immersed in the scent of griddle burgers, crispy fries, and fresh apple pie the moment they walked through the door. The warm lighting reflected off the checkered tile floor. The hum of conversations filled the air.

Grace's gaze swept over the scene, admiring the simplicity of it all—a place where time felt untouched by the outside chaos of the world. Booths were filled with families, old high school friends, and couples sharing dinner.

Rachel leaned in. "Ben's already here. Looks like he nabbed our favorite spot."

Grace followed Rachel's gaze and spotted Ben seated in the corner booth near the windows, the kind that gave a good view of both the streets outside and the goings-on inside the diner. The lighting framed his figure as he flipped through the menu with casual interest. His gaze lifted as they approached, and he stood to greet them.

"Good to see you again, Grace. What have you two been up to today?" Ben asked.

"Nice to see you, too," Grace replied, as they slid into the booth. "We have had the best day talking strategies and marketing plans for the gallery. I think your sister may be a little excited!"

Ben chuckled. "Hmmm. Rachel's dangerous when she gets excited, you know. Sweeps you up in her whirlwind before you know what hit you."

"Hey!" Rachel protested, swatting her brother on the arm with a playful laugh. "I'm not that bad."

Grace, laughing along, shook her head. "Actually, no... he's not wrong. Once you get going, it's pretty hard to stop."

"Well, if that's what I need to do to get this one,"—Rachel gestured towards Grace—"to literally save my business, I'll take it."

Ben quirked an eyebrow, his gaze flicking between his sister and Grace. "So, what's all this about saving the business?"

"Oh, where to begin?" Rachel launched into a lively recount of their afternoon, her hands punctuating the air as she spoke. "First, you should have seen her at the gallery today. I was stuck in the weeds, drowning with no proper direction, and—" she threw an adoring glance at Grace, who blushed, "—she came in like some kind of marketing superhero."

"She's exaggerating," Grace interjected, trying to downplay the praise, though her smile betrayed the pleasure it gave her.

Rachel wasn't having it, though. "No, no. You don't get to be humble. You totally revamped everything—gave me an actual plan! Marketing ideas, social media help... the whole package!"

Ben leaned back, crossing his arms with a thoughtful expression, though a spark of amusement danced in his eyes. "Is that so?" His gaze turned to Grace. "You're pulling off superhero feats now?"

Grace sighed dramatically. "Don't tell anyone. I've been keeping the cape under wraps for a while now."

Ben's laugh was soft but genuine, and Grace enjoyed the flow of banter between them. The relaxed energy between the three felt natural.

Martha bustled over, an apron wrapped around her waist and a notepad in hand. "Well now, if it isn't the Turner siblings and their charming recent addition," she announced with a welcoming smile. "Y'all ready to order, or do you need a few more minutes?"

Rachel was the first to speak. "We'll take two cheeseburgers—mine with chili and Ben with everything except pickles."

Grace glanced over the menu and couldn't help but chuckle. "You two really have this down to a science, don't you?"

"We've been coming here our entire lives," Ben explained with an exaggerated sigh of long-suffering. "I think Martha could order for us without even asking at this point."

Martha gave them all a wink. "You know that's right."

Grace quickly decided. "I'll join the burger party... but make mine with mushrooms and grilled onions, please."

"Oh, somehow I knew you were a mushroom and onions king of gall!" Martha teased as she jotted down their orders. "And of course, y'all will be getting some of my famous fries on the side. Don't think I'd let you get away without 'em. I'll be back with your food in a jiffy!"

"So, about the gallery," Ben started, his voice laced with curiosity. "How big a difference do you think these new strategies will make? I know Rachel can hold her own, but there's been talk among the locals about how hard it's been for smaller businesses here lately."

Grace hesitated for a moment before answering, "Well, to be honest, it's a tough market everywhere right now, but especially so for small businesses. But Rachel has a real advantage—her work is personal. People are drawn to authenticity, especially when it comes to art. And Laurel Ridge has this... charm to it. People come here because of the experience. I think, with the right steps, her gallery will find a new rhythm."

Ben nodded, then folded his arms on the table. "Makes sense. Experiences are what people chase after."

"Definitely. It's that feeling of connection they can't get anywhere else," Grace said.

Ben's eyes studied her for a moment before he spoke again. "You know, speaking of businesses... I've been thinking about expanding mine. I've got acres of land just sitting there that I'm not using. I've been tossing around the idea more since we last talked. I'm thinking of expanding my current building into a lodge and also and adding cabins out in the woods for visitors. Folks are constantly looking for places to stay outside of town."

Rachel leaned in, nodding. "He's being modest, you know. He's got fifty acres out there, and I've got another fifty right next to him. Our parents left it to us when they passed."

"That's a lot of land." Grace's eyebrows rose in surprise as she looked at Ben.

"Exactly! And right now, it's just sitting there," Rachel added, showing her enthusiasm for her brother's plan. "There's so much potential to grow tourism in Laurel Ridge."

Grace's brain, already in creative problem-solving mode, began to churn again. Connecting dots. "You know... with that much land, you could absolutely expand into a lodge or resort-style experience. There's not much out here for tourists besides The Laurel Ridge Inn, and I imagine they're always full during peak tourist season. I'd have to do some research, of course, but that's just my initial thoughts."

Ben's gaze sharpened, his interest clearly piqued by the direction she was heading. "Go on."

Grace's excitement grew, her voice rounding out the idea. "Okay, so hear me out. What if you combined both of your properties—maybe not physically, but conceptually? Together, you both could offer a full-package experience to tourists. Ben first add a few cozy cabins nestled in the woods. Rachel guided art classes along the riverbank. Then top it off with your adventure packages Ben—kayaking, hiking, maybe even add more outdoor activities like zip-lining or horseback riding? Rachel, you could offer a variety of painting lessons. Group or private lessons on the property, with students learning how to draw or paint the gorgeous scenery around them. It would be one cohesive tourist package and destination. Ben, over time you could begin adding on to the Adventures tours building, expanding into a lodge or even building a separate space. Or, if the cabins are a big hit, consider adding more in a variety of sizes, you know, maybe a few that a dozen or so people could sleep in comfortably."

Rachel beamed. "Oh man, Grace, stop giving me goosebumps! That is... that's incredible!"

Ben let out a low whistle, sitting back to absorb it all. "Cabins... more outdoor activities, huh?"

Grace leaned forward, caught up in her idea now. "Why not? You've got the land, the resources, and honestly—despite being a small town, this place has everything a tourist could want."

Excitement crackled at the table, with Rachel practically bouncing in her seat, unable to contain her energy at the thought. "I can already see it, Ben! This is huge!"

Surprisingly, though, Ben didn't jump in on the enthusiasm right away. Instead, he watched Grace closely—his expression more contemplative than excited. After moments of silence, he leaned forward a little, his tone gentle but serious.

"You may be on to something," he said, his voice carrying a deeper tone that commanded attention. "Grace, you've described a dream expansion better than I've imagined."

Grace blinked, taken aback by the shift in his tone and by the realization that, yes—she had rambled off a few ideas rather quickly, but she could clearly imagine it and it could work.

Ben continued, "It's not just a casual idea. It's a real vision—one that could change things here permanently. For this town. For me. For Rachel. And maybe... for you."

Heat rushed to Grace's cheeks at those last few words. "For me?"

Ben's gaze was steady, his tone almost cautious, like he was feeling out the unfamiliar conversation. "What I mean is... everything you've said so far, it makes perfect sense. But if this is going to come together, we'd need someone with your kind of expertise to guide it. You've got the know-how. You've already started helping us with things we didn't think possible. So it makes me wonder..." he trailed off, gathering his words carefully before meeting her eyes, "have you thought about... staying? Longer than you initially planned, I mean. Maybe even making Laurel Ridge your permanent home?"

Stay.

The word lingered in the air between them, enough that Rachel leaned back, her eyes flicking between the two, almost as if she had sensed the change in the mood.

Grace struggled to find words, her mind whirring and her emotions swimming in a strange mix of confusion and temptation.

Rachel broke the brief silence with a playful laugh. "Well, now we're just springing ideas all over the place, aren't we?"

Grace managed a smile, grateful for Rachel's lightness at that moment, but her heart pounded in her chest. Could she stay? Could she make this sleepy, peaceful place—so vastly different from her carefully constructed career life—home? Home for good?

"You don't have to answer right now," Ben said, softer this time. "But think about it. What you've done today, just with Rachel's gallery—that's been more helpful than you know. I'm thinking this town could do with a little more of your expertise."

Martha approached with their dinner plates, breaking the moment with her usual chatty energy. "Here we go! Three burgers piled high. And don't forget, I'm giving y'all extra fries because you've got the biggest smiles in the entire diner."

The table shared an appreciative laugh, and the next few moments were spent passing around condiments and napkins. But Grace couldn't shake the excitement of the possibility of a huge career change, a fresh start. A do-over, right within her reach.

"What you're suggesting... it's big," she said, careful with her words. "Being here... staying here for a length of time... the thought has crossed my mind, sure."

Ben nodded. "Well...just think about it some more. Maybe explore the town a bit more. Even some of the surrounding towns. See if there are ways you could offer your services here. Maybe look into offering your services at City Hall, and help expand tourism."

Grace felt a flutter in her chest at his words. Could Laurel Ridge be more than just a temporary home away from home? The thought both excited and unnerved her. Could she build a business of her own?

"Who knows?" Ben added, "Maybe you were meant to be here all along. Maybe New York was just a pit stop. Sometimes, life has a way of pointing us in unexpected directions."

Grace nodded, mulling over his words.

Ben leaned back, his expression thoughtful. "You know, there's a verse in Jeremiah that's always stuck with me. It says, 'For I know the plans I have for you,' declares the Lord, 'plans to prosper you and not to harm you, plans to give you hope and a future.'" He paused, his gaze meeting Grace's. "Sometimes, the path we think we're supposed to be on isn't the one God has in mind for us. Maybe this detour to Laurel Ridge is more than just a break."

Grace felt a flutter in her chest at his words. The idea of divine guidance on her journey here was both comforting and intimidating. "I... I hadn't thought about it that way," she admitted softly.

Rachel chimed in with a mischievous grin. "Well, I, for one, think it's a great idea for you to stick around, Grace. This town could use someone with your talents." She paused, her eyes darting between Ben and Grace with a knowing look. "And who knows? You might find more than just a career change, too."

Grace felt the heat rise in her cheeks at Rachel's implication.

Rachel's grin widened. "Oh, come on, you two. Don't tell me I'm the only one seeing this... connection here?"

"Rachel," Ben warned, but there was no real heat in his tone. He looked at Grace apologetically. "Sorry about her. She likes to play matchmaker."

Grace laughed nervously, trying to dispel the tension. "It's okay. I'm... flattered." She met Ben's eyes, feeling a spark of... something again. Connection? Possibility?

Rachel clapped her hands together. "See? This is exactly why you should stay, Grace. Think of all the possibilities–for your career, for the town, and maybe," she wiggled her eyebrows suggestively, "for your personal life too."

"Alright, that's enough," Ben said, though he was smiling. He turned to Grace, his expression softening. "But in all seriousness, Grace, I hope you'll consider it. No pressure, of course. Just... keep an open mind?"

Grace nodded, feeling a mix of emotions swirling inside her. "I will," she promised. And as she looked at Ben's hopeful expression and felt the warmth of Rachel's enthusiasm, she realized that maybe, just maybe, Laurel Ridge was offering her more than just a temporary home. It was offering her a chance at a new beginning—in more ways than one.

# Chapter 22

*A few days later...*

The diner's morning rush had ebbed into a comfortable lull. Grace sat alone in a booth, her laptop in front of her, its muted light casting shapes across the pages of her open notebook. She had been gazing out the window for some time, captivated by the sight of Laurel Ridge as it unfolded before her—children darting between striped awnings, neighbors exchanging greetings, and couples strolling hand in hand down the quaint sidewalk. The town buzzed with a charm that felt almost timeless. Yet deep down, Grace was grappling with her own thoughts, trying to pen down the logistics of what it would take to create a business here in this idyllic mountain town.

Her mug of coffee had long since turned cold, but Martha, ever attentive, noticed it sitting neglected on the table. With a knowing smile, she approached, carrying a steaming pot and a fresh mug.

"Need a fresh cup of coffee, sweetie?" she asked.

Grace grinned, more grateful for the interruption than the coffee itself. "Yes, please."

Martha poured the fresh brew, her eyes glinting with that familiar twinkle. "What are you working on? Plotting more of Rachel's world takeover, I reckon?"

Grace couldn't help but laugh. "Something like that. We've made great progress in her gallery, but I was just looking over my notes, tying up a few loose ends. Thinking about a few things…"

Martha set the coffeepot down on the table and slid into the booth across from Grace.

"You've done more in these last few weeks that you've been here in Laurel Ridge than some of us manage in years," Martha said, folding her hands on the table. "You've got the head for it, no doubt. But what's been on my mind isn't what you have up here," she added, tapping one finger gently near Grace's temple, "but what you're holding back here." Her finger shifted downward, a casual point toward Grace's chest.

Grace stared back at Martha, at a loss for words.

Martha's eyes softened as she leaned in just a little more. "Listen, I don't know much about the big city life you've lived, but I've lived enough years to know when someone's restless, caught in a space between what they've left behind and what they're maybe a little afraid to move toward." She paused, her voice growing even gentler. "That's why I want to ask you if you'd come join me at church tonight. We're having a little planning meeting for the Harvest Festival, and I just thought… well, maybe you could lend us some of your talents. You know, join us, maybe meet a few more people. Spread your wings a little."

Grace smiled, grateful for Martha's gentle insight, but hesitant to share too much of her internal conflict. "I appreciate the invite,

Martha, but I have to confess...it's been a while since I stepped foot in a church for anything other than a wedding, funeral, or holiday service with my parents."

Martha waved her hand dismissively, brushing aside the notion. "Oh, darling, nobody's keeping score here! It's all about community, warmth, and fellowship. I can guarantee you'll see some familiar faces. Plus, you're always welcome to stick by my side. Or you could bring along some snacks to charm the crowd!" She winked, her tone teasing and playful.

"I'm not that great at baking. My idea of fancy is cinnamon and sugar toast!" Grace grinned. "So, tell me a little more about this planning meeting for the Harvest Festival? Is it pumpkin spice-flavored everything?"

Martha chuckled. "No, no! We'll probably enjoy a little pumpkin spice coffee this evening. I'm bringing some appetizers I whipped up, and others will most likely bring a few desserts or something to munch on. But the main focus of this meeting is just getting everything in order. If anyone has new ideas or suggestions, we'll dive into those as well. Trust me, Grace, we're a laid-back bunch. All we want is a fun, family-friendly festival, and so far, we've succeeded every year!"

Grace leaned back, her curiosity piqued. "Hmm... the snacks definitely sound tempting, and the company sounds delightful. However, I can't help but feel a bit apprehensive. I'm not a member of your church, and I worry that people might judge me, seeing me as a big-city snob intruding on their festival planning."

Martha leaned in, her expression sincere. "We're not like that here. None of us pass judgment in such a harsh way. You are always welcome in our church—our doors are open to everyone. We don't care if you're down to your last penny or if you're a millionaire. You are not a snob, Grace. I simply want you to come and enjoy an evening of fellowship with us."

Grace raised an eyebrow playfully. "Are you trying to recruit me for some church-side hustle, Martha?"

With a sparkle in her eye, Martha leaned back dramatically. "Well, now that you mention it, I do need someone to help me keep everyone in line! You'll be my assistant with a clipboard, and we can pretend we're in one of those planning montages from a movie. You know the type—cue the upbeat music, camera zooms in on the pie chart, and we both smile at the camera while sorting fall decorations!"

Grace burst into giggles. "That does sound appealing."

Martha let out a warm laugh and shook her head in amusement.

Grace rubbed the back of her neck, feeling a wave of awkwardness wash over her. "I just don't want to feel like a hypocrite, you know? It weighs heavy on my heart that I've sidelined God during my career."

Martha nodded, her tone gentle but firm. "Honey, don't you worry about a thing. It's natural to feel that way, but it's not a judgment call—just a part of life. Church is about embracing each moment, about picking up the pieces and building from there. It's okay to have stepped back; the important part is that you're stepping forward again now. God won't put you to the test for everything you've been through."

"You really think so? That he's not holding a grudge or...plotting some wild scheme for me every time I accidentally skip a Sunday?" Grace said with a grin.

Martha chuckled, her eyes kind. "Not in the slightest, you goof! But seriously, every day is an opportunity for renewal, dear. And here," she leaned in slightly, lowering her voice. "You know what the church crowd has? An endless supply of love and support. You walk in as you are, and nobody bats an eye. They embrace you just as you are."

Grace considered this for a moment, warmth spreading in her chest. "You know you're convincing me, right? I might just show up tonight..."

"Yes! That's the attitude to have, hon!" Martha clapped her hands together

# Chapter 23

Grace eased her car into the gravel lot of the Laurel Ridge Community Church, her fingers tight around the steering wheel, knuckles pale. Ahead, the modest white church stood framed by rolling hills and timeworn trees, its steeple rising with an unspoken grace against the landscape.

Her chest tightened.

It's just a meeting, she reminded herself, not a Sunday service. Just a handful of people planning an event.

With a deep breath, she stepped out of the car, gravel crunching softly beneath her feet. From somewhere behind the church, a ripple of laughter and easy conversation carried on the breeze. Turning the corner, her steps slowed as the scene unfolded before her.

Nearby, under the wooden shelter of a pavilion, a small gathering of people mingled in quiet camaraderie, their voices soft and harmonious, woven seamlessly into the tranquil mountain air. The scene exuded a timeless quality, as if plucked from another era and set gently in motion—organic, unhurried, real. The pavilion itself seemed to rise naturally from the earth, its thick, weathered beams standing sturdy, hinting at years passed. No walls enclosed the space; instead, it invited the cool breeze to flow freely through.

Above, a high, sloping roof of aged shingles blended effortlessly with the mountainside, as though the structure had always belonged there. Beneath it, wooden benches fanned out in a semicircle, offering an inviting space for rest. Strings of warm lights crisscrossed overhead, swaying gently in rhythm with the wind. Beyond the pavilion, picnic tables—draped in modest tablecloths—sat scattered across the grass, their surfaces holding small signs of activity: baskets, clipboards, and handwritten pages catching the glint of late afternoon light.

As soon as Grace stepped closer, she saw Martha, Rachel, and Ben among those milling about, chatting easily with one another and organizing supplies.

"There she is!" Martha waved.

Grace smiled and waved back, making her way toward them. Each step stirred a mix of excitement and unease within her, but the sight of their familiar faces felt like a warm embrace, gradually melting away her initial nerves.

"Glad you could make it," Rachel greeted. Next to her, Ben relaxed and laid back as usual.

"Did Martha twist your arm too hard?" Ben teased, his hazel eyes gleaming with a mix of humor and intent.

"She was actually pretty gentle," Grace said.

Casual chatter about the festival picked up. Grace lingered for a while, listening in on conversations about food vendors, hayrides, and the annual pie-baking contest that apparently held legendary status in the town.

Rachel handed her a clipboard detailing a list of marketing ideas and promotional strategies they wanted to implement for the festival.

It was second nature to Grace, like stepping into familiar waters, except these waters were different, perhaps warmer, more friendly and fun.

"You mind taking a look at that?" Pastor Eli asked as he approached Grace, his deep voice smooth and steady, like the Appalachian rivers themselves. His gray hair was neatly combed and his outdoorsy persona clear in the well-worn boots he wore with his button-down shirt. "Martha mentioned you've got some expertise that might come in handy. We're always looking for fresh ideas."

"Sure," she said, scanning the points written in neat handwriting. "I see you've got some good ideas here already. What do you most want to accomplish with the festival?"

Pastor Eli chuckled. "Well, truthfully? We just want people to come together. For some of them, it's the only chance they get all year to slow down, chat with community members, and let family ties grow a little stronger. We have many families that live on the outskirts of Laurel Ridge and don't have neighbors that live nearby. The festival's about connection—not just with each other, but with God's blessings we tend to overlook when life gets busy." He paused and added, "We try to bring in folks who may have forgotten that they're part of our community. And bringing in more visitors from surrounding towns certainly wouldn't hurt our local businesses, either."

Grace nodded, her thoughts turning. This differed from planning corporate events. It was more heartfelt, simpler, but also more meaningful. "Maybe we could broaden your outreach, try advertising the festival in nearby towns, and get on social media platforms. You'd be surprised how much traction you can get with a few targeted posts."

Pastor Eli raised an eyebrow, intrigued. "Social media, huh? Well, I don't know a thing about it, but if you think it'll help..."

"I'm happy to help," she offered.

As Grace was scribbling more notes onto the clipboard, the soft strumming of a Christian hymn began to play over an old radio that Pastor Eli had brought out. The soft melody of the hymn floated through the air, stirring something deep within Grace, tugging at long-buried memories. It transported her back to a sunlit church pew from her childhood. She could feel her mother beside her, singing the familiar tune in her warm, steady voice, her presence a balm against the restlessness always hovering just beneath Grace's surface. On the other side, Aunt Imogene's hand gently patted her small leg, keeping time with the music. She must have been six or seven then, her legs swinging back and forth idly, too young to stay still for long but soothed by the harmony of their voices.

Her hand froze, fingers hovering above the clipboard she'd been writing on, her focus drifting.

This place—this very church. She hadn't thought about it in forever, but now, standing here, it hit her. She had been here before. Often, actually. How could she have forgotten?

When she was younger, visiting Aunt Imogene every summer, her parents had always made it a point to attend this very church. She could practically feel her small, childlike hands clasped in theirs as they walked together across these same grounds, the cool morning air and the ringing of the church bell almost palpable in her mind.

Back then, the church had felt like its own little world. Even if they only attended a couple of weeks each year when they were in town, it had still felt like home. She could almost smell the polished wood of the pews, remember the soft hum of hymns filling the sanctuary, the gentle rhythm of the congregation's voices blending.

How had she forgotten such a simple joy?

She slipped away from the gathering, finding her way to one of the empty picnic tables set off to the side, letting the soft notes of the hymn wash over her.

How had she forgotten so much from her childhood?

Her fingers traced lazy circles on the smooth wooden surface as her mind wandered back to Sundays from a simpler time—when faith had felt like more than just a word spoken out of habit, and hope was as clear and present as the hymns that filled the morning air.

Ben approached quietly. Grace was so lost in thought that she didn't hear his footsteps. When she finally looked up, he was standing a few feet away, his gaze soft yet steady as it rested on her.

"You okay?" He asked.

Grace smiled. "Yeah, I was just... thinking about Sunday mornings when I used to go to church with my family."

Ben settled next to her, his presence warm but respectful.

"Songs..." Ben said. "They have a way of bringing everything back into perspective, don't they? Things you thought you'd forgotten—the good, the bad—it all swims up to the surface."

Grace nodded.

"You know... whatever you're feeling? It matters," he said.

Grace gave a small nod, the weight pressing on her heart lifting just a little more.

"Alright everyone, let's wrap it up here. Thanks for all your hard work tonight—looks like we're about ready for another great festival!" Pastor Eli said.

The gathering began to shift, people collecting clipboards and baskets.

Martha, smiling as she approached. "Grace, I sure am glad you came this evening."

Before Grace could respond, Martha patted her hand. "Oh, and just so you know, church service on Sundays starts around 10:30. I'd love to see you there if you're free."

"You know what, Martha? I'd like that. I think I'll be there this Sunday," Grace said.

Martha's face lit up. "That's wonderful, hon."

# Chapter 24

Grace pulled open the door to the diner and spotted Ben right away, sitting in the corner booth, flipping through the morning's newspaper.

"No cape today?" Ben teased as she joined him at the booth.

Grace tilted her head in confusion. "Cape?"

He grinned. "Well, last time we met here, we discussed your superhero marketing feats with Rachel. I wasn't sure if we'd be sparring villains before breakfast."

Grace smirked, settling into her seat, as her eyes did a quick sweep of the diner. Martha was standing at the counter, polishing a mug, watching them with one of those knowing smiles.

Grace rolled her eyes, meeting Ben's gaze. "Please, if I had superpowers, I'd start with a bottomless coffee pot and perhaps the ability to dodge Martha's obvious matchmaking attempts."

Ben chuckled, folding the newspaper and setting it aside. "Hey, she means well. Plus, she makes a mean stack of pancakes."

"One I intend to order," Grace replied, stealing a quick glance at the menu, though everything here was familiar by now. "I was thinking chocolate chip. I feel like today calls for chocolate."

"Breakfast of champions. You planning to paint the town with the sugar rush you'll be on after a breakfast like that?" Ben asked with a wink.

"Paint the gallery, actually," Grace responded, picking up the joke and running with it. "Rachel's got me on painting duty today. I'll be covered in lilac and slate gray by noon, guaranteed."

"You using a roller or one of those little stencil brushes?" he asked, voice all faux seriousness now.

"Both," she said, matching his tone. "Because I believe in artistic versatility."

"Brave. If you need backup, just let me know," he said. "I can probably risk a few paint splatters."

"I might just hold you to that."

Martha sauntered over, pad in hand, her eyes narrowing. "Well, well, if it isn't my two favorite customers. Together, again, no less." She clicked her tongue in an exaggerated fashion. "I thought maybe you two would actually surprise me and sit at separate tables today. But, alas, here you both are. Sitting together. Cozy."

Grace shared a look with Ben, smirking as she set down the menu.

"Would it help if we faced opposite directions while eating?" Ben asked innocently.

"Just calling it like I see it." Martha pointed a finger at them as she tapped her notepad with a grin. "Now, are we sticking with the usual here, or are you going to throw me for a loop today?"

"I'll take the chocolate chip pancakes," Grace announced, with a decisive nod.

Martha scribbled on her pad, glancing at Ben with a raised eyebrow. "And you, Mr. Adventure Tours?"

Ben leaned back in his seat, as though pondering an impossible question. Then, with a theatrical sigh, he replied, "I'm feeling adventurous. Give me the... scrambled eggs with sausage and toast."

Martha clicked her tongue. "Oh, I see what you did there." She gave them a wink, then spun around with her usual efficiency, heading off to the kitchen.

As she disappeared behind the counter, Ben shook his head. "Mercy, that woman has more pep before 9 a.m. than most people do all day."

"She truly does," Grace added, glancing over to see Martha chatting with the cook.

"So," Ben began, shifting the conversation. "You're giving Rachel's gallery a facelift today."

Grace nodded. "It's kind of exciting. I love a good before-and-after project. Plus, Rachel's been so easygoing about everything. She's open to all the crazy marketing ideas I throw her way."

"Sounds like Rachel. She'll dive headfirst into anything to do with art, the gallery, or improving either of those."

Grace smiled. "Yeah, I picked up on that. She's got a real vision for the place—I'm just helping her channel it a little more."

"Hmm." Ben paused, eyes trailing back toward the diner's door as a few regulars walked in. "And after the gallery is all painted, what's next on the agenda for Laurel Ridge's resident marketing genius?"

"Retirement, probably," Grace deadpanned. "Open up a small shop that sells nothing but mismatched socks and maybe become a professional napper."

Ben chuckled. "If you're going for an original business model, I'd say mismatched socks just might corner the market."

"Exactly. Every sock comes with a story. 'These were lost in the dryer… these ones never met their mate. Some were abandoned on city streets.' It'll be tragic. People will cry."

Ben's laughed. "You might be onto something."

Grace folded her arms, leaning toward him, eyes gleaming. "What was it you always said? 'People are drawn to authenticity?' Tell me, is there anything more authentic than a mismatched sock?"

Ben threw up his hands in mock surrender. "Alright, you've convinced me. Your entrepreneurial vision is flawless."

"Thank you," Grace said, leaning back with an air of triumph.

Just as Ben was about to fire back with another playful jab, Martha reappeared, balancing two plates.

"Pancakes for the lady," Martha offered, placing the plate in front of Grace. "Scrambled for the gentleman," she said, placing Ben's plate in front of him like it was a formal ceremony. She paused for dramatic effect before placing a syrup bottle on the table and leaning in conspiratorially. "Don't tell anyone, but I snuck in extra sausage. Compliments of the house."

Grace glanced at Ben. "You're getting the royal treatment today."

Martha offered a sly wink. "Just keeping my best customers happy." She straightened, looking pleased with herself, before sauntering off once again toward the counter.

Grace watched her go, shaking her head and laughing.

Ben cleared his throat, drawing her attention back to the table. His hand reached out, palm up, resting on the smooth surface between them. His hazel eyes met hers, warm and steady.

"Grace," he said, "would you join me in blessing the food?"

Grace smiled. "I'd like that."

Her hand slipped into his. Ben bowed his head, his voice quiet but full of reverence.

"Lord, we thank You for this food and for the time we get to spend together," Ben began, his words flowing naturally. "Thank You for the blessings of this morning, this meal, and the community we're lucky to share. We ask that You guide us through the day ahead with gratitude and grace. Amen."

"Amen," Grace echoed.

"You know," Ben said after a bite of his sausage, his voice casual but thick with deliberation, "speaking of... oh, maybe an adventure..."

Grace raised an eyebrow. "Oh boy, where is this going?"

"Serious question," Ben continued, his tone playful. "Have you ever hiked one of the major trails around here? Or do you just observe nature from the comfort of a porch swing?"

Grace tilted her head, pretending to be offended. "While I appreciate a good porch swing, I'll have you know I am more than capable of navigating a trail, Turner."

"Is that so? Alright, then. How about we put that to the test?" Ben said.

Grace's interest peaked with the challenge sparkling in her eyes. "Oh? What exactly do you have in mind?"

"How about tomorrow morning?" Ben said, pausing to let the suggestion hang just long enough to be enticing. "There's this little-known trail up New River Gorge. Nothing crazy—just steep enough to make you feel like you've accomplished something. The view up top? Incredible."

Grace's grin widened as he painted the picture in her mind. "I don't know... I mean, scaling mountains with muscular tour guide types... it's not necessarily what I had in mind for a lazy weekend."

Ben shook his head, grinning. "Oh, it's like that, huh?"

Grace pursed her lips, fighting the smile creeping up her face. "I'm just saying...do you offer oxygen tanks for us mere mortals?"

"No promises on the oxygen," Ben shot back. "But I'll bring snacks."

Grace twirled a fork around her pancakes, pretending to think it over. "Alright. Snacks seal the deal. But if I pass out halfway up, I'm definitely holding you responsible."

Ben's gaze softened, a teasing light still in his eyes. "Deal. I'll even carry you the rest of the way if you collapse from the sheer joy of it all."

Grace almost choked on her coffee, causing Ben to laugh.

"Plus," he added, nudging her plate playfully, "it'll give you a chance to burn off that mountain of chocolate pancakes."

Grace gave him a mock glare. "I'll have you know, these pancakes are fuel. I'm just stocking up before I tackle... whatever ridiculous trail you've just signed me up for."

"I like your style," Ben said, nodding. "You'll need every last syrup-covered bite."

They ate in companionable silence for a few moments, each lost in their own thoughts, comfortable with the pause in conversation.

"So," Ben started again, breaking the quiet, "other than surviving my hike tomorrow, any other weekend plans? Anything new going on with you?"

"Let's see... in addition to painting more rooms in Rachel's gallery, it seems I've been drawn into the mighty orbit of Laurel Ridge's Harvest Festival Planning Committee, for sure, no doubt about it now."

Ben set down his fork, eyes gleaming. "Oh? Martha managed to nab you in one hundred percent?"

"You sound surprised," Grace said with a laugh. "How could I resist free food and a front-row seat to small-town holiday planning?"

Ben grinned, folding his arms across his chest. "Consider yourself warned, then. That means you're about to see some serious pumpkin pie rivalries and hayride politics. Martha runs a tight ship."

Grace feigned horror. "Oh no! What have I done? Maybe I'll have to bow out gracefully."

"I wouldn't let them know you're backing out." Ben gave her a serious look, although the corners of his mouth tugged upward. "There's a very real possibility of being trapped in a 'who makes the best cider' debate for the rest of your life."

Grace sighed theatrically. "Well, it was nice knowing you. I've officially been pulled in too deep."

"You'll make it through," Ben said over the rim of his coffee. "Just keep a backup supply of cookies at all times. It usually smooths things over."

With their breakfast finished, Martha strolled back to their booth, seemingly impressed with how much they'd laughed and bantered their way through it.

"Now, what's this I hear about Grace and our little festival committee?" Martha teased, stopping beside their table and propping her hands on her hips.

Grace raised an eyebrow, trying to act serious as she caught on to Martha's lingering tone. "I suspect it's all a plot to get me to bake something."

Martha winked. "Oh, darlin', you don't know the half of it. By the time we're done with you, you'll have butchered a pumpkin with your own hands and made the best pie in all of Laurel Ridge."

Ben's grin stretched wide as he leaned back in his seat. "She's fast-tracking you to the elite pie-makers' circle. Good luck with that."

"Well, in that case," Grace said, "I suppose I have no choice but to accept the challenge."

"There's the spirit." Martha beamed, picking up their empty plates and shaking her head. "Ben, make sure you don't wear Grace out too much on that hike. A girl's gotta have energy left for decorating scarecrows."

"Noted," Ben replied with a mock salute. "She'll survive. I'll make sure she's returned in one piece."

Martha grinned, then bustled toward the kitchen.

Ben shook his head as Martha walked away. "She hears better than a hawk. There's nothing that escapes that woman!"

As they rose from the booth, Grace gathered her things, smiling at Ben. "Should I pack a first-aid kit for this hike tomorrow, just in case?"

"Nah, we'll be fine. Worst case, I'll just sling you over my shoulder."

"Great. I always dreamed of being carried off into the wilderness," Grace shot back with a smirk.

Ben laughed, but gave a shrug. "Hey, maybe I'll use it as my marketing tagline: 'Adventure Tours—Guaranteed to Carry You When the Going Gets Rough.' Think it'll sell?"

Grace nudged him playfully. "You joke, but that actually might work."

# Chapter 25

Grace adjusted the strap of her day pack, glancing towards the trailhead with a mix of anticipation and nerves.

"I still expect you to take it easy on me, Turner. That was the deal, remember?" Grace said, feigning a stern look.

Ben chuckled, his hand tightening on the worn strap of his own pack. "I promised snacks, didn't I? That's basically mountain-posh hiking. You'll be fine."

Grace shot him a sideways glance, grinning despite herself. "Snacks are non-negotiable. But I'm still deciding how forgiving I'll be if there's no coffee waiting at the finish line."

Ben snorted and shook his head. "Well, if you need coffee at the top of a mountain, you might be more high-maintenance than I thought."

"High-maintenance?" she asked, eyebrows lifting high. "I'm embracing nature, okay? Look—" She waved her hands dramatically around her. "I'm breathing fresh air, I'm walking on dirt, and I haven't demanded Wi-Fi yet."

Ben let out a hearty laugh, the sound echoing into the forest. He gave her an apologetic grin as he started up the trail. "Alright, alright, my bad. You are doing just fine. We'll get you that 'I survived the woods' merit badge when we're done."

Grace rolled her eyes, but smiled as she followed him. The trail stretched before them, a mixture of packed dirt, rocks, and tree roots forming a natural staircase leading deeper into the forest. Birds flitted overhead, their songs lilting through the trees. Sunlight, dappling the path in speckled patches of gold.

They settled into a steady rhythm, Grace in step just behind Ben. He moved easily over the terrain, his movements sure and practiced. She, on the other hand, stumbled a few times, catching her foot on a stray root here, wobbling on a loose rock there. Every time, she'd throw Ben a theatrical glare, muttering something about "nature being out to get her," and each time, Ben would just grin over his shoulder and keep them moving forward.

"How long have you been coming to this trail?" she asked, breaking the silence.

Ben looked back at her briefly as he navigated around a rock. "Since I was a kid. My dad used to bring me up here. We'd hike up, camp near the top a night or two, and then hike back down. It's... always been a special place for me."

Grace slowed her pace, considering his words. "It feels... timeless here. Like the outside world doesn't quite touch it."

Ben nodded. "Yeah. That's what I like about it. It's like... the deeper you get, the less the world matters."

The trail grew steeper, winding its way up the side of the mountain, but Grace kept pace, determined not to let Ben see her faltering, though she felt herself slowing down.

Ben must have sensed it. "Not too much further. I promise the view at the top is worth it."

Grace took a deep breath, trying not to sound too winded. "I'm holding you to that."

Ben looked back and grinned.

"So, ...any mountain lions I should be aware of?" Grace asked.

Ben chuckled and shook his head. "Hopefully not...maybe a few curious squirrels or raccoons, if you leave any granola around."

They continued upward, the trail bending sharply until the mountain began to level out. Ben halted in front of her, turning around with a grin while extending a hand toward her. "You made it."

Grace took his hand, letting him pull her up the last step of the trail. She stumbled and crashed into him.

"Don't act so impressed," she panted. "I made that look way harder than it needed to be."

Ben's grin softened, and without pulling his hand away, he nodded toward the view just past them. "Now look."

Grace turned—and her breath, already labored from the hike, caught in her throat.

Spread out before her was the vast expanse of the New River Gorge, snaking its way through the valley below like a ribbon of emerald and blue, glittering under the late morning sun. The mountains around the river towered into the sky, their peaks silhouetted against a backdrop of rolling clouds. The world below felt so distant. The air seemed fresher, cleaner—like it had filtered through miles of forest just to greet them at the top.

"Wow," she said, her voice barely audible.

"Told you," Ben murmured beside her.

Grace blinked, still stunned by the beauty that stretched out in front of her. "It's... incredible."

"So?" he said. "Was it worth climbing all the way up here?"

Grace nodded. "Yeah," she said. "Okay, Turner. You win this round. This was definitely worth it."

Ben bumped her shoulder playfully. "Glad to hear that. Now come on, time for snacks."

He pulled off his day pack and swung it onto the ground, rummaging inside. Grace sat on a large flat rock near him, enjoying the cool mountain breeze sweeping across her face.

"You know," she said. "I think I could get used to this whole hiking thing."

Ben smirked, raising an eyebrow. "Does that mean I get to take you on more hikes in the future? Or should I retire while I'm ahead?"

Grace laughed, unwrapping a granola bar. "Careful now. I might surprise you and become an extreme outdoor enthusiast. Then where will you be?"

"Pulled into the great outdoors every weekend?"

"Exactly. Consider yourself warned."

Ben shook his head, laughing as he took a bite of his granola bar. "Guess I better start planning more trips then."

"Just, you know," Grace added between bites, "keep the snacks coming. And maybe next time, there'll be some of that 'mountain-posh hiking coffee' at the top."

Ben grinned. "I'll keep that in mind."

Grace tilted her head back, closing her eyes for a moment. The fresh mountain air filling her lungs.

"Thanks, by the way," she said. "For bringing me up here. I needed it. More than I realized."

Ben's voice, when it came, was low and steady. "Sometimes getting away from everything helps put things into perspective."

"Yeah," Grace agreed. "It really does."

"I come here now and then. When I need to clear my head, reconnect with... everything. Nature has a way of grounding a person." Ben said.

Grace nodded, wondering what "everything" might mean for Ben. There were still so many things about him, she didn't know, despite how easily they seemed to get along. He was steady, sure—but there were currents underneath the surface, just like the river below.

"So..." Grace started, her tone casual but with a hint of mischief, "I have to ask, Ben—how are you still a bachelor? I mean, surely some lucky woman must have tried to lock you down by now."

Ben hesitated for a moment, his gaze dropping to the ground as he gathered his thoughts. He turned to face Grace with a quiet, deliberate resolve in his eyes.

"There's something I need to share with you," he began, his voice low but steady, almost as if he was carrying the weight of what he was about to say.

"I like you, Grace," he admitted, the honesty of his words hitting with unexpected clarity. "I really enjoy spending time with you, and I've been thinking a lot about... what's happening between us. There's something real here, something I want to explore, if you feel the same way."

His hazel eyes, searching, but not pushing. "Before we go any further, though—and I realize this is a big if—but if we're both hoping to walk down this path together, there's something I need to tell you. Something important."

Grace nodded, encouraging him to continue without words.

"There's a part of my past I don't like to talk about," he continued. "Not because I'm hiding it, but because it's... difficult. And before anything between us becomes deeper, I think you should know about it. I want to be open and honest... I owe that to you."

# Chapter 26

Grace watched Ben wrestle silently with his thoughts, his eyes fixed on the horizon as if the vast expanse of the New River Gorge might offer him the words he couldn't yet find. The tension in his posture was barely concealed, each breath measured, like he was preparing to defend something personal and fragile. Whatever he was holding onto, whatever demons he was about to release, it wasn't easy for him.

"You don't have to say it right now if it's too hard," Grace said. "If you need more time—"

Ben shook his head. "No, Grace, this... it's important." He shifted his position, sitting more upright, and faced her fully. "I don't want to keep this from you any longer."

Grace held his gaze, searching his warm hazel eyes. His expression had changed—not the playful, easygoing Ben she'd come to know, but something deeper, more serious.

Ben cleared his throat. "When I told you I've been through some things that shaped who I am today, I didn't just mean little challenges here and there... this goes way back, Grace. Back to when I was just a teenager."

His voice stayed calm, but Grace could feel the tremor beneath it.

"My parents," Ben began. "I was sixteen when they died. It was sudden, a freak accident. They were driving home from visiting my dad's family in another town. The weather had taken a bad turn—heavy rain, one of those mountain storms where the roads switch from dirt to mud so fast you barely have time to react. There was a landslide. Their car..." He trailed off for a moment, sucking in a deep breath as if he could pull himself out of that memory. "Their car went off the side of the mountain."

Grace inhaled hard. She didn't dare speak.

Ben's voice, thick with restraint, continued. "The impact... killed them instantly. At least, that's what they told Rachel and me. I don't know if that was meant to comfort us, but nothing about their deaths felt comforting."

Grace didn't hesitate. She reached for his hand, her fingers curling over his.

"They were everything to us," Ben said, his voice lowering. "My dad... taught me everything about the outdoors. My mom? A faith so strong you couldn't shake it. Sundays at church, family barbecue afterward. That kind of life." He looked up at the sky. "When we lost them, for a long time, we lost everything."

Grace's throat tightened at the depth and loss in his words.

Ben squeezed her hand back, managing a sad smile. "The thing about loss...there aren't any words that fix it. Time doesn't erase it. You just..." he shrugged, "you learn to live with it."

"We moved in with Martha after that," he continued. "She and her husband—they didn't blink. They took us in without so much as a second thought. But Rachel and I? We weren't easy to deal with. We were angry—at the world, at God, at ourselves.... especially God."

Grace remained quiet, but leaned closer.

"I dropped out of church altogether," Ben admitted, his voice flat. "Felt too hypocritical to even step back into those pews. Everything we'd been taught—that God was good, that he had a plan, that everything happened for a reason—it all just felt like a lie. Rachel was going through her own version of it. Pushed everyone away. We were lost in our own ways."

The heartache in his voice echoed through Grace. She had seen her own version of lost days—feeling like she didn't know who to trust, retreating into herself when the corporate scandal hit. She felt that sting of betrayal, too, but here was Ben, who had lost so much more—and with none of the privilege she'd had to even prop herself up.

"I started hanging out with this crowd, you know? A bunch of other guys who told me they understood. There was drinking...drinking seemed to drown the pain. And for a while, that helped—or at least I thought it did. Until I made the worst decision of my life...I drove drunk one night," Ben said, his voice faltering. "Lost control... hit a tree. Wrecked the car. The front end was smashed to pieces, and I ended up in the hospital. Broken ribs, bruises... but I survived." His eyes closed again. "Barely."

Grace's heart squeezed as she imagined Ben in that hospital bed, surrounded by the wreckage of his life, both literally and figuratively. She spoke, unable to hold back her feelings. "I can't even imagine how scared you must have been. What made you turn things around?"

Ben took a deep breath, his expression softening as he glanced off into the gorge, his face flickering between grief and gratitude. "Martha. She's the one who pulled me through. Not in any dramatic way. She didn't lecture or drag me to church, though maybe she had every right to. She just... stayed steady, you know? Quiet. Patient. She let me come to terms with my own mess, but she didn't have to say much. Her faith... she lived it. And somewhere along the way, I started paying attention. Started thinking maybe I could believe again."

Grace swallowed hard. "That takes a lot of strength. To take that step back toward faith when you feel like it's deserted you."

Ben looked at her long and hard, something unspoken but intimate passing between them. "I stopped running. And eventually, I found my way back to God... because of her."

Grace admired this man more with each word, but a shadow hovered at the edges of her thoughts. His honesty didn't just reflect his pain—it reflected the kind of deep-rooted faith she was struggling to reclaim. But here, right now, his story wasn't just about him—it was about them. Could she handle where this conversation was leading?

Ben shifted and cleared his throat. "There's more," he said, his voice gentle, but there was caution. "It's about... Anna."

Grace blinked, her thoughts fractured by the unexpected shift. "Anna?"

Ben nodded. "We met not long after I came back home to God—after I started piecing things together again. She was incredible, Grace, and I loved her. Really loved her." He looked down into his hands, tracing invisible lines. "I thought she'd be the one—my future. We talked about marriage, planning a life right here in Laurel Ridge. There was just one problem. After that accident, the doctor told me that there were complications. From the car crash, internal injuries." Ben paused, his jaw tightening. "It's unlikely I can have kids. Not impossible, but... not one hundred percent likely."

Grace's breath caught in her throat.

"When I told Anna, I thought we could get through it. She was supportive at first... but eventually, Grace, she realized what that meant. Anna wanted a family—a house full of kids. And I couldn't guarantee that. Not the way she wanted. And it... it ended us."

He delivered the words so plainly, but Grace saw the tautness around his mouth, the flicker of pain behind his eyes. This wasn't just a piece of his history—it had been a devastating loss, another piece of his heart that had been broken and left behind.

Grace inhaled, keeping her eyes on him—steadying herself. "That must have been so hard, Ben. I can understand someone wanting that... but walking away from something so real? I don't know if that would have been my choice."

"It was hers. I didn't fight it. I wanted her to have the life she dreamed of."

"Ben..." she hesitated, her voice quiet but clear. "Thank you for telling me this. For sharing all of it with me."

Ben's shoulders visibly relaxed, as if he had braced for a different reaction.

"I know," Grace continued, her voice stronger now, "that kids, or the possibility of not being able to, that can make things complicated for some people. But..." She shifted closer to him, their legs now touching slightly as she sought his gaze again. "You know that doesn't change how I feel about you, right?"

Ben's eyes searched hers, his expression unreadable for a moment. "I wasn't sure. I didn't know if it'd be... something you'd want to walk away from..."

Grace leaned in, reaching up to touch his arm. "You have been through so much, Ben. Your strength and your faith? They're part of why I admire you so much. These things, these challenges—these losses—they don't lessen who you are to me." She smiled. "If anything, they make me care about you more."

"You're really something, Grace," he said. "Thank you."

They sat in silence for a while as the endless view of mountains and flowing rivers stretched before them, but Grace felt the air between them shift once more—this time, lighter, easier, as though something vital had been settled in the quiet rhythm of their conversation.

Grace cleared her throat. "So...I guess this means I'll have to get used to you opening up to me from time to time?"

A small grin tugged at Ben's lips. "I guess you'll just have to get used to that."

"And here I was, thinking this relationship was all about mountains and granola bars..." she teased, shoulders brushing his.

Ben chuckled, the sound easing the tension that had once pressed on them. He leaned down, resting his forehead briefly against hers in a kind of quiet, unspoken promise. "For the record," he murmured, "it's so much more than that."

# Chapter 27

"Since we're being honest with each other..." Grace pressed her palms against her thighs, trying to gather her thoughts. *Where do I even begin?*

"What you've been through, Ben... it's heavy." She tilted her head, her eyes soft but sincere. "And I just want to say thank you for being brave enough to share all of that with me. My past..." She paused, looking down at her hands as her fingers fidgeted slightly against the fabric of her pants, "Well, it's not as tragic—not in any way, really. But that doesn't mean I don't have my own messes."

Grace tugged at the corner of her lip with her teeth, exhaling a faint laugh, as if trying to release the tension building inside her. "You know... when I was fresh outta college, I thought the world was just waiting for me to conquer it. New York was everything I'd ever dreamed of. Fast-paced, exciting, full of possibilities." She gave a small chuckle, more to herself than anything. The sound was tinged with the slightest edge of bitterness, "But what I didn't realize was how easy it was to let it all consume me."

"I was good at what I did—no, I'm not being modest. I was good, and I loved the challenge of it. I loved the ideas, the innovation, the thrill of being at the top..." She leaned forward, elbows resting on her knees, eyes scanning the horizon as she recalled the life she had been so enamored with. "But being at the top comes with a cost, you know? You start measuring everything by success. By accomplishments, awards, promotions... and that's where I got lost, I guess. I started letting the world around me define me instead of some deeper purpose."

She caught Ben's eye, the understanding there soothing the knot in her chest. "I stopped making time for what really mattered. God became an afterthought. Someone I occasionally prayed to when I really needed something, or when things got rough. I was just... too busy to fit Him into the timeline of my high-profile, glamorous life." She let out a sarcastic laugh. "Somewhere along the way, I convinced myself that it was okay to put Him on the back burner."

Ben gave her a soft, knowing smile. "Yeah. That's easy to do sometimes, especially in a world that pulls you in every direction but the one that matters most."

"Exactly," Grace murmured. She traced her thumb across the small scar on the side of her neck, her mind flickering briefly to the little girl she had been—the one who once believed anything was possible with the strength of her faith alone. How far removed that girl seemed from the woman she had become.

She straightened, casting a playful glance Ben's way to lighten the mood just a fraction. "And sometimes it felt like the entire measure of success in New York could be boiled down to who had the flashiest clothes or the most 'Instagrammable' brunch." She shook her head, scrunching her nose a little. "And trust me—I am not proud of the fact that I once got roped into a four-hour conversation about avocado toast trends."

Ben snorted, a hearty laugh falling out as he nudged her gently with his elbow. "Sounds traumatic."

"Oh, absolutely. I think it should be classified as an emotional hazard," Grace shot back, her smile widening as she appreciated the levity. The humor made it easier to talk about the serious parts. The cracks beneath the professional mask she had worn for so long.

"But seriously, Ben. Somewhere in all of that—between the deals and the deadlines and the... well, brunch-talk—I lost myself." She paused, then added, "And I lost sight of God. Of what really matters."

Ben's face was calm, reflective. He turned his attention back to the gorge, digesting her words with the same thoughtfulness he gave to everything. She loved that about him—how he didn't rush through things, how he allowed moments to exist without forcing a resolution.

"So," she began again, shifting in her seat as her thoughts traveled down a new path. "I really do want to stay here. West Virginia..." She tilted her head, gazing past the horizon. "It feels like home, more and more every day. But there's this part of me..." she trailed off, furrowing her brow before trying again. "There's this part of me that needs to be absolutely sure I'm ready to leave New York behind. I don't want to walk forward carrying a bunch of what-ifs on my back. I need to know—deep down—that it's done."

"I might need to go back for a little closure," Grace admitted, chewing on her bottom lip. "Wrap things up for good. Not because I'm looking for an escape—not because I want back into that life. I just need to make peace with the part of me I left there."

Ben's gaze was steady, unwavering, but there was no hint of judgment in it. He leaned his elbow on his knee and looked over, his hazel eyes locking with hers. "I get that, Grace. I do." He paused, considering for a moment before adding, "But just so you know—I'm not in any rush. I want you to be all in... not feeling like you left something unfinished behind."

Grace felt her chest tighten, not with fear, but with gratitude. The fact that Ben saw her so clearly—understood her even when she wasn't entirely sure she understood herself—well, it was something she hadn't expected. She hadn't realized how much she needed that reassurance until this very moment. "Thank you," she said with a grateful smile.

Ben shrugged, the corners of his mouth tugging up in that small, inherent smile of his. "I'd rather wait for you to be certain than have you diving headfirst into something while you're still figuring things out."

"Good," she said, the corner of her mouth quirking up. "Because there's a very real possibility I'll pick up a million-dollar latte while I'm back in New York."

Ben laughed aloud, the sound bright and full of warmth. "I'll allow it, but only if they top it with some ridiculous Instagram-worthy foam art."

Grace nudged him with her shoulder, chuckling as she shook her head. "Deal."

After a moment, she looked back out at the gorge, the vastness of it grounding her thoughts as she spoke. "There's something else I need to ask of you."

"Go on," he said.

Grace exhaled, hands fidgeting in her lap.

*Don't be afraid to be honest, Grace.*

She took a deep breath. "I want to build this relationship on faith, trust, and God." Her voice faltered, but she pressed forward. "But... I need time when it comes to the God part. I've spent so many years having faith take this back seat in my life... I let my career be the thing that drove me. I put God second—third, even. I want—no, I need—to change that. But I need you to know this..." Grace paused, feeling the earnestness rise in her chest before continuing. "I need you to be patient with me, Ben. Because finding my way back to God is... well, it's not something I can fix overnight. I need time."

"I'm not in this for the short game, Grace. I'll walk that road with you—however long it takes," he said.

"Thank you," she said. "And not that I'm expecting a crash course or anything, but you might occasionally get texts from me with random questions about faith. You know, basic 'God 101' kind of stuff."

Ben chuckled, shaking his head with amusement. "I'm always available for 'God 101.' Just be sure to throw in some humor along with the questions. Can't have boring faith talks."

"Oh, don't worry," Grace teased. "I'll be sure to make it amusing."

Grace felt a spark of hope. It was different from the excitement she felt in the business world. This was real. This was discovery. Maybe faith wasn't so hard to reclaim after all... not if she had someone to guide her through the wilderness. Someone to remind her what really mattered.

They sat in reflective silence for a minute longer, the vastness of the natural world around them echoing how small their worries seemed to be in the grander scheme of things. And yet, in this small corner of the world, their hearts carried weight.

Grace broke the silence with a cheeky grin. "You know, dating is kind of like PR."

Ben arched an eyebrow, amusement twinkling in his eyes. "Oh?"

"Yep," she nodded confidently. "It's all about communication, problem-solving, and... let's face it, a lot of damage control after the first 'meet-the-parents' moment."

Ben laughed, loud and bright, his head tilting back. It was a full-bellied laugh—the kind that made Grace's heart flutter because she'd shared it with him. He shook his head, disbelief clear in his eyes. "So... should I expect a color-coded, highly detailed PR plan for this relationship?"

Grace raised her brow. "Oh, absolutely. I'll have an Excel spreadsheet and a PowerPoint ready for you by the next hike. Complete with relationship strategies."

"I'd be disappointed if you didn't," Ben replied, grinning.

They stood, stretching slightly after sitting for so long.

She turned to Ben with a half-smile, motioning toward the trailhead they'd climbed earlier. "So, turns out hiking is easier when you're not lugging your emotional baggage with you."

Ben let out a low chuckle as he nudged her gently with his shoulder. "I think that's what they call progress."

# Chapter 28

"**G**race! Right on time, as always," Ben called, beckoning her over. His trademark grin etched deep into his face. There was an openness to his posture that invited her to join without hesitation. Like he'd missed her.

"Well, you know me," she said as she walked closer. "I aim to please."

"I'd never doubt it, Anderson," he teased, shaking his head.

Ben slid over on the bench, making room and patting the empty spot beside him. "Best seat in the house," he said.

Grace accepted the seat, feeling the slight brush of his arm as she settled in.

She liked this feeling. The closeness. Not just physically, but... emotionally.

"Hey you!" Rachel said, with the enthusiasm of someone two cups deep into a latte.

"You're right on time, honey," Martha said, enthusiasm dripping in every word. "We were just finalizing the vendor walkthrough real quick."

Grace smiled. Being here, now—it felt like the pieces of her life were slowly finding their place again. "Sounds perfect."

"Okay, everyone!" Martha's called. She stood clipboard in hand, her presence a beacon of enthusiasm. "We've got four days left until the Harvest Festival, so let's make sure we're all on the same page before things kick into overdrive."

A ripple of nods and murmurs of agreement passed around the churches' lawn.

"Rachel!" Martha called. "You're in charge of decorating the vendor booths, right?"

Rachel smiled and flashed Grace a wink. "Yep, I've got it mostly under control. I've lined up some seasonal decorations from the gallery—lots of vibrant autumn colors, pumpkins, mums, things to make people feel like they're walking into a picture-perfect postcard."

Grace nodded, flipping through the clipboard she held to check the vendor maps. She surprised herself by feeling a surge of excitement sweep through her at the sight. Here was a blueprint she could follow, something tangible and clear. This was something she could... improve.

Martha glanced back toward her, eyes twinkling just so. "Now, Grace. Have you given any thought to ways we might fill up the remaining time slots for the festival?"

"Actually, yes," Grace said, feeling her voice strengthen as she spoke. "I was thinking... You've already got some great vendors lined up, but what if we held a special event that highlighted some local talents—like Rachel could do a live painting demonstration? We could even invite some other artists for a quick pop-up booth. Could be a great way to get folks involved in ways they weren't expecting."

Rachel perked up, her hand reaching out to nudge Grace on the shoulder. "I love this plan. I absolutely do. I can do the painting. And you're right—we could ask the other artists. It would be a hit!"

"I knew you'd come up with something brilliant, Grace," Martha said. "I'll take care of contacting the local artists to see if they're interested."

Pastor Eli, seated off to the side, nodded thoughtfully. "That's a fine idea, Grace. Very fine, indeed." He rubbed his chin, his eyes tracking down his clipboard. "Doesn't look like we'll have much in the way of overlap, either. The artists can set up in the space between the pie tables and Beth's clothing booth."

Beth, who had been proud of her mini-boutique pop-up ever since they'd announced the festival dates months ago, grinned. "That's perfect for me. I'll be right there in the thick of things." She leaned in, hand on her hip. "You know, I'll be up on stage this year too, giving that good ol' pie contest speech. And I'll be expectin' y'all to cheer when I announce the winner."

That elicited a round of uninhibited laughter from the group. Beth was notorious for her spirited speeches, especially where pies were concerned, and everyone knew full well she'd treat the award ceremony like the grand finale of a Broadway show.

"Well, I've got all the volunteers lined up to help with the games," Leslie chimed in, waving her clipboard. "We've also got a few extra activities set up for the kids—hayrides, pumpkin painting, a bounce house, and face painting. I think people are going to love it."

"Perfect," Pastor Eli said. "The bounce house came through, then?"

"Yup!" Leslie confirmed, looking as pleased as ever. "It's going to be the hit of the festival."

As the conversation carried on, Grace became engrossed in the details—the schedules, logistics, and minor adjustments that needed to be made to make the day perfect. Though this wasn't a polished corporate event, the improvisational nature of small-town planning had its own charm, and the eagerness in the voices around her was infectious. She bounced ideas back and forth with her new friends, their laughter drifting into the cool air like soft music.

Minutes turned into an hour, and as the group continued to swap tasks and nail down specifics, Grace felt more and more like a vital part of the team. Not just an outsider dipping her toe into the water, but someone who belonged here, someone who offered something only she could give.

"We're almost there," Pastor Eli declared, rising from the bench with a stretch. "Everything looks wonderful, folks. It's going to be a great Harvest Festival this year."

Grace sat back and smiled.

After the final walkthrough of the festival timeline, when everyone was gathering up notes and posters for the last tasks to be done before the big day, Grace remained seated, just breathing it all in—the camaraderie, the excitement, the warmth.

Ben lingered beside her, clearly in no rush.

"You did really well tonight," he said, glancing at her.

"Thank you," she replied. "It feels... good. To be a part of this."

Ben nodded, a quiet understanding in his expression. "You're not just 'A' part of it, Grace. You're a big part of it. You've helped to shape this whole thing in ways you don't even know."

She smiled, feeling the connection between them grow a little deeper in that shared moment of understanding.

"Ben!" Rachel called from the pavilion, waving a pile of festival flyers over her head with dramatic flair. "You've got pie pickup duty

Saturday morning, right? I'll be in the gallery or in my booth finishing last-minute details, but I need you to swing by the bakery to grab the pies for the potluck dinner that day."

Ben groaned, rolling his eyes. "Yeah, I can grab them."

Rachel grinned, clearly enjoying his reluctant agreement. Before Grace could make any comment on the matter, Rachel turned her attention to her. "Grace, you're coming by the gallery tomorrow, right? We're doing some last-minute touch-ups to the displays inside, and I could use your design expertise."

Grace chuckled. "Design expertise? Is that what we're calling my scribbly little notes now?"

"Oh, I've promoted you to full-on creative consultant," Rachel replied, though the twinkle in her eyes gave her away. She sauntered across the pavilion with the confidence of someone who had just won a minor victory. "Go on, now. Don't make me beg."

Martha gave everyone a final round of thanks before closing the meeting. "I think we're all set for the festival," she called. "But don't forget, we're a team—we'll keep things flexible if we hit any bumps in the road. Let's just focus on making it an event to bring everyone together, celebrate our community, and enjoy the Lord's blessings."

# Chapter 29

### 4 Days Later

Grace stood at the edge of the town square, her breath forming a visible puff in the crisp autumn air. The Harvest Festival was in full swing. The town buzzed with energy. The sweet scent of caramel apples and cinnamon rolls filled the air.

Fall had always been her favorite season, but there was something about it here, in this little corner of West Virginia, that made her appreciate it all the more. Everything about the scene before her spoke of warmth, community, and tradition.

A gentle gust of wind tossed a few leaves around her feet, and Grace shivered, pulling her jacket closer. She checked her phone for the festival schedule she'd typed up two nights ago—timed reminders set for herself so she didn't forget any of the big events or let something fall through the cracks.

"Grace! There you are!" Rachel's voice rang out, clear and tinged with the excitement she was trying—and failing—not to show.

Grace turned to find Rachel jogging up, bundled in an oversized cardigan, her hands stuffed in her pockets. Her eyes radiating nervous energy, like at any moment, she might either burst into laughter or tears. Maybe both.

"Well, good morning to you too," Grace said with a knowing smile. "Ready for the big day?"

"I think so? Maybe?" Rachel's hand fluttered around as she spoke. "I mean, you know, I've only been obsessively rearranging everything in the gallery for three days straight, no big deal."

Grace chuckled, looping her arm through Rachel's as they took a brief stroll toward the gallery. "You're going to do great. I'm sure the gallery looks spectacular, and people will love what you've set up. Seriously, Rachel, you've built something wonderful here. Today is just the world catching up to it."

Rachel sighed, the tension in her shoulders loosening. "I just hope people continue to show up. I don't want to be that artist whose biggest customer is her aunt."

"Lucky for you, you have more charm than you think. And hey, I'm sure Martha wouldn't mind buying your entire stock just for the bragging rights." Grace winked, and Rachel laughed, an infectious sound that seemed to carry warmth into the chilly morning.

They arrived at the gallery, where sunlight gleamed off the charming glass windows. Rachel's stunning outdoor display for the festival showcased paintings in autumn hues of reds, oranges, and gold that evoked serenity and passion. Hand sculpted clay pottery was strategically placed here and there. She had artfully arranged mums in burnt reds, oranges, and purples, with pumpkins and fodder shocks scattered throughout.

Rachel placed a nervous hand on one of the painting's frames.

"I couldn't have pulled any of this off without you, Grace," Rachel said. "I thought I knew how to run a business, but you've really shown me how to elevate it without changing who I am."

Grace looked at her, surprised by the raw honesty in Rachel's voice. "You're the talent here. I just helped you see it."

Rachel smiled. "Still, I'm glad you're here. More than you know."

Grace's heart swelled at the sentiment. She squeezed Rachel's arm in quiet understanding.

***

By early afternoon, the town square was even busier. Stalls lined both sides of main street, and the scent of caramel apples, roasted chestnuts, and cinnamon rolls floated through the air, wrapping everything in a comforting cocoon. Tourists and locals mingled together, their laughter and conversation blending in a vibrant hum of activity.

Grace moved between booths, tapping into her PR expertise to ensure everything was running as smoothly as possible. She double checked signage, suggested ideas to vendors who wanted to draw more attention to their stalls, and even fixed a few flyers that had been posted askew. But the usual high level stress she would have felt back in New York was non-existent. Instead, there was something deeply satisfying—knowing that her skills had contributed to something meaningful, something bigger than herself.

This was community.

She was so lost in thought, she hadn't noticed Ben approaching until he spoke.

"Over here saving the entire festival again, huh?" He asked.

"You caught me. Next, I'm thinking of taking on world peace," she replied.

He laughed, an easy, warm sound. "Should've known. Always the overachiever."

Grace rolled her eyes good-naturedly. "Someone has to keep this town running."

"Oh, that someone's definitely you," Ben teased, then leaned in, his voice dropping to a soft conspiratorial tone. "Speaking of which... I've got a surprise for you."

Grace raised an eyebrow, tilting her head as she studied him. There was that mischievous twinkle in his eye she adored. "A surprise?"

Ben grinned and guided her toward his Adventure Tours booth. "See for yourself."

Her eyes flickered over the sign he'd posted: "Moonlit Tour & Art Along the River Experience" with illustrations of kayaks on brilliant moonlit water alongside easels and paint brushes.

Grace's heart skipped a beat. The idea she had casually mentioned during one of their conversations, the blending of outdoor adventure with Rachel's artistic talents, was now a reality. She blinked up at Ben. Emotion clogged her throat.

"I—Ben..." she stammered. "You... You really did it?"

Ben's grin softened into something more genuine, his eyes warm and steady on hers. He shrugged modestly. "Of course I did. You've got good ideas, Grace."

Her heart thudded in her chest, warmth flooding her as she looked at him. It wasn't just the gesture; it was the way he listened, the way he paid attention to the little things. No grand declarations, no over-the-top romance like the kind she used to dream about. This simple, sincere act meant more than any bouquet of roses or ritzy dinner ever could.

Grace spent the next hour visiting other vendor booths, helping where she could, but her thoughts kept circling back to Ben's gesture and the swell of emotions it had sparked inside her.

The sweet smell of kettle corn and hot apple cider filled the air. Children ran by, their laughter echoing around the booths, and though the temperature dropped with the setting sun, the warmth of the community seemed to intensify.

Grace drifted back to Ben's booth.

"How're you holding up, world saver?" he asked, his voice low and calm in the surrounding chaos.

Grace sighed, her eyes drifting over the bustling scene. "I'm... good. Great, actually."

Ben seemed content with that, his quiet approval lingering between them as the night crept closer. The lights strung above the town square had just come on, casting a soft glow that brightened the area like stars.

The last event was about to begin—the fireworks display.

# Chapter 30

The townsfolk gathered by the river's edge, spreading blankets across the grass and setting up lawn chairs, their quiet conversations and laughter filling the air. Families huddled together as the evening grew cooler. Off to the side, a little removed from the crowd, Grace and Ben stood shoulder to shoulder, taking it all in. Their breath showed in soft, misty puffs against the crisp night air. Above them, the sky was a dark canvas dotted with stars, like scattered diamonds, while the river flowed steadily nearby, its surface reflecting the faintest glimmers of light, mysterious yet serene.

"Ready?" Ben asked in a soft voice, his hazel eyes glowing in the twilight.

The first firework shot into the air, trailing a hiss before exploding in brilliant blue. Then another, this time gold and glittering, illuminating the river's surface. Grace's breath hitched at the beauty of it, her eyes wide as the night sky danced with vivid color.

Amidst the bursts of light and sound, she felt Ben's hand slip into hers, and it spread warmth through her entire body.

Grace's heart fluttered, a mix of excitement and nerves blooming within her as her hand instinctively tightened around Ben's. The firework's glow painted his face in bursts of color, his features illuminated momentarily before fading back into the shadowed softness of the night. She turned her head, tilting her chin up toward him. The air between them seemed to hum, like the space around them had pressed pause on everything else just for this moment.

Another firework burst above, casting bright shades of green and gold across the sky, reflecting in his eyes, and for a heartbeat, all she could do was stare at him. It wasn't just the fireworks, or the perfect stillness of the night, but the way he looked at her—like she was as essential to him as the air they were both breathing.

Ben's gaze flickered over her face, the corner of his lips curling into that soft, knowing smile that had a way of melting the world around her. Without a word, he moved closer, closing the remaining space between them, his hand still warm, grounding hers in a quiet reassurance.

Grace's pulse thrummed beneath her skin, echoing in her ears. Her breath caught, and her eyes darted from his lips to his eyes and back to his lips again, anticipation surging in her chest.

"Grace," he murmured, her name like a secret only the two of them shared.

She didn't respond—not with words, anyway. She didn't need to. Instead, she moved ever so slightly closer, her eyes holding his, the world around them dissolving into the background, as the sounds of the town and firework show dimmed to nothing more than a soft whisper. Her heart raced, feeling that magnetic pull between them.

Ben leaned down, slowly, almost cautiously at first, his breath warm against the coolness of the night. Time seemed to stretch endlessly, each heartbeat echoing through her chest as his lips inched closer. And then, without hesitation, he closed the remaining distance, his lips brushing against hers in a tender, heart-stopping kiss.

The kiss was soft—tentative and sweet, as if they were both savoring the newness of it. Grace felt that warmth spread through her, not just from the touch of his lips, but from the realization that everything she had been searching for—the peace, the belonging, the sense of finally finding where she was meant to be—was wrapped up in this moment. In him.

She kissed him back, letting her free hand reach up to cup his jaw gently, feeling the slight roughness of his stubble under her fingertips. The world blurred into nothing—just the soft hum of his presence, the steady beat of her heart in time with his.

When they finally pulled apart, it was slow, reluctant, as if neither really wanted to leave the warmth the kiss had created. For a second, their foreheads touched, breath mingling in the space between, eyes still closed, as if grounding themselves in the seriousness of what had just happened.

Ben's thumb gently brushed over her hand, still holding it in a firm but gentle grip. "I've wanted to do that for a while," he whispered, his voice low and filled with quiet sincerity.

"Me too," she whispered back.

# Chapter 31

Later, after most of the town had packed up for the evening and headed home, Grace lingered in front of the Laurel Ridge Community Church, her hands stuffed in her jacket pockets as she tried to process the whirlwind of feelings that had swirled inside her all night. The stained-glass windows of the church glowed in the moonlight, their colors muted but still beautiful.

She hesitated, unsure whether to step inside the church or head to her car and call it a night.

Her life had taken so many unexpected turns lately. She no longer viewed these changes with apprehension, or as detours from the grand plan she had once envisioned for herself. New York, with all its noise, hustle, and accomplishments, felt like a distant memory, one that no longer held any power over her. This small town—Laurel Ridge—had claimed her heart. She could honestly say this was home and where she wanted to be. This new chapter of her life wouldn't be shaped by her career, but by something far more lasting—love, community, and faith.

And then there was Ben.

Just the thought of him stirred the deepest parts of her heart. His steady encouragement, his quiet way of seeing her when she wasn't even sure she wanted to be seen, and his ability to face his past without pretense. Being with him wasn't the grand, intense whirlwind of emotions she'd once craved in her past relationships. It was something deeper: a quiet, abiding confidence that whispered, you can rest here. And what surprised her even more was her desire to rest—in him, with him.

But that also brought with it its own set of questions. Grace bit her lip, tugging her jacket just a little closer as her mind swirled with uncertainty. How could she build a future with someone, even someone as steadfast as Ben, when there were still questions she didn't have answers to? Not just about him, but about herself?

She climbed the church steps and pushed the heavy wooden door open. The church glowed inside, bathed in the warm, dim light from the sconces that lined the walls. The lighting gave the space an ethereal warmth, inviting but quiet, a hush that penetrated straight to her soul.

Her footsteps were soft against the worn wooden floor. Her fingers brushed lightly against the back of the pews as she passed by—each one telling the story of generations that had sat there before her. Families, singles, the young, and old, all coming to this place to talk to God. To find Him again. Or to simply sit in His presence. To rest.

She took a deep breath and slid into a pew.

The dim lighting wrapped around her like a comforting embrace, and the silence sank into her bones, grounding her, making her feel anchored in this moment. She allowed herself a moment just to sit. To breathe. To be. No more bustling, no more expectations, no more proving she was capable or strong or worthy.

She closed her eyes.

Grace let the stillness wash over her. She sat with her face upturned, as though waiting for heaven to offer some glorious, tangible sense of clarity or peace.

But the answer didn't come in a voice. It came in the soft, rhythmic thumping of her own heartbeat, steadying itself against the buzzing worry in her chest. It came in the quiet, unspoken realization: she was not here just for answers. She was here for something deeper.

She had come for God.

Her hands, folded loosely in her lap, now came together. The world outside the church was cool and breezy, but here, within the church's walls, Grace felt warmth—the kind that seeps into the soul rather than just the skin. It was a warmth she needed.

She opened her mouth to pray, pausing as the magnitude of everything she was feeling caught in her throat. But she took a breath—deep, slow—and let the words flow from her heart, raw and honest.

"Lord…"

She paused, the word resonating in the quiet.

How long had it been since she'd called on Him like this? Really opened her soul and laid everything bare before Him?

"Lord," she breathed again, steadying herself, her words becoming more confident. "I don't even know where to start. So much is happening in my life right now, and I'm amazed… You've blessed me in so many ways. Things I never expected… returning to Laurel Ridge and finding the town welcoming me with open arms. The wonderful people you've put in my life. I didn't realize… how much I needed to get away from New York. Away from… well, everything I thought was important."

Her eyes stung with the beginning of tears. She blinked them back, steadying her voice again.

"And Ben..." She paused, her breath catching on his name. "I wasn't looking for him. And I didn't think I was ready for him, either. But yet, You brought him into my life. And now..."

She exhaled, her fingers tightening around themselves as new doubts slid in. "Lord, help me to understand. To know. Please give me wisdom. I don't want to make decisions based on feelings alone. I don't want to rush into something without Your guidance. Because Ben... Ben is special. And I don't mean because he's good, and kind, and all those things. I mean, he feels like..." She faltered, a tear rolling down her cheek as she whispered, "He feels like home."

The sound of her own voice was so small in the cavernous silence, but the confession felt huge—like a mountain she'd been struggling to climb. Ben was not just a fleeting thought anymore. He was rooted somewhere deep in her heart. He'd grown there, quietly, steadily—just like those towering trees outside her cabin, the ones she'd come to love.

But still, ... doubt lingered, and around the corners of her thoughts, darker questions remained.

Grace let out a shaky breath, leaning into the next prayer.

"But Lord... what about children?"

Her voice, though soft, cracked with a pain that startled her. She hadn't realized how deeply Ben's confession—the one he'd shared just days ago—had shaken her until now. It wasn't that she loved him any less, knowing about his past. Far from it. But she had always dreamt of being a mother. Of having a home buzzing with the laughter and chaos of little ones. A life filled with tiny hands grasping onto hers, the sweet smell of baby shampoo, and the joy of snuggling with her own children before bedtime.

It was everything she'd wanted. But Ben... he couldn't promise her that life. It might be possible, yes, but...

Grace closed her eyes tighter, feeling the ache in her chest as she confronted this desire. "Lord, give me the strength to accept… to understand that Your plans are beyond what I can see. If I never have children of my own, help me to trust You—to see that You have a purpose far greater than anything I've imagined. And help me to know if Ben and I are meant to walk this road together."

Her hands trembled now, but her resolve deepened as her heart called out in an almost desperate plea. "Help me, Lord, not to make this decision based on what could be or what I think I need. Help me to make this decision based on what You want for me."

Grace sat there, motionless, letting the silence wrap around her prayer.

The steady flicker of light from the sconces on the walls in the sanctuary caught her attention, and she looked toward them—the light illuminating the simple wood cross.

It was comforting, that cross. So humble, so grounded in the truth of what Jesus had done for her.

And Grace remembered that she didn't have to figure all of this out tonight. She didn't have to shoulder the weight of these decisions on her own. God had brought her this far, and He wasn't about to abandon her now. He hadn't brought her to Laurel Ridge only for her to be confused and uncertain. He was still here, guiding her through each step.

Grace let out a long breath, her heart softening as she spoke her next words—simple, but saturated with earnest hope.

"Lord, give me clarity. Let me see Your plan unfold before me, one step at a time. Help me to trust not in my own understanding, but in Yours. Guide me toward what You have in store for me, whether it be here in this place, with Ben, or… wherever You may lead next. I'm ready to follow You again."

She sat there a few moments longer, grounding herself in the quiet stillness, letting the peace of the moment wash over her.

It wasn't a sudden, earth-shaking revelation, but something deep within her spirit settled—quiet, still, but present. Like a seed planted beneath the earth, just beginning to take root.

Slowly, Grace opened her eyes, blinking back her tears.

# Chapter 32

The last day of the Harvest Festival arrived, and an air of anticipation hung over Laurel Ridge. A palpable energy flowed through the crowd, a blend of local voices and out-of-town visitors who had ventured to experience the charm of this secluded sanctuary. Their laughter, lively conversations, and occasional contented murmurs filled the air in a harmonious hum.

Grace strolled leisurely through the town square, pausing at each booth to offer a warm smile or engage in a brief chat. The festival had come together perfectly, each detail seamlessly falling into place. Rachel's gallery booth was alive with vibrant displays of local talent. Martha's cinnamon rolls had attracted a line that snaked halfway down the street. Ben and Rachel's moonlit art excursions were fully booked. Everything was a resounding success, beyond what Grace had ever imagined.

Rachel approached, elbowing her. "I literally cannot feel my feet anymore." Her voice carried the undercurrent of contained excitement. "I think I've talked to more people today than in the past three months combined!"

"Well, all the buzz around your gallery and the moonlit art classes are clearly paying off. You're going to need a bigger space at this rate, Rachel."

Rachel made a face, half disbelief, half excitement. "I just... I really hope people actually show up for my classes."

"Rachel, you'll be fine. You're going to knock it out of the park," Grace said.

Rachel sighed, although she looked calmer, her face softer as she glanced around the square. "I guess we both went and created something really amazing for the future of my gallery, didn't we?" Her dark eyes flickered to Grace's, knowing and grateful.

Grace reached out, squeezing her friend's hand. "You did it, Rachel. I just gave a little push."

As Rachel disappeared back to her booth, Grace glanced toward the Adventure Tours tent and a familiar figure caught her eye, standing tall and steady. Ben. He was adjusting a miniature kayak on display outside his booth, smiling as he talked with a group of people gathered beside him. He looked completely in his element. The man defined peaceful contentment.

Their eyes met across the square, and for the briefest moment, the rest of the festival noise faded. That connection—the understanding that had been growing between them—hung in the air like a whisper only they could hear. Ben smiled, and Grace felt it down to her toes.

Just as Grace was about to head toward Ben, a hand landed on her shoulder. She turned to see Martha, a mischievous glint in her eye and a grin across her face.

"There you are, my dear! Thought I might have to send a search party for you," Martha teased, glancing toward the booth where Ben stood, clearly aware of where Grace's attention had drifted.

Grace chuckled. "Ah, you know me—just trying to enjoy the day, and make sure everything's running smoothly."

Martha waved a dismissive hand. "Oh, please! This festival couldn't have gone smoother if we greased it ourselves. And besides, you've done enough work for ten people these past few days. It's about time you took a break and had some fun."

"Fun, huh? I figured being on duty and keeping things organized was enough for me," Grace responded.

Martha shook her head, laughing. "Oh, honey. If we can't pull you away from your duties for at least a few minutes, then I'll be forced to declare this festival a partial failure on account of you not soakin' it in like the rest of us!" Her eyes twinkled as she grabbed Grace's hand, giving it a light tug.

Before Grace could protest, Martha winked dramatically. "Come on, let's go have some fun before you wear yourself out with all that efficiency."

Grace couldn't resist. "Alright, alright. Lead the way, Martha."

The two of them strolled across the square, weaving through clusters of festival-goers. Martha guided her toward the large family arts and crafts tent, which stood across from Ben's booth. Colorful banners fluttered in the breeze above the tent entrance, and the air was filled with the sound of giggling children.

Inside, the craft tables were bustling with activity—kids painting pumpkins, gluing leaves onto construction paper, and furiously coloring in pages from oversized coloring books. The vibrant mess of glue sticks, paint, crayons and tiny, determined hands was a scene of controlled chaos.

Martha's face lit up instantly. "Now this is what pure fun looks like! Creativity run wild." She laughed, her eyes dancing in delight as she took in the sight of children fully engrossed in their projects.

Grace smiled. There was something beautiful in the simplicity of it all—the way these kids expressed uninhibited joy through the messiest, but most beautiful, methods.

"Come on," Martha said, grabbing a paintbrush from a nearby table. "Let's be kids again and have some fun. How about we spruce up a few pumpkins! You ever been much of a pumpkin painter, Grace?"

Grace laughed as she picked up a brush of her own. "Oh, well... my artistic talents may not compare with Rachel's," she began, glancing at the impressive handiwork of the nearby children, "but I'll give it a shot."

Martha leaned in, as if imparting a grand secret. "Here's a trick—these kids will love whatever you do. It's about the fun more than the masterpiece."

Before long, the tent was filled with even more splatters of paint, glue-covered hands, and youthful chatter. Grace picked up a small pumpkin, her brush gliding over its surface to create a swirl of autumn-colored patterns.

One little girl, who had come up beside Grace, giggled at the streaked lines of bright orange and purple.

"Your pumpkin is so pretty!" the girl exclaimed, her eyes wide with admiration.

Grace smiled, her heart swelling a little at the child's genuine praise. "Thank you! I think you might need to paint one for me next—you're the real artist here."

"Martha!" a boy shouted from across the tent as he waved a glue-covered hand in the air. "Can you help with my leaves?"

"I'll be right there!" Martha called back, flashing Grace an amused look as she grabbed a bottle of glitter glue and made her way around the table to help with some reorganizing. "You see?" she said to Grace. "We're in high demand in here!"

Grace laughed as she settled into the rhythm of the moment, her ease and delight growing the longer she stayed. She continued painting alongside the kids, all the while laughing at Martha's animated commentary. By the time they finished their pumpkins, Grace's fingers were covered with streaks of paint and the tips of her fingers threatened to stick together from all the glitter glue she had used. It didn't bother her, though—she was too caught up in the easy joy of the craft tent.

In between handing out fresh supplies and offering snippets of encouragement to the small artists surrounding her, Grace caught the eye of a mother helping her two young children with a vibrant collage. The woman's grateful smile said it all. Being here didn't just make her feel like part of the community—Grace was part of the heartbeat driving it forward.

As the kids scrambled to show off their creations, Grace crouched down to their level, commenting on each one. "That's beautiful! I love the way you used all those leaves," she said to one little boy. To another girl, she whispered conspiratorially, "I think your pumpkin might just be the most glittery in all of West Virginia!"

The joy on their faces lit up Grace's day, a reminder of the innocence found in creating happiness through simple pleasures—paint, glue, and laughter.

Ben stood outside his own booth, his attention drawn to the sight of Grace with the kids. There was a softness about her—that quiet, gentle smile she offered them, the way she leaned in, truly engaged with their mess of colored leaves and glue. She wasn't just humoring them; she was there. Present. Enjoying it.

Ben's chest ached a little as he watched her laugh, the lines around her eyes crinkling as she helped a child straighten their leaf creation. The joy on her face—it was genuine, unfiltered. It reminded him of the conversation they'd shared not long ago, about the future, about the possibilities that might lie ahead. He'd been honest with her, laid it all out, not wanting to leave any illusions about his past or what his future might look like. But in this moment—he couldn't help but wonder if he was witnessing a part of Grace he hadn't fully thought about before.

The thought tugged at him.

The undeniable joy Grace exhibited in spending time with kids. The way her face lit up when they proudly held up their creations. Ben couldn't ignore how his heart tightened—not with worry, but with the growing realization that Grace wasn't just experiencing this moment... she was thriving in it.

And that's what made him pause.

He sensed what this kind of life—a life filled with children—could mean to Grace. It was written in the lines of her smile as she laughed alongside Martha and the children. It was clear in the way her eyes softened when a child would run past, their laughter echoing against the rhythm of the festival. Kids... they brought a light to her face.

Even from where he stood, he could see how effortlessly she clicked with the little ones, the way her natural warmth seemed to draw them in.

Was it fair? Was it fair to move forward if, in the end, what she deserved... was something more than what he may be able to give?

The sound of children's laughter continued to fill the space as Grace dug her fingers into a bin of pom-poms, giggling alongside Martha at a particularly enthusiastic boy who was now attempting to fling glitter glue onto a pumpkin. Grace's joy was radiant, spilling over into everything and everyone around her.

Ben kept watching, unable to pull himself away. There was something irresistible about the sight of Grace fully immersed in the innocence and wonder of the children's arts and crafts tent.

Grace glanced across the square and locked eyes with him. She smiled—one that was full of pure, unspoken affection—before returning her focus to the excited children nearby.

Ben's chest tightened again. That look...

# Chapter 33

Ben and Grace stood side by side in the busy pie-baking competition tent. Warm apple, spiced pumpkin, and sweet pecan scents—filled the air. The atmosphere buzzed with anticipation as the crowd's chatter rose. Families huddled together, children happily munching on caramel apples and cotton candy, while older couples shared intimate, murmured conversations from nearby benches. All eyes were drawn to the judges seated at the head of a long table, the tantalizing display of pies before them promising a sweet finale to the festival. The air was thick with excitement, each person waiting for the big announcement that would crown the day's winner.

Ben leaned down, whispering in her ear. "You ready to see who's going to take home the coveted pie trophy?"

Grace raised an eyebrow. "Is there an actual trophy?"

Ben's smile widened. "I think you'll be pleasantly surprised."

"Alright y'all!" Beth's voice boomed with a mixture of enthusiasm and delightful flair that commanded attention. She stood proudly on a small platform, hands poised as if beginning the world's most important speech. "Gather 'round, because it's time for the moment you've all been waiting for—the official declaration of who makes the best pie here in Laurel Ridge!"

The crowd chuckled, drawn in by Beth's infectious energy.

Beth grinned mischievously, scanning the gathered faces. "Now, before I announce the winner, let me remind y'all of the stakes here. This isn't just about any ol' pie baker winning a little ol' prize. Oh no, no, no." She lowered her voice dramatically, causing more chuckles to ripple through the crowd. "We are talking legendary status, folks. Bragging rights for the entire next year. Every meal, every church potluck, Thanksgiving... oh honey, even Christmas dessert tables. This baker will hold their head high, knowing they've got the golden touch when it comes to pie crusts and fillings!"

Another round of laughter erupted from the audience as she waved a finger at the friendly pie competitors. "Oh, I see y'all over there pretending to be nervous—uh-huh! We all saw how confident you were when you dropped off those pies earlier. Now let's see who takes home the trophy!"

Beth wasn't done. "Now, I've tasted more pies today than–well, let's just say someone might have to roll me home if I don't pace myself for the rest of the day. I tasted classics like your apple and cherry, some bold moves with toasted pecan, and even a surprise key lime in there. And honey, let me tell you what heaven tastes like.... my goodness. Not a one of these bakers disappointed my taste buds today. I can say with all certainty, Laurel Ridge has the best bakers. Full stop."

A smattering of cheers and playful whistles followed her declaration. She tapped her chin thoughtfully before continuing, narrowing her eyes dramatically. "But, alas... though my heart wishes I could hand out trophies to every one of you, the rules say there can only be one winner."

She paused, milking the anticipation for all it was worth, the tension so thick it could be sliced—much like a perfect piece of pie.

Beth peeked at the card in her hand, giving the audience a teasing grin before drawing a deep breath and letting it out slowly. "And the winner of this year's Harvest Festival Pie-Baking Competition is..." she stretched the words, dragging the suspense through the crowd like a fishing line. Every person leaned in.

She held the audience for a beat longer—just to see the way folks were fidgeting—and then let the words break free.

"... Lucille Widmore's legendary apple pecan pie!"

The square erupted into lively applause as Lucille herself—every bit as proud and exuberant as Beth was grand—rose from the crowd, a wide, beaming smile on her face. Lucille strutted forward, waving to the crowd like a pageant queen, her cheeks pink with pride.

Beth clapped herself, her voice rising above the noise. "Now, y'all know Lucille and this apple pecan pie of hers—this isn't her first rodeo! She's been perfecting this recipe since some of you were barely knee-high to a grasshopper! Heaven's gonna have to make room for this pie because it's divine!"

As Lucille approached the platform, Beth picked up the sizable gold and silver trophy. It gleamed in the late afternoon sunlight, an oversized tribute to the bake-off's deep-rooted tradition.

With a playful wink and warm admiration, Beth handed the trophy to Lucille. "Well, Lucille, you've outdone yourself, honey! I don't know how you crafted such a perfect pie, but now you'll have folks begging for that secret recipe all year long."

Lucille let out a hearty cackle and spun in place, proudly hoisting the oversized trophy high above her head. It nearly dwarfed her, drawing laughter from the gathered crowd. "Thank you, thank you, everyone!" she called, grinning from ear to ear. With a mischievous glint in her eyes, she added, "The secret? It's in the spices, y'all! Oh, and plenty of love... and a whole lotta butter!"

The crowd chuckled and applauded louder. Everyone caught up in the good-humored spirit of the event.

Beth, clearly delighted with the event's success, leaned into the microphone, her voice brimming with enthusiasm. "Let's give another big round of applause for Lucille Widmore and her incredible apple pecan pie, folks!" The crowd erupted in cheers as Beth joined in, her face beaming with pride. "And don't forget—if you want a slice of Lucille's award-winning pie, you better be quick! Plenty of pies from the competition, along with a variety of other homemade dishes, are waiting for you behind the church at our potluck dinner. Now let's all go enjoy the delicious food our amazing community has prepared!"

"You weren't kidding about the trophy," Grace said as she leaned toward Ben, eyeing the trophy that was the size of a small toddler clasped lovingly between both of Lucille's hands.

Ben chuckled, shaking his head. "I know, a little over the top, but hey, it's all in good fun."

It was such a simple thing—an oversized trophy for the best pie—but somehow it was a reminder. Life wasn't about achieving the world's biggest goals. It was about the small victories, the gentle joys. The laughter shared between loved ones.

***

Ben guided Grace to the picnic area behind the church, where the tables—draped in mismatched checkered cloths—were alive with the murmur of conversation and laughter. The air was rich with the comforting aromas of home-cooked dishes: steaming chicken and dumplings, crisp fried chicken, tender green beans, freshly baked bread, and the tempting sweetness of pies and cakes that lined the dessert table. It was a gathering filled with the simple joy of community, where stories were shared and hearts were full.

After loading their plates, they settled at a picnic table beneath the shade of an old oak tree, the distant notes of folk music wafting through the air from the town square where the festival was winding down. Grace cut into a slice of Lucille's apple pecan pie, took a bite, and let out a soft, contented sigh.

Ben watched Grace, a playful glint in his hazel eyes. "I'm not sure if it's the magic of the festival or if Lucille has a secret ingredient stashed away, but I don't think I've ever seen someone look quite so blissful over a slice of pie."

Grace raised an eyebrow, a playful smirk tugging at her lips as she dabbed the corner of her mouth with a napkin. "What are you trying to say, Turner? That I don't usually look this blissful?"

Ben's mouth quirked up in a teasing grin. "Oh, no. You're always positively glowing."

Grace chuckled, nudging her plate toward him. "Here, have a bite and get in on this blissful action. You won't want to miss it."

Ben grinned as he took a deliberate forkful of pie, chewing with mock seriousness before letting out a satisfied hum. "Now that's good. Really good. But between us," he added in a conspiratorial tone, leaning in slightly, "Martha's pumpkin pecan? It's always been my favorite, hands down. Just... don't tell Lucille. The last thing this town needs is another pie rivalry."

Grace laughed, shaking her head. "Oh, the stakes just get higher around here every day, don't they?"

"High stakes, low stakes," Ben shrugged. "Depends on whether we're talking pies... or—"

Grace cocked her head and gave him a wry look. "Or?"

Ben paused for dramatic effect, setting his fork back down. "Pumpkin painting. That's another competitive Laurel Ridge affair."

She let out a groan of laughter, tossing her napkin at him. "Oh, don't even go there. You saw my pumpkin earlier—it was abysmal next to those kids' masterpieces! You should be grateful I didn't ask for your critique."

Ben laughed, catching her napkin midair. "I noticed that swirl of colors you were working on. Not bad at all."

"Oh please," Grace waved dismissively. "Between Martha and the kids, I think they were more charmed by my paint disasters than my actual talent."

Ben leaned in. "You know... you looked like you had a lot of fun with them. The kids, I mean. I've never seen you laugh like that—playing around with them, covered in glue, paint, and pom-poms, as if you didn't have a care in the world."

Grace hesitated, the lightness of the moment slowing, her smile softening as her eyes drifted down to her nearly empty plate before meeting Ben's again. "You know," she began, tone slightly more thoughtful, "it was a lot more fun than I thought it would be. Being in that tent, getting covered in glitter and smearing paint—it kind of felt like being a kid again. No stress. Just... pure, simple fun."

Ben studied Grace's face, the flicker of emotion in her eyes that she hadn't yet put into words.

"I could see that," Ben said softly. "You were... glowing."

Grace's smile lingered, but a deeper thought clouded it for a moment. She glanced away, her eyes following a family of four walking hand-in-hand across the picnic area. She watched the young boy, maybe five or six, excitedly point to the dessert table before his mother knelt down, smiling, and ruffled his hair.

"Something on your mind?" Ben asked gently.

She hesitated, biting her lip before shaking her head, "No, just thinking back on the day. How fun it was. So, tell me what are your plans for tomorrow? I was thinking maybe I would meet you at church and then afterward we could pack a lunch and take a hike, or maybe you could show me how to white water raft. What do you think?"

Ben took his time before responding, his eyes wandering over the churchyard where friends and family enjoyed their dinner, laughter and conversation filling the evening air. Finally, he turned his attention back to Grace, his voice thoughtful. "You know...I don't miss church often, but I'm thinking I'll head out on a solo camping trip tomorrow morning. Just for a few days, up into the mountains. I need some...time—just me, nature... and God."

Ben's easy-going demeanor softened into something more introspective. He glanced off toward the mountains and continued, "Just need to get away—clear my head, reconnect with God, you know?"

Grace set her fork down, her mind working through the layers behind his words.

This wasn't just about a casual few days in the woods, was it? No, there was something deeper lurking beneath the surface.

"Is everything okay?" she asked, searching his face for any sign of what he might be thinking. Her brow furrowed as she tried to catch his gaze again, feeling as though there was a crack in the smooth veneer of the day.

"Everything is fine... it's all good, Grace." His lips twitched into a smile, but something about it didn't quite reach his eyes. He exhaled, running a hand through his tousled hair.

Grace shifted in her seat, crossing her arms instinctively as the warmth from earlier began to ebb. "Okay... What does that mean?"

He paused, rubbing the back of his neck as if searching for the right words. "Grace, don't take this the wrong way. Everything's good, really. I just feel like I need to head out into the woods for a while, camp for a couple of nights, clear my head. It's nothing serious, just... you know, one of those things guys sometimes do to reset."

"Okay," Grace said, her voice calm but a little surprised. "I'm not upset. You just caught me off guard, that's all. But I get it."

"But..." Ben gently prompted, leaning forward.

"I guess... I don't know," she admitted, tilting her head as she tried to gather her thoughts. "I guess I wasn't expecting you to want space so soon, especially when—we've just started figuring this thing out... together." She sounded more vulnerable than she intended, and the rawness of it tugged at her. "I'm not finding fault with it, I just... it caught me off guard, that's all."

"Grace, the last thing I want is to make you feel like I'm pulling away. That's not it at all." He reached across the table and took her hand, his rough, calloused fingers warm against her skin. "I'm not running, I promise," he said, his voice low, meant for her and her alone. "But... there are things I need to think through."

Grace stared at his hand in hers, her heart torn between understanding and... something deeper. A tiny voice, quiet but persistent, echoed in the corners of her mind.

*Why is he retreating now, just when things were feeling so real?*

She inhaled slowly, keeping her expression measured. "I respect that, Ben," she said. "I trust you. I...get it."

# Chapter 34

The familiar creak of the cabin's old wooden door welcomed Grace as she stepped inside. After attending service this morning at Laurel Ridge Community Church, she felt a lingering joy, the kind that often hung around after genuine fellowship. The smile from Pastor Eli's closing prayer was still on her lips. The morning had been refreshing, filled with the simple comfort of Scripture and the gentle hum of hymns that settled her spirit.

Grace kicked off her heels by the door and set her leather purse on the table in the living room. She filled the coffeemaker with water and scooped in a fragrant pumpkin spice blend she'd recently picked up at a little shop in town. As the machine hummed to life, the warm, autumnal aroma began filling the air.

Her thoughts flickered to Ben. His absence was a shadow she had tried to ignore during the service this morning—especially when Pastor Eli spoke of trust in God's timing, in plans that weren't always visible right away. Even sitting in that pew, Grace had felt her mind wander—wondering why Ben had chosen now to leave, why he needed a solo trip when things between them had been falling so naturally into place.

She headed into her bedroom, swapping her lavender floral dress for a soft, oversized t-shirt and her favorite pair of leggings, the comfort seeping into her as she let go of the day's formalities.

She padded back to the kitchen and poured herself a mug of coffee, inhaling the rich, familiar scent.

With the steaming mug of coffee in hand, Grace picked up her laptop and phone from the counter and stepped out onto the back porch. The porch swing calling her name, its inviting sway offering a quiet reprieve from her thoughts on this crisp Sunday afternoon. Around her, the sky was a clear blue, and the air carried the scent of sun-warmed pine. The sound of the New River, flowing beyond, created a natural soundtrack.

As she settled into the swing, she took a slow sip, letting the coffee's warmth spread through her body. The gentle creak of the chains holding the swing added a soothing rhythm that paired well with her thoughts. Across the valley, she saw specks of kayakers paddling along the river, their bright-colored gear contrasting against the deep silvery blue waters. Even from where she sat, she could hear their faint shouts of laughter carried by the breeze.

But despite the peaceful scene in front of her, her mind kept circling back to Ben.

Staring off into the distance, the river's curves hypnotizing her thoughts. She knew Ben well enough to understand his desire for solitude—he wasn't someone who made impulsive decisions. So why did his choice to head off on a solo camping trip feel like a jolt to her system?

She replayed their conversation from the day before in her mind.

*"...I need to head out into the woods for a while, camp for a couple of nights—not for any reason other than just me, nature... and God,"*

Grace had nodded, told him she understood, and that she didn't take it personally. But now... here alone on the swing, with no rush of life to distract her, she wondered if maybe that wasn't entirely true.

*Why now?* She questioned silently. Just when... just when something between them had begun blossoming in a way that felt real—tangible.

She sipped her coffee. The breeze cooling the warmth on her cheeks.

This wasn't about some big fight, or miscommunication, or doubt. There was no trace of drama in Ben's actions. On the surface, his plan for a camping trip made perfect sense. He had confided in her before about how he found peace in God's creation—in hiking through the Appalachian mountains, or sleeping under the stars, away from everything. It wasn't about her. If anything, it spoke to who Ben truly was—a man who sought God in the quiet places, the stillness of nature, in ways that went deeper than most people would imagine.

But knowing all that didn't stop a small voice in the back of her mind from asking: Is this a retreat because of me? Is he unsure about us?

She shook the thought away and set her coffee mug down on the porch's small wooden table.

Ben wasn't like anyone she had dated before. He was thoughtful, genuine, the kind of man whose presence made you feel calm and cared for without a single word. And yet, she realized, there was a part of her that wasn't used to this—to someone walking through life independently of her, making their own space without relying on her for stability.

Just as she picked up her coffee again, a shrill ring intruded on the peace of the moment.

Her phone.

Her heart gave a strange, startled jolt—a reflex from how the sharp sound clashed with the serenity of the morning. She reached for the phone and saw the name. Jack.

A part of her wanted to ignore it. Her thumb hovering over the screen. But she knew this conversation couldn't wait any longer, especially since Jack had already left half a dozen missed calls and messages.

"Jack," she answered.

"Grace! Finally!" Jack's voice cut through, loud and brimming with barely contained exasperation. "I've been trying to reach you for days. What's going on? I've called, I've emailed... I thought we had an understanding about this opportunity."

His words immediately brought her back to a place she wanted to leave behind. The fast-paced, head-on collision of her corporate world life. She could practically hear the noise of New York buzzing. The image of towering skyscrapers flashed in her mind, along with the suffocating elevator rides and endless strategy calls.

"I'm sorry, Jack," Grace said, her voice calm, but knowing where this was heading. "I've been—well—soaking in a quieter life lately. I haven't checked my emails or kept my phone on much at all."

There was a pause on his end, a beat of disbelief, before his voice softened only slightly but remained urgent. "Grace. You haven't checked your... emails? This position—it's huge. You understand that, right? President of Communications, Grace. Leadership on a level you've been working toward for years. I... I don't think you realize how big this is."

She bit her bottom lip. Of course, she realized how big it was. The old Grace would have leapt at the chance, packed her bags, signed the contracts, and thrown herself right back into the beast that was corporate New York.

The words from church that morning—about trusting God's guidance—resurfaced quietly at the back of her mind.

"I know, Jack. I understand. It's a massive offer."

"Then what's the problem? I pulled more strings than you can imagine to get this offer on the table for you. And the salary package…" He paused, clearly thinking this would hammer home the point. "It's way beyond anything you've probably ever been offered before, Grace. We're talking seven figures, top benefits, the works. This is more than you could've dreamed of when you came to New York all those years ago. And it's yours if you just say yes."

Grace took a deep breath, staring out at the river. She could see the sparkles of sunlight reflecting off the surface, feel the coolness of the breeze brushing her cheek.

"Jack… I appreciate everything you've done. Really," she replied, her voice steady. "But I can't accept the job."

For a moment, there was stunned silence on the other end of the line. She could practically see Jack sitting at his desk, staring at the phone, completely dumbfounded.

"You… what?" His question came out slowly, like he hadn't quite heard her right. "Grace, you can't be serious. Have you lost your mind? You've built your career around moments like this."

She leaned back on the swing, watching a group of birds take flight in the distance. Jack's incredulity didn't surprise her. She knew walking away from something this big was unthinkable for many people.

Her definition of success had changed. Once, success was defined by titles and paychecks. By who noticed her in a boardroom meeting or what next-level project she was leading? Now, success looked a lot more like peace. Like community. Like the quiet, intimate connections happening in a place where there wasn't always a need to strive.

"I know what it looks like, Jack," she continued. "And I get that it might not make sense to you, or to anyone who knew me back in New York. But that doesn't matter. What I do or what I choose is my business and mine alone. I've changed. I want something different for my life. Titles and seven-figure contracts... they don't have the same pull over me anymore."

He didn't answer for a moment, and she could hear his breath coming out in a slow rush through the phone. "Anderson, you can't be serious?"

"The name's Grace and yes, I am quite serious," she said, easily this time.

Jack sputtered on the other end of the line, clearly still trying to wrap his mind around what she was saying. "Look, I get that this whole 'finding peace in a small town' thing. But Grace, you're giving up..."

Grace interrupted him, "I'm not giving up anything, Jack. I'm gaining something far better than I ever found in boardrooms and skyscrapers. Look, I'm grateful. I can't tell you how much I appreciate the offer—really, I do," she said, her tone softening as a smile spread across her face. "But the job you're offering me, and my life back in New York—it's not mine anymore. I don't want any of it."

Another long silence followed. Grace could hear Jack shifting in frustration on his end of the line.

"Grace... seriously, take a minute and think this through—really think about it. Opportunities like this don't come around every day. And trust me, the higher-ups? They're already starting to wonder if you've lost your edge by not jumping on it right away. If you pass this up, Grace... people will remember. And not in a good way. There's no coming back from a decision like this. Saying no to an offer like this—it's career suicide. This isn't just some job, this is THE opportunity, and walking away from it? That's just... it's unthinkable."

"I have thought about it, Jack," she said simply. "And I'm sure what you've said is true... in your world. But in the life I'm creating for myself now? Edge doesn't matter as much as having peace does. And I wouldn't trade that for all the titles or bonuses in the world."

Jack's breath hissed out on the other end, his frustration finally bubbling to the surface in such an overt way. "I can't believe this. You're walking away from everything for what? Some cabin in the middle of nowhere?"

"Yes, a cabin in the middle of nowhere, where I wake up to the river flowing outside my window. Where I actually know people when I walk down the street. Where I've made connections, Jack—real connections that don't hinge on deal negotiations or strategy meetings. Things that actually matter. This is where I belong now. And it doesn't change what I've done in my career. This town—it's become home," she said, her final words soft but firm. "And I can't say the same for New York."

Jack exhaled again sharply. "Your nuts. You're making a mistake, Grace. You'll see it sooner or later."

"I'm sorry you feel that way. But I know what I'm doing. Thank you, Jack. I really do wish you the best."

And she ended the call.

Grace lowered the phone, staring at it for a minute longer before setting it down on the porch table.

She stared out at the river, feeling the cool breeze ruffle her hair. She had made the right choice. It wasn't the kind of decision she would have found herself making a year ago. But Grace could feel the steady assurance bloom within her chest.

This life—right here, in this tiny corner of West Virginia—had given her more clarity than any fast-track promotion ever could. It might not have been the life she had mapped out once upon a time. But that was okay.

The world kept moving—all around her the sounds of nature and the passing of time, as constant as the flow of the New River. As she relaxed again, Grace knew one thing for sure.

She was home.

# Chapter 35

*Later that afternoon...*

Grace sat on the porch swing, her laptop balanced on her lap, as a soft afternoon breeze played with her hair. The steady creak of the swing's chains added a soothing rhythm in the background as she clicked between realtor websites, skimming profiles, reading reviews, and jotting down names. Her fingers moved with purpose, but her thoughts wavered, distracted by the familiar pull of the river's steady flow, its waters glistening in the late afternoon sun. Even the simple task of list-making—something she had once done methodically, almost compulsively in her corporate life—failed to provide satisfaction.

She hadn't fully expected the mix of emotions that washed over her while searching for someone to sell her condo. It wasn't just an address she was preparing to part with—it was the last tangible tie to the life she'd thought she would lead forever.

Back in New York, that condo had been her sanctuary in a world of high heels and power suits. It had witnessed her triumphs, her moments of quiet exhaustion, and now... she was ready to let it go.

Grace skimmed through another realtor's website, but before she could scroll past the polished headshot splashed across her screen, her thoughts were pulled away by an unfamiliar sound. The crunch of gravel under tires—a vehicle coming up the driveway. She frowned slightly. She wasn't expecting anyone.

Setting her laptop down, Grace rose from the swing and walked to the front of the cabin. As she turned the corner, her breath caught.

Stepping out of a white Jeep were two familiar figures: Martha and Rachel.

"Martha! Rachel!" Grace exclaimed, her surprise quickly turning into genuine excitement.

"Well, don't just stand there, honey—we come bearing gifts." Martha's eyes twinkled as she lifted a large, checkered picnic basket.

Rachel grinned, brushing a few stray strands of hair from her face. "Took us a while to pack all of Martha's gourmet goodies, but we figured you could use some girl time. You didn't think we'd let a gorgeous day like this go by without showing up, did you?"

Grace blinked, momentarily speechless. She knew the last time Martha had visited the cabin was when her Aunt Imogene had been alive.

"Well, this is a surprise," she said, chuckling as she moved to kiss Martha on the cheek and give Rachel a hug. "I guess it's a good thing I didn't slip into my pajamas earlier, like I was tempted to."

"I almost wore mine," Rachel said as she leaned into the jeep to grab a cooler.

Martha swatted at Rachel with the back of her hand, laughing soft-ly. "She's kidding. You know I'd never allow that. Too much dignity to uphold, even out in the middle of nowhere."

Grace smiled as she watched the two women. She realized just how much she needed this—this simple, unexpected display of friendship.

They took the food around to the back porch, where the breeze was gentler, and the view of the river was perfectly framed by rustling pines. Martha set out a tablecloth on the porch floor while Rachel popped open the cooler. Sweet tea sparkled in the sunlight as Martha poured it into plastic tumblers, garnished with lemon slices because, of course, Martha did everything right down to the details.

"We thought you might not be eating enough home-cooked meals," Martha said with a wink, taking the cap off a mason jar filled with chilled potato salad. "And since I knew this old place so well—well, I couldn't resist the chance. Brings back memories."

Grace smiled, her heart softening as she glanced around the porch. Her aunt and Martha had probably sat in these very chairs on count-less summer evenings, sipping sweet tea and swapping stories. The nostalgia tugged at her, bittersweet.

"Thank you both for coming," she said, taking a sip of the tea. "You have no idea what this means to me."

Martha waved away her thanks with a playful roll of her eyes. "Nonsense, honey. That's what we're here for. Besides, I live for stuff like this. Nothing better than porch sittin' on a good Sunday after-noon, eatin' and gossipin'."

The meal was laid out—crispy fried chicken, buttery rolls, a jar of Martha's homemade preserves, and the infamous apple pecan pie that had won over the entire Harvest Festival crowd just yesterday.

As they settled into their seats, the conversation flowed easily, punctuated by laughter and good-natured teasing. Rachel excitedly detailed the upcoming art workshops, sparked by the success of her gallery's booth at the festival. Martha regaled them with tales of past festivals.

But as the afternoon light began to mellow into the soft golden hues of early evening, the conversation naturally shifted to more personal topics.

"So," Rachel said, her tone adopting a teasing edge, "how're things going with our dear Ben?"

Of course, the topic of Ben would come up—it wasn't a subject that could be avoided easily, not with Rachel being his sister and Martha being, well, Martha. Still, it caught her a little off-guard.

"Oh, you know..." Grace hesitated before opting for honesty. "It's going... good. I think."

Martha shot her a knowing look. "Mm-hmm. You sure about that, dear?"

Grace forced a laugh, leaning back in her chair. "Well... he's on one of his solo camping trips—out in the mountains. He mentioned something about needing time to clear his head, and..." She bit her lip. "I don't know. I've been trying to figure out whether it's me, or if it's something else."

Rachel chuckled, her fork pausing midair over a piece of pie. "Oh, Grace, you're over-analyzing it. Ben does this. It's a man thing. The moment life feels heavy or if he's thinking something through, he disappears into the woods like some kind of caveman."

Grace laughed at the image Rachel painted. "Is it really that simple?"

"Oh, absolutely," Rachel said with a grin. "I can't count the number of times he's gone MIA because he's mulling over some big decision—whether it's about business or anything else. He comes back looking like he just had a heart-to-heart with a tree, but it clears his head. You'll see."

Martha, in her infinite wisdom, chose that moment to weigh in, her voice low and steady. "Rachel's right, darling. Ben's an old soul—very much in tune with what he needs, and he doesn't rush anything. Not unless he's sure. It's a good quality, but it can leave you wonderin' sometimes. The best thing to do is give him space. Trust the process."

"He's always been this way," Rachel added, scooping another spoonful of potato salad onto her plate. "And honestly, he wouldn't just run off if he didn't feel something serious about you."

Grace's heart gave a tiny flutter, though she tried to keep her expression neutral. "What do you mean?"

Rachel eyed her. "Oh, come on, Grace. Haven't you noticed? He's all in, whether or not he's said it. The man practically glows when you're around."

Martha nodded in agreement, a smile playing at her lips. "That's true. I've seen it. Reminds me of how my late husband Scottie was. Men don't always blurt out what they feel, but it shows, plain as day." She patted Grace's hand gently. "Trust it, dear heart. Ben's figuring out how to make sure he's ready for what could come next. And I'm sure it'll be worth the wait."

Grace leaned back in her seat, letting the words sink in while staring out at the sun setting on the horizon.

"I guess you're both right," she mused. "I just don't want to mess anything up."

"You won't," Rachel said, her tone leaving no room for doubt. "You're exactly what he needs—whether or not he knows it. And if he needs a few days in the woods to realize that? Let him."

Their conversation shifted to lighter topics, peeling away the layers of heavier discussion about Ben. Laughter fluttered back into the air, their banter bouncing freely between bites of delicious food and sips of sweet tea.

Rachel, ever the natural storyteller, leaned back in her chair with a gleam in her eye and a mischievous smile playing on her lips. "Okay," she started, raising an eyebrow. "I'm going to tell you about the time Martha here—bless her heart—played matchmaker at during our Thanksgiving dinner a couple of years back."

Grace sat up straighter in her chair, sensing that a good story was brewing. "Oh, this sounds promising," she teased.

Rachel grinned wider in response. "You have no idea. Picture this," she began, raising her hands dramatically as if setting the scene. "It's Thanksgiving. There I am, minding my own business, ready to dig into a perfectly cooked dinner, when Martha, in her infinite wisdom, decides that this is the day to push me into the arms of—wait for it—the town pharmacist."

Grace nearly choked on her tea. "The pharmacist?" she repeated, eyes widening in disbelief as a smile crept across her lips.

"Oh yes, the town pharmacist," Rachel confirmed with a tragic sigh and a shake of her head. "John Henry... the man who hands me allergy meds and sinus spray in a brown paper bag."

Grace couldn't help but giggle at Rachel's theatrical flair, but Martha, seated on Rachel's other side, simply waved a hand dismissively.

"Well... the man liked you!" Martha jumped in defensively, though a mischievous twinkle danced in her eyes. "If you'd look beyond the mashed potatoes, you'd have seen it, too."

That line hung in the air for exactly one second before Rachel dissolved into a fit of laughter.

"The mashed potatoes?" Grace said, her curiosity getting the better of her. "Okay, you're going to have to explain now."

Rachel took a moment to compose herself. "Oh, I'll explain, all right. So, there I was, plotting my escape from what could only be described as an extremely awkward dinner conversation, when dear John Henry gets overly enthusiastic about passing me the mashed potatoes. In his nervousness—"

Rachel paused for dramatic effect, her eyes widening as she relived the moment.

"In his nervousness?" Grace leaned in, her expression alight with curiosity.

Rachel nodded, throwing a pointed glance in Martha's direction. "In his nervousness, he dumps the entire bowl of mashed potatoes right into his lap."

Grace gasped, but before she could react, Rachel continued.

"There was just this brief second... this second of silence where everyone froze. I promise you, it was like a scene out of a sitcom on television."

The three women burst into laughter, the sound filling the valley and mingling with the soft rustle of the surrounding trees.

"Oh, but wait, the situation—it got even worse," Rachel said, trying to catch her breath between bursts of laughter. "I couldn't stop myself—the words just spilled out before I even knew what I was saying." She paused, still laughing as she recalled the moment.

"What did you say, Rachel?" Grace asked, still laughing, eager to hear the punchline she knew was coming.

"Oh Lord, forgive me for my mouth," Rachel said, raising her hands toward the sky as if appealing for divine intervention. "Poor John Henry, there he was mashed potatoes all over himself, and the words just came out of my mouth without thinking...I said, 'well...I guess we won't be needing the gravy tonight, Aunt Martha'... Grace...I was so embarrassed for him and myself after saying that. I still can't believe I said it!"

Martha gave a playful shrug and chuckled. "Oh, come on now—it was just a little mishap! That doesn't change the fact that he was head over heels for you, Rachel."

Rachel shot Martha a mock-offended look. "Mishap? Martha, You had me seated right next to him, and he filled his lap with mashed potatoes, and he was trying to act like nothing happened. Eighteen people at the dinner table, all trying to stifle their nervous laughter---it was ridiculous!"

That image set them off again, a cascade of giggles falling from their lips as they clutched at their sides, helpless to stop the onslaught of laughter.

Martha shook her head, still chuckling softly. "Well, maybe if you had given the man a little more of your attention, you wouldn't be sitting here single now. Pharmaceutical advice and mashed potatoes? That's a solid deal, if you ask me."

Rachel tossed a smile in Grace's direction, as if throwing her an olive branch amid the teasing. "See what I'm dealing with here? She's still ready to marry me off to the local pharmacist."

Grace wiped at her eyes, giggling. "I can see the argument for it. Sounds like he was into you, Rachel."

"Sure," Rachel drawled sarcastically, crossing her arms dramatically. "Because nothing screams 'romance' like 'Would you like a side of penicillin with your potatoes?'"

Laughter swelled again, the easy camaraderie between the three women filling Grace's heart with a warmth. Sitting here with Rachel and Martha, it was like falling into an old rhythm—the rhythm of friendship that didn't need words to be understood.

Grace glanced between Rachel and Martha, her chest swelling with tenderness. The simple joys of this moment, the laughs between friends over something as silly as a botched mashed potato handoff, filled her in places that had long been empty. Grace knew this laughter, this safe harbor of shared stories and friendship—was exactly what God had intended for her when He brought her back here to Laurel Ridge. To a cabin tucked away on a ridge. A place far removed from the cutthroat world of public relations.

"So tell me," Martha said, punctuating her words with a knowing smile, "Have you really started to see Laurel Ridge as home?"

Grace leaned back, the sun warming her face. "Yes," she replied, a smile playing on her lips. "I really, truly have. In fact, just before you both arrived, I was actually making a list of realtors. I'm ready to sell my condo in New York for good."

Martha grinned as she reached for her glass of sweet tea. "Well, it's about time, honey. You've found something special here—something a bustling city can't offer you, no matter how many perks come with it."

Rachel nodded, her smile broadening. "I should've told you weeks ago: Sell that condo already, toss the cell phone in the trash, and donate those business suits to Goodwill."

Grace chuckled.

After an easy lull in the conversation, Martha let out a small sigh, catching both Grace and Rachel's attention. She stretched her arms out above her head, her movements slow and deliberate. "Well, I suppose I should head home pretty soon. These old bones can only handle so much."

"I'll help you pack up, Aunt Martha." Rachel began to gather the leftover food, stacking jars and reusable containers into the picnic basket.

Rachel paused and looked over at Grace. "Things with Ben will work themselves out," she said quietly, the humor of earlier replaced with a resolute calm. "He's stubborn sometimes. I might not understand some things he does, but he's a good man. Don't worry too much."

"I know he is," Grace said, her voice soft but resolute. "I'll do my best not to overthink it."

Grace helped tidy up the remnants of their meal and walked with the women toward the Jeep.

"You know, you won't be rid of us this easily. Expect another visit soon," Rachel said as she placed the cooler in the jeep.

Grace laughed, rolling her eyes with affection. "I wouldn't dare complain. Next time, though, I'll promise to cook."

Martha chuckled as she set the picnic basket in the jeep, her movements deliberate but swift. "Well, darling, if you do, make sure it's something you've learned from this side of town. We don't want any of that big-city takeout sneaking in."

Grace grinned. "I think I've said goodbye to city takeout for good, Martha."

Rachel gave Grace a quick squeeze. "Don't overthink things with Ben, okay? He likes you more than he knows how to say. Trust me."

Grace smiled, grateful for the reassurance again.

"I'll try my best," Grace replied. "Thanks, both of you, for everything."

"Grace, how 'bout you come down for breakfast at the diner tomorrow?" Martha said with a twinkle in her eye.

"I guess I could," Grace said, "though I hadn't really thought that far ahead. Why?"

Martha grinned and nodded, her eyes sparkling with mischief. "Don't you worry about the 'why,' honey. I have a surprise in store for you. Just be there for breakfast, alright? I'll see you then, ya hear?"

"Alright. I'll see you for breakfast in the morning," Grace said, laughing.

The two women climbed into the Jeep, and as the engine rumbled to life, they exchanged waves before disappearing down the winding road, their laughter leaving a lingering trace of joy in the air.

As the sound of the Jeep's engine faded into the distance, Grace was left standing in the quiet, her heart full.

# Chapter 36

G race inhaled the mouthwatering aroma of warm, buttery biscuits and savory sausage gravy as Martha set the plate before her with an expert flourish. Without even asking for her order, the diner owner had appeared from the kitchen carrying a tray brimming with food too tempting to refuse. Flaky, golden biscuits smothered in rich, creamy gravy, perfectly crispy bacon, hash browns... perfection—Grace could hardly believe her eyes.

"Oh my," Grace said, blinking at the feast, her stomach growling in anticipation. "Martha, did you really have to bring out half the diner's menu for me?"

Martha chuckled and waved her off. She winked, her bright blue eyes sparkling as she folded a napkin and placed it beside Grace's coffee mug. "I know what you need, dear, before you do!" With a pat on Grace's shoulder, she moved off to tend to another customer, her laughter trailing behind her.

After a quick glance down at the realtor websites opened in multiple tabs on her laptop screen, Grace set her work aside. Eating felt more important—especially when it involved a meal this rich.

She ate her breakfast and enjoyed the quiet conversations of the breakfast crowd floating around her. Her laptop sat to the side, notifications blinking, but Grace resisted the pull to dive back into emails and logistics, knowing this breakfast demanded her full attention.

Once Grace had eaten all she could, she wiped her mouth with the napkin, and moved her laptop back in front of her, letting the world of real estate tug her back into focus. A few taps on the keyboard, and she resumed her search for a realtor who could sell the condo. Even the thought of it—letting go of that last piece of her old life—felt so odd, yet exciting.

Soon, Martha approached again. "Are you finished?" her voice, though soft, held an edge of seriousness that made Grace look up. Martha stood with both hands on her hips.

Grace blinked. "Oh, yes. Thank you, Martha. The meal was incredible."

Martha said nothing at first, her eyes narrowing slightly as she studied Grace in that way only Martha could—seeing past all the polite words. The kind of look that made you sit up straighter without even meaning to.

Grace clicked her laptop closed, taking another sip of her coffee to stall. Had she done something wrong?

Martha pointed to the closed laptop. "Wrap that up for now."

Grace hesitated. "Wrap it up?"

"You heard me," Martha said, crossing her arms. Her usual bright smile had softened into something a little more playful. "We've got other business to tend to."

Intrigued, Grace powered down her laptop, unsure of where this was going. "Did I miss something?"

Martha grinned a little, her eyes twinkling as she nodded toward the kitchen. "Follow me."

With a look of confusion, Grace slipped out of the booth, tucking her laptop back into her bag, slinging it over her shoulder. "Where are we going?"

"You'll see," Martha said, already marching back toward the kitchen, her sturdy frame passing easily through swinging doors. Grace followed without hesitation, her curiosity piqued. The diner's kitchen was usually off-limits.

The moment Grace stepped inside, the atmosphere shifted. She was met with the aroma of fresh bread dough baking inside warm ovens. The kitchen was an organized choreography of gleaming stainless-steel pots hanging in neat rows, and the steady hum of an industrial-sized refrigerator. Grace had never been back here before, and it amazed her how pristine and professional the kitchen was. It was the heartbeat of the diner, and somehow, it reflected Martha—the perfect mix of control and chaos.

Grace smiled and gave a nod to the cook working behind the griddle, a familiar face at the diner.

He nodded back, flashed a quick grin, and continued to clean the griddle.

Grace returned her attention to Martha. "What's this about, Martha?"

Martha gave her a stern look, combined with a quirk of humor on her brow. It was clear she had something planned. "Miss Grace, you've been in Laurel Ridge long enough. It's time you learned one of the essentials if you're gonna stick around. You're gonna learn how to make biscuits and gravy."

Grace's eyebrows shot up. That had been the last thing she'd expected. "Biscuits and gravy? Me? But who's going to watch the diner?"

"My sister-in-law Ruth will be here in a few minutes. She can take care of any customers that might stop by." Martha nodded, her expression serious but with a glint of mischief again. "Now...if you're gonna live here, honey, you need to know your way around a proper kitchen. And biscuits and gravy? That's the heart and soul of any true Appalachian meal."

Grace crossed her arms, a smile playing on her lips. "And I take it you're going to be my cooking instructor today?"

"You better believe it," Martha answered, already gathering a flour sack from one of the lower shelves and tossing it onto the counter. "Now, apron up. Let's get to work," she said as she tossed Grace an apron.

Grace chuckled, still not quite believing this was happening, but she tied the apron Martha tossed her around her waist.

Learning how to make biscuits and gravy from a diner legend, this ought to be interesting.

Martha cleared her throat, gathering a series of bowls and measuring cups before setting them down on the counter with deliberate care. "All right, now the key to perfect biscuits isn't complicated. First things first..." She grabbed the flour and measured a careful amount into the bowl in front of her. "You start with the basics: flour, salt, baking powder, and some real good buttermilk...fresh if you can get your hands on some. Most folks like to overthink this next part, but that's where they go wrong."

Grace watched as Martha began sifting flour into the bowl, the way her hands moved surely yet gently, the flour pouring through her fingers like dust caught in a breeze.

Martha paused, catching Grace's gaze. "There's a lot about life that's like making biscuits, Grace." She began measuring once more, her tone growing softer. "You can't rush it, can't over-handle the dough, or you'll toughen it up. And the best things take time. Patience."

The words lingered in the air for a moment, leaving Grace to simmer on their meaning. Was she talking about biscuits still... or something else?

Martha mixed the flour and buttermilk mixture deftly with her hand. "Now, you give it a try. Don't be shy."

With a deep breath, Grace tentatively reached for a bowl, measured the dry ingredients just as Martha had done. Sifted it a little with her hand, then measured the buttermilk into the center of the bowl, and blended the ingredients together, trying not to fumble through the process. If Martha noticed her hesitance, she didn't call her out for it. Instead, she offered warm, steady encouragement.

"That's right," Martha said, leaning slightly against the counter, one eye still on Grace's hands. "Biscuits, much like life, don't respond well to over-managing. There's a reason you leave the dough room to breathe before you bake it. It's got to grow on its own."

Grace tried to suppress a smile, the dough clinging to her fingers. She now understood this was more than just a cooking lesson.

"It's kind of like some people I know," Martha continued, her eyes piercing but still warm. "Like you and Ben, for instance..."

Grace leaned back, her fingers sticky with biscuit dough, pausing as the weight of Martha's words settled over her. She raised her brows, her voice laced with curiosity. "Oh?"

"Relationships take time, just like making a good batch of biscuits. You can't rush them or push too hard, honey. If you handle that dough too rough, if you knead instead of gently folding it together, all you'll end up with is tough biscuits. And trust me, nobody likes a tough biscuit."

Grace couldn't help but chuckle. "I suppose you're right. Ben... he does need some breathing room."

Martha leaned back, smiling as she watched Grace. "He's one of the good ones, but that boy's got a lot running through his mind at any given time. But men—they don't always talk about what they're feeling. Doesn't mean they're running away or tryin' to avoid anything... it just means they need a quiet moment to clear their head. You understand?"

Grace nodded slowly, her hands working more rhythmically now. "I have to admit... it's hard not to worry."

Martha waved a hand at that notion, making a soft "tsk" sound under her breath. "Trust me, Ben's not going anywhere. He's just like this biscuit dough you're working with—it takes time to mix and blend the ingredients. But just 'cause you can't see what's happening under the surface doesn't mean God isn't at work."

Grace paused, letting the words settle like fresh snow. This was all true—it wasn't just about patience or understanding. It was about trust. Trust in Ben, yes, but also trust in God's timing and ways.

Martha smiled, dusting her hands off. "Let's get that dough cut into biscuits next and get them in the oven."

The door of the kitchen swung open, and a woman—about Martha's age—walked in with a warm smile that lit up the room. She made her way straight to Martha, wrapping her in a hug like an old, cherished friend. As they pulled apart, the woman's gaze shifted to Grace, her sharp eyes softening into something both welcoming and amused.

"Well, if it isn't the famous Grace Anderson," the woman said, her tone full of friendly warmth. "I've heard quite a bit about you, young lady. It's nice to finally meet you—welcome to Laurel Ridge."

Grace smiled, feeling the genuine kindness in the woman's words wrap around her like an embrace.

"Nice to meet you as well," Grace said with a smile on her face and a fair bit of flour dust on her face.

"Grace is doing a fine job, Ruth," Martha said. "You wanna join us, or would you rather stay up front in case any customers wander in?"

"Well, there ain't a soul in the dining room needin' my attention—just ol' Earl sitting there, and I'm sure he's capable of pourin' himself another cup of coffee if he runs low," Ruth quipped with a laugh. With one swift motion, she tied on an apron, grabbed a bowl, and began expertly mixing up another batch of biscuits.

"Well, aren't we quite the team, making biscuits together?" Grace said with a playful smile. "This is an Instagram moment if I ever saw one."

"Well honey, I'm not exactly sure what this Instagram thing is, but if you say so," Ruth said with a hearty laugh.

"All right then, now we're going to pat this dough out and—" Martha's instructions were interrupted by a burst of laughter.

All three women turned toward the window to see Rachel standing there, grinning from ear to ear, her phone raised as she snapped pictures. "Well, well, well," she teased, "looks like we've reached the biscuit-making initiation. Should I send a few of these photos to Ben? You know, just in case he has cell service and wants to see what his girl is cooking up with ya'll in the kitchen?"

"Now listen here, missy," Martha said, wagging her finger at Rachel, her tone both teasing and firm. "You had your chance with

John Henry and you let that opportunity slip past, but mark my words... your time's still comin'. Just you wait!"

"Now, Martha," Ruth said with a teasing smile, "give her some time. She'll find herself a good man soon enough."

"Y'all enjoy yourselves. I'm just here to grab some cookies—I've got to get back to work," Rachel said with a cheerful wave before heading out of the diner.

"Mark my words, ladies," Martha said, shaking her head with a knowing smile. "One day, someone's gonna come along, catch her eye, and calm that one down just a bit. We all need a little of that in our lives from time to time. But Lord help the poor man who falls for her—that girl's a handful for sure. Now where were we..."

Grace laughed as turned her attention back to Martha.

"All right now... You want to work the dough gently, not too rough," Martha explained, her voice firm but filled with that gentle warmth Grace had grown to love. Martha expertly patted the biscuit dough on the lightly floured counter top, using gentle pressing motions. "It's all about touch. You don't need to manhandle it—just enough coaxing to get it to do what you want."

Grace nodded, mimicking Martha's motions, her fingers sinking into the cool, soft dough.

"See how smooth that is now?" Martha said, pointing out the even texture. "That's when you know it's ready."

Grace glanced up, a small smile tugging at her lips. Martha had done this a thousand times, maybe more, and yet the older woman handled the dough with the reverence of someone experiencing the art for the first time.

Ruth stood just to the side, leaning comfortably against the counter, offering the occasional nugget of wisdom as they worked. "You know, biscuits are like life. You gotta find the balance between doing too much and doing just enough. Too much pressure, and things can get tough. Take your time, but don't overdo it, or you lose the magic."

Grace chuckled at Ruth's words. There was that wit and wisdom again—so simple on the surface, yet deeply resonating beneath. She never imagined biscuit making could teach life lessons.

Martha reached for the biscuit cutter, pressing it firmly into the dough with a crisp, satisfying smoosh sound. "See? Just like that," she said, effortlessly lifting the neatly formed round of dough, placing it onto a baking tray. "The trick is to not overthink it. Press straight down, lift the cutter clean—don't twist it, or you'll mess it up and the biscuit won't rise like it should. Then, place that biscuit right on the tray, and move on to the next. Smooth and steady."

Following suit, Grace finished pressing out the dough gently with her hands and then cut and lifted a dough round, marveling at how perfect it looked.

Ruth grinned as she watched Grace. "You've got a knack for it! Some people fuss too much, tryin' to create perfection. You? You're letting the biscuits come naturally."

"Maybe I have good teachers," Grace teased.

Martha smiled. "You're a quick learner, that's for sure."

Before long, trays were filled with dough rounds, perfectly shaped and arranged for baking.

Martha slid each tray into the oven and wiped her hands on her apron, standing back with an approving nod. "Well, now they're in God's hands. Let's see what He cooks up, hmm?"

Grace grinned, feeling a warmth in her chest that had little to do with the oven's heat. She was learning more than just the art of biscuit-making today. Learning to trust. To embrace the process, whether it was in love, life, or biscuits.

Ruth chuckled, glancing at Grace. "Well, sugar, you may not need fancy New York bakers in your life after this. You're a natural! You've got an Appalachian heart in you, that's for sure."

Grace smiled as she stepped back, watching the golden tops of biscuits rising in the oven. The simple warmth of the kitchen, the friendship, and the little moments of flour-dusted peace filled her up inside.

"Now we can work on the gravy." Martha said as she grabbed two skillets and started heating them on the stove.

As the sausage began to sizzle and the fat rendered down, Martha and Grace worked side by side, adding a bit of milk or flour here and there until the creamy, delicious consistency of sausage gravy started forming.

"Grace, let me tell ya something 'bout life and gravy." Martha gave her a sideways glance. "Gravy is like love. You don't just throw everything into the pot and expect it to work. It takes a balance—patience. You add things a little at a time."

"The same's true with Ben, right?" Grace asked with a smile, grateful for Martha's unwavering way of mixing humor with truth.

"Ben, your faith, your calling here—all of it," Martha confirmed. "You two are building something solid, bit by bit. Slow and steady. You've got to trust that each ingredient—the good times, the challenges, even those moments where you're tempted to overstep and take control—are part of something bigger. That's what makes the gravy perfect, girl."

"And if I mess up the proportions?"

"You fix it. Sometimes, you just add more flour. Or a little milk. Or you scrap it and start again." Martha shrugged. "But you don't quit."

"Don't forget the stirring, honey," Ruth chimed in with a twinkle in her eye. "Now listen, Grace, you gotta keep a steady hand when you're working that gravy. Stir it nice and gentle, but don't back off for a second. You take your eye off it for too long, and before you know it, it'll start to clump up, gettin' all lumpy on you. And worse—Lord help us—it might even burn."

Martha chuckled, nodding her head in agreement as she worked beside Grace. "She's right. Stirrin' gravy's not just about keeping everything smooth in the pan," she said, her Southern drawl stretching across her words. "It's kinda like life if you think about it. You gotta keep tending to things, even when you're tempted to step away or rush through. If you don't give it the attention it needs, trust me, you'll feel the burn later—one way or another."

Grace smiled, feeling the gentle weight of their words settle within her.

More than just biscuits... more than just gravy. Grace was beginning to understand a deeper truth: everything in life—whether love, faith, or even healing—required careful tending. It needed time to take shape, a delicate stirring to ensure the right balance, and the patience to nurture it through its messier moments. Rushing would only ruin it. Life could toughen up if handled too roughly. Love—whether in relationships or in one's spirit—needed room to breathe and grow. Like the slow rise of dough or the thickening of gravy, the process demanded care, a watchful eye, and the wisdom to trust that, eventually, the right flavors would emerge.

They finished making the gravy, and the biscuits were ready, golden brown and warm.

"You did it, girl," Martha said, standing back, folding her arms. "Now, let's see if it tastes as good as it looks."

Grace plated one of her biscuits, split it open, and spooned the warm gravy liberally over the soft bread. With Martha and Ruth's watchful eye on her, Grace took her first bite.

It was perfect.

"Well?" Martha asked, her hands on her hips, a knowing smile on her face.

Grace smiled, licking a bit of gravy from her fingertips. "Delicious."

Martha grinned, her eyes twinkling with satisfaction. "I knew it!" She wiped her hands on the towel she'd been using and turned toward Ruth with a knowing look. "Well, Ruth, what do you think of Grace's first go at biscuits and gravy?"

Ruth held up a perfectly baked biscuit, eyeing it critically for a moment before taking a generous bite. She chewed thoughtfully, a small smile curling at the corners of her lips as she let out a soft hum of approval. After a dramatic swallow, she looked over at Grace and Martha; her smile spreading wide.

"Well now," Ruth began, "if I didn't know better, I'd say you've got yourself a natural in the kitchen, Martha." She set the biscuit down on a plate and wiped her hands on her apron, glancing at Grace. "Grace, honey, these biscuits are as good as any I've ever tasted! And this gravy..." She spooned a generous amount of gravy over the biscuit and licked her spoon clean, shaking her head in approval. "I tell ya, it's got me wantin' more. Might need to keep a close eye on you, or you'll be taking over for Martha here at the diner."

Grace laughed, her cheeks flushing slightly under the praise. "Oh, I don't know about all that, but I have to admit, this was a lot more fun than I expected. And... well, I think this is the first time a meal I helped make hasn't ended in disaster." She glanced down at the biscuits, still amazed that she'd had a hand in creating them. "Honestly, I was a little nervous I might mix too much and end up with hockey pucks for biscuits."

Martha chuckled, shaking her head. "See? Wasn't so hard, now, was it? You just needed a little patience and the right guidance. You're lucky, though," she added with a wink. "Not everyone makes a good biscuit on their first try. I had a feeling you'd take to it."

Grace grinned. "I have good teachers."

Ruth tilted her head toward Grace, her smile gentle. "Don't underestimate yourself, dear. Some people spend their whole lives never realizing that biscuits aren't just about the ingredients—they're about love!"

# Chapter 37

*A few days later...*

Grace blinked, tangled up in her quilt, feeling the last remnants of sleep ripple away. Her bed, far less pristine than it had been the night before, reflected her restless tosses and turns throughout the night.

Ding... Ding... Ding

The soft musical chime of her phone floating from the bedside table. She stretched, fumbling clumsily to reach it.

She swiped the call open and pressed the phone to her ear.

"Grace, sweetheart! Good morning! I'm not waking you up, am I?"

Grace chuckled. "No, Mom. I'm up." Not technically a lie—though her feet hadn't quite touched the floor yet.

"Good," her mother replied. "It's been a few days since we last talked, you know. I just wanted to check in, make sure you were still alive out there in the wilderness."

Grace rolled her eyes affectionately. "Mom, I'm not in the wilderness. I have electricity and running water, you know."

"Well, okay, whatever you say," her mother responded, a teasing lilt coloring her words. There was the faint clatter of dishes in the background—her mom cleaning up breakfast from earlier, a habit she'd never outgrown, even though it was just her and Dad now.

Her mother sighed softly. "I just want to make sure you're not letting that corporate mess keep you hidden away forever. You're meant for big things, Gracie."

Grace took a deep breath as she padded her way into the kitchen.

"I know that, Mom," she replied, grabbing her favorite mug, the ceramic "World's Okayest Boss" mug that made her laugh now every time she used it. "I've been thinking a lot about things... and I've made a decision." She flicked on the coffeemaker and the machine hummed to life.

"Oh? What kind of decision?"

Grace shifted her feet, leaning a hip against the kitchen counter. "I'm putting my condo up for sale, Mom. I've decided... I'm going to stay here in Laurel Ridge, at least for the foreseeable future."

Her mother was silent for a few seconds—just long enough to make Grace instinctively bite her lip. Louise was never someone prone to long bouts of quiet, even when processing something meaningful. But as Grace waited, her heart thumping lightly in her chest, her mother's soft voice returned through the crackle of the phone line.

"Well... I suppose that makes sense," her mother said, though there was a hint of uncertainty in her voice. "You've always been independent, Grace. But this is a big step, and I don't want you making any decisions just to run away from things, you know?" The maternal concern came through clear as day.

Grace poured herself a mug of coffee, the warm steam rising alongside her internal reflection. She had considered that worry, of course—whether she was running or choosing to plant roots. It wasn't

New York that she was leaving behind, but rather that person she once believed she had to be. Someone caught in boardrooms and running on deadlines, trying to craft the perfect image.

"Mom... it just feels right here. I can breathe. I can think without the city noise constantly pressing in around me. I'm happy. I can see building a career here. I have faith I can make it happen," Grace explained as she moved toward the back door.

Louise's voice was soft when she responded. "That's all I want for you, Gracie. To be happy. To feel settled. No matter where that might be."

Grace could hear the love in her mother's words, even if they were tinged with the inevitable sadness that came when a parent realized their child would always be building their own life apart. Pushing open the back porch door, Grace stepped outside into the early morning air, the sounds of the river in the distance making her heart feel light.

She was halfway to the porch swing when her steps faltered. At first glance, she hadn't noticed it—her mind too focused on the continuing conversation with her mom.

A bundle of roses.

Her heart skipped a beat.

Lying across the worn wooden boards of the porch swing was a beautiful bouquet of deep red roses. A note wound around the stems, tied neatly with a simple piece of twine.

"Mom," Grace breathed, her voice caught somewhere between soft disbelief and joy, "hold on just a second."

"What is it, sweetie?" her mother asked, clearly surprised by the shift in Grace's tone.

"It's... nothing, just give me a second."

Grace set her coffee down on the small side table near the swing, her hands trembling ever so slightly as she stared at the bouquet.

"Grace, what's going on?" Louise pressed.

"There's a bouquet of roses on my porch," she said.

Her mother's laughter floated through the phone, warm and knowing. "Someone's being romanced, huh?"

Grace smiled and reached for the note wrapped delicately around the stems. The simple twine fell loose under her fingers as her heart sped with anticipation. She tugged the paper free and unfolded it carefully.

I'm back. I missed you. Let's catch up later.—Ben

Her breath caught as she read it once... twice. The words were simple, but full of meaning. He had missed her. Ben had returned after his quiet time away, and somehow, the thought of him thinking of her during that time, missing her, made her heart pulse.

"They're from Ben, aren't they?" her mother teased, but Grace could hear the tenderness behind her question.

Grace smiled, unable to hold it back any longer. "Yes."

"And a note, a card? Anything? What did it say?!" Louise exclaimed, her laughter bubbling with a soft edge of triumph. "Oh, honey, that man is a good one. I can just feel it! Your father and I can't wait to meet him."

Grace's smile widened. "He's... amazing, Mom. He left a note saying he's back from his camping trip, and he missed me. Nothing dramatic or overly romantic. Just... sweet."

Louise let out a happy sigh. "Simple is good. In fact, simple can often mean more. Please tell me you're going to see him soon?"

"Oh, I plan on it," Grace answered, a soft, giddy chuckle escaping her.

"Good. I think, Grace, ... for once in your life, you're letting yourself be still long enough to actually feel what you need to feel. And this—Ben, Laurel Ridge—I think it's all part of what God wants for you."

"Mom..." Grace paused, her voice softening. "You're right. I think God has more planned for me right here. I didn't see it right away, but I don't need to keep proving myself in the way I always thought I did."

"Oh my dear girl. You've never needed to prove anything to anyone but Him, and you know that in your bones. He loves you, honey. Let Him lead."

Grace smiled. "Thanks, Mom. For always knowing how to point me in the right direction."

"I'll always try, sweetheart. I love you."

"I love you too, Mom."

They ended the call, Grace's mind still swimming. She read the note in her hand again.

"I'm back. I missed you..."

She tucked the note back into the bouquet, inhaling the soft perfume of the roses as she settled herself down on the swing, cradling her mug of coffee in her hands.

Grace leaned back in the porch swing, her heart filled with hope, gratitude, and the quiet excitement of knowing that whatever came next—with Ben, with this place—God's hand was in it.

# Chapter 38

race stepped through the door of Adventure Tours, her eyes scanning for Ben.

Behind the counter, a man she didn't recognize was unpacking a box of what appeared to be fishing lures. He was tall and stout, his tan skin suggesting countless hours spent in the sun.

"Good morning," Grace said, stepping forward, offering her warmest smile.

He looked up, smiling back. "Morning! Need help finding anything?"

"Well, actually..." Grace hesitated, glancing around once more before refocusing on him. "I'm looking for Ben. I thought he might be here."

"Oh, Ben?" The man chuckled softly. "Nah, he's not working today. Smart man...he's taken the day off. Told me if we need him to just call his cell."

"Oh…any idea where he is?" Grace asked, trying to keep her tone casual. She didn't want to sound too eager, but the note in her pocket was all the encouragement she needed.

The man paused and gave her an amused look. "Oh, well, if I know Ben—he's out on the dock near his place, fishing."

Grace's brow furrowed slightly. "I've never been to his house. How do I get there?"

He grinned, extending a hand over the counter. "I'm Andrew, by the way, Ben's assistant manager. You must be Grace."

She smiled and shook his hand. "Yes, I'm Grace. Nice to meet you, Andrew. So, Ben's place?"

"Real easy, actually," Andrew said. "Just head out past the back of the store, take the trail that runs through the woods. It's kind of a natural path—the trees get real thick, but there's a bit of a clearing near his place. Follow it straight, and you'll end up by his cabin. You won't miss it. The cabin overlooks the river. Beautiful spot."

Grace nodded, trying to map it out in her head. "Thanks, Andrew."

"Anytime. Oh, and one more thing—don't let that serious look of his fool ya when you get there. Fishing is Ben's way of unwinding. He might look deep into it, but he'll be all smiles when he sees you. Trust me on that."

She couldn't help but feel excitement spread from her chest down to her toes as she exited the building.

The path beneath her feet behind the store was soft with fallen leaves. Walking amidst these towering oaks and maples calmed her nerves.

After a few minutes, the path began to open up, just as Andrew had promised, revealing a wide, sprawling view of the New River. A clearing ahead, showcasing the most picturesque cabin Grace had ever seen. Ben's home was breathtaking.

Her eyes landed on the dock.

And there he was.

Sitting in a blue camp chair, one hand lazily holding a fishing rod while the other rested in his lap, Ben looked entirely at ease.

This was Ben, alone in his element. The rugged beauty of it all struck her deeply.

And then, her gaze caught on something else: the stubble lining his jaw. He hadn't shaved. A small smile tugged at her lips. He was usually so cleaned up, even for a man who spent most of his time outdoors. But she liked this look on him. It was unpolished, real.

As she walked toward him, Ben's head turned, and his warm hazel eyes found hers. A slow smile spread across his face, the kind that made the world around her stop.

"There you are," he said.

"Here I am," Grace answered, walking up to the dock with a mix of trepidation and certainty.

Ben chuckled, looking unapologetically comfortable in his camp shirt and faded jeans. "To what do I owe this surprise visit? Looking for a fishing lesson?"

"Oh, definitely not," she shot back with a grin and a teasing eyebrow raised. "I don't see a single fish in your bucket," she said as she pointed to the empty bucket sitting nearby.

Ben laughed, running a hand through his tousled hair. "The fish are shy today. I blame the weather. Or maybe my casting technique's slacking off." He paused, taking her in. "Though I'm guessing you didn't come all this way to critique my angling skills, did you?"

Grace shook her head. "No, I guess I didn't." She hesitated for a moment. "Got your note... and the flowers, by the way. That was really sweet. Thank you"

Ben's smile softened, and he glanced away for a second, as if suddenly shy in her presence. "I missed you. Thought you'd like 'em."

Grace felt her pulse quicken. She liked how Ben never made a big deal out of things, but every word he spoke carried weight, intention.

"You were right," she said. "I do like the roses."

"Come sit," Ben said, gesturing to the other chair next to his. "And yes, I brought out another chair, just in case...ya know?"

She laughed, sinking into the camp chair.

"So...?" Ben said, flashing her a grin.

"I missed you too," Grace said.

Ben smiled.

"You know," she teased as she settled beside him, "I think I like this new look you've got going on... it's rugged. Works for you."

Ben chuckled. "You mean the 'roughing-it-out-in-the-woods-didn't-shave-for-a-few-days' look?" He said as he rubbed his chin, a twinkle in his eye. "I wasn't sure I could pull it off, but if you're giving me the seal of approval, maybe I won't rush to shave it off just yet."

Grace's laugh was warm. "Don't get too used to the praise. I've got to keep you on your toes."

Ben chuckled again. "Well, I'll take what I can get. But, just for the record," he added, his voice softening, "I've missed this—missed you."

He glanced at her with a playful glint in his eye. "So... I hear you've been busy in the kitchen. My sister sent me some photos—looked like a full-on biscuit-making masterclass with Martha and Ruth."

Grace laughed, her cheeks flushing slightly. "It was an experience. I'll say that much."

He leaned back in his chair, casting the line out again, the quiet splash of the lure dissolving into the river's rhythm. "Martha's biscuits and gravy are legendary."

"I picked up way more than just biscuit and gravy skills," Grace said with a playful grin. "But something tells me I could use a few more kitchen lessons... for, you know, the future."

"Really?" Ben said, his lips curving into a playful grin as he turned toward her. "More cooking lessons? That's... interesting."

"So, Mr. Turner," Grace teased, leaning back in her chair. "Tell me about this camping trip of yours. Did you master any new wilderness survival skills? Make any life-changing revelations while out there?"

"I just might have," he said, his voice warm, his gaze locking onto hers with a quiet intensity. "Care to hear the rest?"

"Oh, do tell," she prompted with a playful gleam in her eye.

Ben chuckled and nodded, reeling the line in with an easy motion before setting the fishing rod aside, letting it rest gently on the dock.

"I spent a lot of time thinking," he began, his voice measured, thoughtful. "Out there in the woods, away from everything. And, well, I realized something..."

Grace leaned forward. "What did you realize?"

Ben rubbed the back of his neck, searching for the right words. "I came to understand something out there," he began, his voice calm yet sure. "We're going to be okay, Grace. You, me... us. I handed it all over to God—every doubt, every worry—and now, I'm trusting in His plan, whatever that looks like. No more second-guessing, no more hesitation. When it comes to you, I'm all in."

Grace smiled, "I'm all in too."

Ben's smile widened, his eyes crinkling at the corners.

"Well, then," Grace said, standing up with a newfound lightness. She glanced over at the empty fishing bucket, hands on her hips. "What do you say we catch something today, huh? Because that bucket is looking awfully empty."

Ben threw his head back and laughed, standing up alongside her.

"Show me your technique, Mr. Wilderness Expert," she teased.

Ben shook his head, still laughing, and grabbed the fishing rod. He stepped behind her, guiding her hands on the reel. "Okay, first things first."

# Chapter 39

G race nestled comfortably in the oversized recliner by the fireplace, a cup of coffee cradled between her hands. She loved the way the flames danced in the hearth, casting flickering shadows across the wooden beams overhead. The space felt like a cocoon tonight, a little world of her own where time seemed to slow, leaving her with nothing but the pleasant reminder that she was home.

Home. The word fluttered warmly in her chest, more familiar now than it had ever been.

The unexpected knock on her door jolted her out of her thoughts. Glancing toward the door, curiosity tugged at her. Who would come by at this time of night?

Setting her coffee down with a soft clink on the side table, she stood and crossed over to the door.

Ben. He wore the simple blue flannel shirt she'd grown to love on him.

Ben...who looked as though he had just stepped out of the West Virginia wilderness, a mountain man, every inch steady and sure. His hands were stuffed casually into his jeans' pockets, as if the cool air didn't faze him.

"Ben?" Grace blinked, a surprised smile teasing at the edge of her lips. "What are you doing here?"

"You busy?" he asked with that small, teasing grin of his.

"No..." She leaned against the doorframe. "I mean, no plans. Why?"

He tilted his head, a flicker of amusement dancing in his eyes. "How do you feel about a little adventure tonight?"

"Adventure?" Grace echoed, raising an eyebrow. "You do know it's almost dark out, right?"

"I'm aware," he said, smirking. He stepped a little closer, the autumn breeze rustling his hair. "I have a surprise for you, and I think you'll like it."

Grace smiled, leaning into the moment. "A surprise? Care to give me a hint or two?"

Ben's smile widened. "Nope. You'll just have to trust me." His hand slid behind his back for a brief second before he produced a bandana from his back pocket. His eyes sparkled with humor as he dangled it in front of her. "Think you can handle being in the dark for a little while?"

Grace laughed, her heart doing something funny in her chest. "Okay," she said. "As long as you promise no spiders ... or snakes."

"No spiders, no snakes ... got it," Ben confirmed, his grin playful as he stepped forward and gently slipped the bandana over her eyes. His fingers brushed against her temple, soft and warm, and her heart fluttered.

"Now what?" she asked, feeling the grin on her own lips, a mixture of nerves and excitement bubbling inside her.

"Well," Ben's voice was low and calming, right near her ear, "next comes the easy part. I pick you up."

Before she could react or protest, one muscular arm slid behind her back, the other under her legs, sweeping her off her feet. Her heartbeat kicked up as she let out a surprised gasp. "Ben!"

Laughing, Ben adjusted her in his arms. "Don't worry."

"If you drop me, there will be severe consequences," she said.

"Noted," he replied, his voice light with humor. She could feel the steady hum of his heartbeat where she rested against his chest.

The night air swirled around them as he carried her toward the truck. She listened to his footsteps crunching over fallen leaves, and she relaxed into his arms.

Ben's voice broke the silence as he gently placed her on the passenger seat of his truck, his hands lingering just a fraction of a second longer than necessary. "There. Nice and safe."

Grace chuckled, both nervous and giddy with whatever this plan of his might be.

"Is this the part where you ask if I trust you?" she teased as she heard the driver's door open and his seat creak with the weight of him. "Actually," his voice came closer as he started the engine, "I already know the answer."

"Do you now?"

"Mm-hmm. It's written all over that smile of yours," he said.

"Ben, did you forget something?" she asked, a teasing lilt in her voice.

Ben blinked, confused but amused. "What?" he asked, tilting his head, genuinely trying to piece together what he might have missed.

Grace chuckled, shaking her head. "I think you'd better go put out the fire in the fireplace before the entire place burns down while I'm gone," she said with a grin. "Oh, and closing the cabin door might be smart too—I'd rather not come back to a house full of bears, thinking an open door is a warm invitation."

Ben's eyes widened, and he burst out laughing. "Ah, right—can't have any bear parties while you're away," he joked. "I'll take care of it."

***

"You're not going to give me even the slightest hint about where we're going?" Grace asked.

"Nice try," he said, amusement thick in his voice. "But no. You're going to have to wait."

"You're holding out on me, Turner." Dropping her head back against the headrest with dramatic flair, she let out a long, exaggerated sigh. "Not even a guess?"

"Well, the moon's out tonight..."

Grace's mind ticked over the possibilities. "Hmm... my next fishing lesson?"

Ben's shoulders shook with laughter. "Wrong." There was a pause as his voice dropped a little lower, softer. "But don't tempt me."

The truck came to a halt, and Grace's curiosity spiked, her heart already racing. She heard Ben step out, his boots crunching on the gravel. A moment later, the passenger door opened, and she felt his hands—steady and sure—helping her out. The cool night air wrapped around them, carrying the scent of the river and nature. Everything was still, save for the soft whisper of the river nearby.

This time, there was no nervousness as Ben lifted her into his arms once more and began walking. Instead, her heart raced with a playful excitement, the anticipation bringing a smile to her lips.

"Okay," he murmured as he set her gently on her feet a few moments later. "Ready for the reveal?"

Grace nodded, breath hitching with the kind of anticipation that spiraled high inside her chest. Slowly — so slowly it was almost agonizing — Ben's fingers loosened the knot on the bandana and the soft fabric slid away.

And when her eyes focused, her breath faltered.

Before her, candles — hundreds of them, it seemed — flickered gently along the wooden boardwalk of the dock, casting light across the water that shimmered like polished glass. Their flames danced in time with the subtle evening breeze, creating an ethereal warmth that wrapped around Grace like a tender embrace. The river itself was so still, reflecting the moon and stars from above, as if the heavens had bent down to kiss the earth.

"For me?" Her voice was barely a whisper, a tremor of awe threading through it as she turned to face him.

Ben's eyes, deep pools of hazel under the candlelight, held hers steadfast. "For us," he said, his voice quiet but rich with meaning, as if those two words alone carried the weight of a hundred unsaid things. "You deserve something special, Grace. Something beautiful."

Grace's heart swelled, and for a moment, she had no words.

A long, slow breath escaped her, and when she found the courage to speak again, her voice trembled, but only with joy. "I love it."

Ben's lips curved into that soft smile she knew was just for her, and just like that, he extended his hand. "Come see the rest."

Her pulse quickened again as she followed him. The dock creaked gently under their weight, the river whispering secrets beside them.

Resting at the end of the dock, bobbing quietly on a slight ripple in the river, was a tandem kayak.

Grace let out a soft laugh, momentarily lost for words again. "We're going on the water?"

Ben chuckled beside her, walking her over to the kayak. "You catch on fast."

They drifted across the water, guided by Ben's steady paddle. The world hushed around them. All she could hear was the gentle splash of water against the boat and the soft hum of his voice as he occasionally murmured something low, quietly reassuring in the stillness.

And then—like a painting coming to life—a glow in the woods along the riverbank.

A soft, twinkling light filtered through the trees ahead. As they paddled closer, the glow revealed an unexpected sight: easels—classic wooden artist easels—neatly arranged along the riverbank. Familiar faces bent toward their canvases, brushstrokes coming to life under the glow of hundreds of fairy lights strung overhead. Countless lanterns had been thoughtfully placed all around, their gentle flicker adding to the enchanting atmosphere.

Martha. Pastor Eli. Claire. Ruth. Leslie. Beth. Grace's mom and dad.

All of them, laughing, painting together as though the world around them had paused for a moment of pure creative joy. Rachel stood nearby, paintbrush in hand as well as she instructed her group of students, her expressive face filled with an excitement that was unmistakable even from this distance.

"Oh my word," Grace breathed, heart swelling with disbelief and awe.

Ben chuckled softly, his voice full of affection. "The Moonlit Tour & Art Along the River Experience...it's all because of you, Grace. Your vision brought this to life."

Grace's lips parted in a soft gasp before laughter bubbled from her chest. She turned to face Ben, her eyes wide with amazement. "You've really outdone yourself, Ben Turner. How on earth did you pull all this off? Even my mom and dad were in on this?"

"Well, I had to meet your parents sooner or later, didn't I?" he said with a playful grin.

Grace glanced back at the moonlit art class before her, amazed to see the effort everyone had put into this entire evening adventure.

Rachel caught her eye with a conspiratorial grin and waved her brush with exaggerated glee, her spirit as infectious as ever.

"I love it," Grace said, her words a whisper carried on the breeze.

"You deserve nights like this," Ben said, his voice as steady as the river.

Eventually, they drifted past the lights, leaving behind the laughter and creativity, sinking once more into the deep stillness of the river. Only the moon, the stars, and the quiet rhythm of Ben's presence.

***

By the time they returned to the dock, the candlelight still flickering softly, Grace felt like her heart had expanded beyond what she ever thought possible. Ben helped her out of the kayak, his hands firm but tender.

Grace opened her mouth to thank him again, but before the words could take flight, he said, "Grace..."

His words hung in the air, lingering, sweet and intimate, as he reached into his pocket and sank to one knee.

Ben looked up at her, his hazel eyes catching the candlelight, making them shine in a way she had never seen before. Leaning forward, he held up a small burgundy box.

"Grace," he began, his steady voice thick with emotion, "I love doing life with you." He opened the box, revealing a ring—simple, elegant, and every bit a reflection of the man who was offering it. "Will you marry me?"

Grace felt her world tilt. Her heart stumbled, then soared as tears blurred her vision. She took a step toward him. She leaned down, cupping his face, and breathed out, "Ben... I love doing life with you, too. Yes... Yes, I will marry you."

The smile that spread across his face stole her breath away. Rising, he slipped the ring onto her finger, sealing the promise. When their lips met, it was not hurried, not frantic. It felt as if the whole world had paused just for them to exist in this moment.

Their friends and family—Martha, Ruth, Rachel, Claire, Pastor Eli, Leslie, Beth, Grace's mom and dad—all clapping, cheering, and hollering with excitement. Rushed over in a flood of joy and congratulations, enveloping them in a whirlwind of love.

But even in the midst of the laughter and cheers, for Grace and Ben, no one else existed. They stood there, at the dock's edge, in their own little world, hearts aligned—doing life together.

# Leave A Review

If you enjoyed this book, please consider leaving an honest review on Amazon or Goodreads.

Visit Our Website:
www.tarabaisden.com

Visit Our Amazon Author Page HERE


Find Us On Social Media:

Facebook

Instagram

TikTok

Pinterest

GoodReads